WORLD OF DINOSAURS ANTHOLOGY

Edited by
Jonathan M. Thompson
Alana Joli Abbott

APEX: WORLD OF DINOSAURS

"Horizon Alpha: High Wire" copyright 2016 by D. W. Vogel. First published in *Future Worlds: A Science Fiction Anthology*, edited by Future House Publishing, Utah, August 2016.

"Just Like Old Times" copyright 1993 by Robert J. Sawyer. First published in *On Spec: The Canadian Magazine of Speculative Writing*, Summer 1993.

"Forever" copyright 1997 by Robert J. Sawyer. First published in *Return of the Dinosaurs*, edited by Mike Resnick and Martin H. Greenberg, DAW Books, New York, May 1997.

Published by Outland Entertainment LLC
3119 Gillham Road
Kansas City, MO 64109

Founder/Creative Director: Jeremy D. Mohler
Editor-in-Chief: Alana Joli Abbott
Senior Editor: Gwendolyn Nix

ISBN: 978-1-947659-80-3 (Print)
ISBN: 978-1-947659-85-8 (eBook)
Worldwide Rights
Created in the United States of America

Editors: Jonathan M. Thompson & Alana Joli Abbott
Additional copy editing: Gwendolyn N. Nix
Cover Illustration: Herschel Hoffmeyer
Cover Design: Jeremy D. Mohler, Michelle Dreher, & Angie Bayman
Interior Layout: Mikael Brodu

Printed and bound in China.

Visit **outlandentertainment.com** to see more, or follow us on our Facebook Page **facebook.com/outlandentertainment/**

Dedicated to Victor Milan.

— TABLE OF CONTENTS —

— FOREWORD —

My kids don't always get excited about my work. There's not a lot that's exciting about sitting in front of a computer and typing, especially for my five year old, who'd rather have me watching *Dino Dana* with him than working on story development or copyediting (though I think that's fun!).

When Outland Entertainment started working with Herschel Hoffmeyer on the *APEX Therapod Deck-Building Game*, however, I got to be a Cool Mom. "Come see the new pictures for the game we're doing!" I'd call out, and my younger kiddo, who knows more dinosaur names than any five year old has a right to know, would come running to look at the giganotosaurus or spinosaurus on my computer screen.

I will admit that I had lost my passion for dinosaurs as an adult until I became a parent. My older daughter could not get enough *Dinosaur Train* when she was little, which is how I learned that troodons are the smartest dinosaur, and that therapods are the ancestors of modern birds. (Even *Sesame Street* is sharing that information these days; when I was a kid, I'm pretty sure we were still being taught they were reptiles!) I've started clicking through on dinosaur-related news any time it comes up in my feed. I had wrongly assumed, for a long time, that we pretty much knew everything there was to know about these extinct creatures. Dinosaur books when I was a kid had maybe thirty or forty types of dinosaurs. We now regularly read from dinosaur books that feature over a hundred different species.

Did you know that the triceratops actually lived closer in time to humans than to the stegosaurus? Dinosaurs were on earth for so long that the end of their era was closer to the start of our history than it was to the beginning of theirs. It boggles the mind.

Over the course of the last decade or so, I've become a huge dinosaur fan again, which is why it was such a joy to work with Jonathan to bring together the authors for this anthology. We didn't give them many boundaries: we wanted stories about dinosaurs, and we wanted to see what they'd come up with. In these pages there are funny dinosaurs and terrifying ones, dinosaur partners and dinosaur threats. Some talk. Some are no smarter than animals. Some are only smarter than animals because humans interfered—and some were smarter than us in the first place.

I hope that wherever you are in your own journey with dinosaurs that you enjoy these tales. I hope some of them give you a good jump-scare in the style of *Jurassic Park*. I hope others give you warm fuzzies as people (and creatures) come together, or make difficult choices about their futures or their loved ones.

Most of all, I hope you share in our joy in bringing you these stories. Dinosaurs may be extinct, but their legacy lives on.

Alana Joli Abbott, co-editor and author
September, 2020

— INTRODUCTION —

Ever since William Buckland discovered the first fossil in 1818, humankind has been fascinated by Dinosauria. It is a subject that has permeated our hearts, minds, and souls for generations. Every kid knows they have a favorite dinosaur, and so do a lot of adults. It is a subject that transcends age, gender, race, and creed. These creatures appear as movies, television shows, and books. They have spawned a science dedicated to the study of dinosaurs—and of course, there are those that make a living from fictional dinosaurs doing things, like you'll find in this anthology.

When I was a child, I fell in love with the triceratops. To me it is the most beautiful animal to have ever walked the Earth. This started a lifelong fascination with these creatures, most of them as deadly as they were beautiful. As I got older we learned more and more about these creatures. Even now there seems to be a popular theory that some dinosaurs had feathers (while I am sure is true, but after forty years, this still looks a little silly—but we are all capable of adjusting our perspective on things.)

Being invited to be a part of this anthology made me happy, and the thought of getting to work with my co-editor and the other authors of this book always brought a smile to my face, even in the midst of tragedy. While I was working on this book, I was struck by a fire in my home that displaced me for almost a year. The fire killed some of my beloved pets and destroyed my ability to work (since it started in my home office) and about a quarter of my collectibles. The people that are Outland Entertainment are the best people. They and the other authors were able to look past the issues I was having and continued to have me as a part of this project. I am very grateful.

My story, "A Boy and his Dog" is set in the fictional universe of "The Dinosaur Protocol," a setting for the Savage Worlds game engine, written by Christopher Halliday and me. The world is not unique as a post-apocalyptic setting, but it is one where Earth itself has survived anything that could have been done to it. It is a world where dinosaurs exist, much like Apex itself.

Dinosaurs literally fill my world. I have several on my desk currently as I type this introduction. They are my wallpaper on my computer, and they are seen everywhere in my office and home. Dinosaurs bring out the kid in all of us, and it is said that the *Jurassic Park* movie from 1993 created a resurgence in the field of paleontology. It made people excited about dinosaurs again and sparked their limitless imaginations.

I know I have rambled on, but remember this. The kid in all of us needs to be with the adults that we generally are. To do otherwise and fail to enjoy life makes it cease to be worth living. Dinosaurs are one of the many things that let us be free.

So, in my conclusion, I want to thank a couple of people. Robert J. Sawyer, who has stories in this book, agreed to allowing us to reprint his work. Robert is a lover of dinosaurs, and he has several novels about them. Secondly, I want to spend some time thanking my friend, Victor Milan. Victor was a dinosaur nerd, and one of the best people I have ever had the privilege of knowing. Victor has been gone for a few years now, but his dinosaur legacy lives on my mind, in my heart and with his books. If you need something additional to read, be sure to look these two gentlemen up. I promise you won't be sorry you did.

Thanks to everyone for letting me be part of this work. I look forward to a second one of these anthologies—maybe we can convince the bosses at Outland that it is worth it!

Jonathan M. Thompson, co-editor and author
September, 2020

— SMILE —
by LaShawn M. Wanak

L et us start first with the news article.

Lab Technician Turned Arsonist Sentenced to Fifty Years in Prison

A judge today sentenced 46-years-old Alma Patterson in her alleged role in the 2056 explosion of a laboratory at the University of Oregon that destroyed research vital to the Velociraptor Revivification Project, where Patterson had served as Lead Technician.

"Justice was served in the sentencing," Michael Rooks, Director and Distinguished Professor, said at a press conference after the ruling. "But our department has been struck a blow that we may never recover from. Years of research have been destroyed, the eggs, the genetic material, the methods we used. It's all gone. It is the extinction of the dinosaurs all over again. Our only hope is that—"

Unfortunately, this was all I was able to recover from the data files, but I do have a video clip to go with it.

Alas, there is no audio, but here we get to see Alma Patterson in the flesh. There she is, dressed in all gray—gray shirt, gray pants, gray nubs of short coiled hair. We can't see her face right now because she must face the judge during her sentencing. But let us admire how straight and stiff her back is, how her head is tilted back to look the judge full in the face. She knows what she's done, and she has no regrets. I dare say her very posture is that of a queen, not a destroyer of arguably the most important find of the twenty-first century.

And now, look, there—the guards are in the act of pulling her away. She sags in their grip, her defiant fire dwindling down at last. But as they turn her around to lead her out the courtroom, we can finally see her face.

Why, yes, what a great observation. That is indeed a smile on her face.

This is just the beginning. I happen to have the most extensive collection of memorabilia from that crucial time period when the raptors were discovered and brought back to life. Patterson figures prominently in most of my collection. Unfortunately, we don't know much about Patterson herself, but I do own the earliest clip we have of her. Shall we have a little watch?

The camera flashes on to show a small box sitting on a clean steel table. The box is opened to show it holding several trays of what appear to be oblong eggs, about a foot in length. A heat lamp shines at the top of the box, showing that it is an incubator. A figure enters the view, covered from head to toe in white, wearing white gloves and a white mask around the nose and mouth. As the eyes crinkle, we see that it is Alma Patterson. She beckons the camera closer.

"You need to get this," she says. Her voice is a light tenor bordering on baritone, and it is breathless with excitement. She reaches into the incubator and takes out one of the eggs, cupping it carefully in her hands. "Come here. Closer. We're viewing history here—oh look! Here it comes!"

The camera zooms in on the egg, which is cracking at the top as whatever is inside pokes and chips at it to free itself. As pieces of shell fall, a bright fuzzy head wiggles its way out of the hole. Despite its orange and green feathery fuzz, it is not a bird—more lizard-like, with tiny black eyes and a long beak of a mouth. It yawns, showing rows of miniature teeth.

"Hello, my friend," Alma speaks softly, almost reverentially. "Welcome. You're a long way from your original time. Welcome to our age."

Why yes, that is indeed our very first view of a raptor chick. Note how Alma's brown eyes widen with surprise, then fills with—what is it called? Warmth.

Hardly the killer of the entire velociraptor race, is she?

The eggs? Ah yes, how did they get the eggs. Unfortunately, I don't have any video or audio from that auspicious discovery, but I do have this. Back then, they called it a "plushie." This was supposed to represent the raptors, but made of the softest materials, even the teeth, so people could give these fearsome predators to their children to play with.

Reach inside its mouth. Go on. It won't bite. Hah, yes, a little joke. You feel something? Go ahead and pull it out. That oblong lump is indeed supposed to represent an egg.

Ironic, isn't it?

It had been a momentous discovery. Excavators had been draining a marsh in what used to be known as Mongolia when they came across a momentous find—a clutch of large salamanders that had died in the marsh, fully preserved. These salamanders were known to have a curious method of survival. During periods of extreme drought, they would burrow down into the earth and secrete a mucus that hardened into a protective shell. They would then go into a hyper-hibernation state until the rains would come to revive them. Unfortunately, those rains never did come for those salamanders.

Radiometric dating on the tissue determined that they came from the Cretaceous Period. Furthermore, scientists were able to examine the contents of their stomachs. Each salamander contained an egg, perfectly preserved and intact. To the scientists' amazement, the eggs were indeed raptor eggs, to be specific, *Velociraptor mongoliensis,* with enough DNA intact to cultivate a full genome.

This was an even more momentous find. Up until that moment, dinosaur DNA only came in fragments too fragile to do anything with. But the DNA in these eggs were stable enough that the scientists felt they could use it to revive the raptors. So they injected the raptor DNA into chicken eggs stripped of their own chromosomes. And what emerged was…well…let's watch another video.

Alma Patterson stands in a room similar to the first room, though there is no furniture here. She is still dressed in a white lab coat and white sneakers, but her face is bare. She is walking around the room in a zigzag pattern. Every few steps, she pauses to bend over and laugh, hands on her knees. The camera jerks, as the wielder also laughs. A male's voice calls out off-screen, "Just like a mama duck!"

The camera blurs out of focus, zooms to focus by Alma's feet. A train of seven raptors amble behind Alma, their bodies covered in feathery orange and brown fuzz. They are the size of large apples. Their forelimbs are clasped almost as if in prayer. Their eyes are large and round as they gaze about, steadying themselves on their legs. As Alma steps forward, they chuff—their vocalizations reminiscent of tiny alligators, but with a longer squawk—and scurry to keep behind her.

Alma leads them in zigzags and circles, laughing until tears stream down her face.

Watch the raptors follow Alma around. Watch the smile spread across her face. Her bare, brown face. Fixate that in your mind. Good. Now here. Take this.

Yes, that is exactly what you think it is. What you're holding is one of the raptor chicks. Don't worry. It's not contaminated. It's been encased in what they called an acrylic block—they used this method to preserve specimens. Pick it up and examine it. Look at how tiny it is. Judging from the size, this chick would have been three days old when it was encased like this. Don't worry, it was already dead when they preserved it.

We also have a video from Patterson at that time. Here:

Alma Patterson sits in what appears to be a desk in an office. Files and books are stacked behind her. She's not in her lab coat, but wearing a green t-shirt. She dabs at her reddened eyes with a tissue. "Five minutes ago, the last raptor chick died. We tried everything, but it just…weakened and died. Just like the others. We didn't even have the chance to give them names."

She takes a deep breath, rolling her head on her neck. She sounds tired. "The best we could determine is that their immune systems were probably in shock, despite everything we have done to prepare them up. But the fact that they were able to live for three days tell me that the DNA is indeed viable. We just need to boost the immune systems. We'll be dissecting the raptors to determine the cause of death; I've already received permission to cultivate a new batch of eggs—"

I have it on full confidence that this raptor had been one of the early chicks in the laboratory. What made the chick die? We believe it was a host of factors, but you can't help but admire the tenacity of Alma Peterson. That's a product of the human condition, to never give up when faced with failure.

I have more raptor blocks here. Note these three is larger—I estimate this one is a week old, and this one is one month. We have no data on how many generations they were able to produce, but these samples are dated months apart. That and the video logs show that they were indeed able to increase the lifespan of the raptors, at least up to three months.

It just so happens that I was able to whip together a small model of what their laboratory looked like. I've cobbled this from the video logs. See, in this room cages where they kept the raptor cages. This room was where they allowed the raptors to run and exercise, as well as feed them meat pellets. This room was for training the raptors to go through certain tasks to test their memory and intelligence. This room was where they quarantined the sick, and here is where they dissected and took samples when the raptors died. This room held the thermocycler, the water baths, the bio safety cabinets, and the desk space to amplify and tweak the DNA. And this room is the incubator room, where they kept fresh eggs ready for the DNA to be inserted.

So many steps. A form of breeding without breeding. It was creative, I'll give them that. The raptors were not yet matured to an age where they could mate, so they selected the raptor that lived the longest and used it to create the next generation of raptors.

Imagine this room filled with bustling people. Imagine the cages, the raptors inside. They must have been, hmm, about three months old now? They're not quite teenagers, our raptors. But they still have teeth, and they are sharp.

And imagine Alma Patterson, directing the workflow, writing up procedures, examining tests results, writing reports, meeting with her supervisor. Do you think the raptors still saw her as their surrogate mother? Did she still appear at their hatching, bending over to smile at them, letting them nip at her heels with their tiny teeth?

I wanted you to see this model of the laboratory. I want you to keep it in mind as we watch the next video. I want to know your thoughts.

Alma Patterson is walking down the hall following another woman whose back is to the camera. The woman, who has short, spiky blonde hair, pauses to punch a code next to a closed door, and they both enter. In the center of the room is a low pen, about knee high. A group of four or five raptors stand within in a huddle, but disperse as the humans stride into the room.

Alma says, "Okay, what exactly am I seeing?

The spiky blond moves offscreen. "Just watch. You'll see."

The camera zooms onto the raptors. They can no longer be considered chicks, but taller, lankier. They have shed their baby fuzz and now bear actual feathers colored muted browns and greens. Their tails are longer, and their arms are shorter, ending in claws. They appear almost as large as wild mature turkeys, albeit slenderer with longer snouts that split when they yawn, showing rows of sharp teeth.

The woman offscreen makes a chuffing sound. One of the raptors turns in a circle, flaps its arms almost as if it plans to take off in flight, then gives an odd squawk, something between a cough and a roar. The rest of the raptors watch, then perform the same action, right down to the odd squawk. The blond woman comes back into view, holding a sack. She dips her hand in and pulls out a handful of kibble, tossing it into the pen. The raptors scramble to gobble them up.

"That's a nice trick," Alma says.

The woman turns to her. There's a gold ring embedded in her right eyebrow, as well as in her right nostril. "But that's just it. I hadn't taught them that trick. I've asked the others, and no one has taught them how to do that. It's something we had taught the previous batch, but not this group."

Alma frowns, moving closer to the pen. "Wait, are you saying that this group 'remembered' this trick even though you hadn't taught it to them yet? That can't be. They must have learned it another way."

"I can get you the printout of all the tests we've done so far."

"Do that."

Let's freeze the video here. See Alma looking down at the raptors. The pen's walls come up to their necks, but they've made no move to jump over the pen's walls, so Alma doesn't consider them as a threat. Yet.

The raptors don't consider Alma a threat either. Look at them, cocking their heads to peer at Alma. Are they hoping she would give them more food? Do they remember her being at their hatching?

Ah, you're right. Not all of them are looking at her.

That one. In the back. It's not watching Alma.

It's watching the blond woman enter the code to leave the room. It's *watching* her.

This next item is just a scrap, I'm afraid. But I estimate this one took place a few weeks after the last video I showed you.

Grad Student in Hospital After Raptor Attack

Portland, Oregon. 26-year-old Nicki Ramirez was taken to the hospital today after being mauled by one of the raptors in the Raptor Revivification Project. Ramirez had been serving on the project writing a thesis on how the raptors could be trained to do certain tasks when one of the raptors attacked her, clawing at her chest and arms while biting her in the face. The project is being put on hold--

It was called an accident. It happens. Grad students back then worked long eighteen-hour shifts. Things can get forgotten or lax. Procedures that are meant to be followed strictly can start to loosen up. There's a drift in morals and ethics. Standards begin to loosen. Flasks aren't put up and cleaned right away. Hands are left unwashed. A grad student forgets to close a door behind her.

Alma posted a video about it:

Alma collapses in her chair in her office. A smear of blood streaks across the right half of her t-shirt. She drags her hand across the top of her head. "Well, that was a fucking train wreck."

She sits up straighter, shifting the camera in her hand. "I had to argue to keep this raptor alive because it attacked Nicki. This had been the longest one to survive yet—three months, two weeks. The others sickened and died last week. He was the only one left. I argued that it would be useless to kill him if he was to die anyway.

"We're still not sure how that raptor was able to get out of its cage. All the cages were locked as well as the door to the raptor room. We're sure of it. And yet, somehow, the raptor got out and headed into the laboratory. How did it know how to head there?"

She stares at the camera, wide-eyed, as if it would give her answers. It doesn't.

This one takes place the next day.

The video jumps and jerks as it rushes down a hallway. Footsteps pound on the tiled floor. Occasionally, the camera swings to show the Alma's back and head, her lab coat flapping as she runs.

Off camera, a male voice cuts in midsentence, "—wouldn't have bothered, but this was so strange, I had to get you."

Alma huffs, "You did the right thing."

They run into the raptor cage room. There are other people gathered around, looking down at one of the cages. Alma pushes her way through. The camera swings over shoulders and nudges aside heads and backs until it zooms down to show the face of the cage.

Alma squats down, pressing her hand to her mouth. After a moment, she speaks, "When did this happen?"

Someone replies, "Last night. Riley found it. It was their turn to clean the cages."

Inside the cage, a long, wet brown log lies on cage's floor. It's as big as one of the raptors, slick and glistening with wetness. Parts of it inflate, then relax. It looks like something took a long dump right in the cage.

The raptor that is supposed to be in the cage is nowhere to be seen.

Someone off camera mutters, "That looks like a mucus shell we found the salamanders in."

Someone else: "But there's no evidence that the raptors have this ability. Is this a hidden trait or is it something else?"

Alma stares at it for a long time before saying, "This is the raptor that attacked Nicki yesterday." She hadn't asked it as a question, but there are some murmurs of agreement among the group. Alma rubs her brow, then rises. When she looks at them, her expression is hard. "All right, I want this cage to be quarantined. Put a twenty-four-hour watch on it. And someone needs to go contact the hospital so that Nicki gets observed as well. Do it now."

She pushes forward, and as she does, a thought occurs to her. "And someone get me a DNA sample on those salamanders," she barks. "I need to see—" She looks directly at the camera, and her expression changes. "From here on out, no more video logs."

Her hand fills the view until the camera shakes, then shuts off.

I'm freezing it just before she shuts off the camera. See how her brow bunches together? See how there's steely resolution in her gaze? I believe it is right here, at this moment, that she started to suspect what was going on. She can't articulate what's unsettling her; it's just a vague uneasiness in her mind right now.

I love this moment, right here. Because this is when Alma Peterson began to change her mind about the raptors.

Unfortunately, I have no record of what was in that mucus shell, nor do we have anything to show what tests were done to it, or what happened to it.

What I can tell you is that a few days after that incident, Alma Peterson tried to shut the whole project down. We know that she had written a proposal to her supervisor to halt the research and store the eggs away until a larger facility with better resources was found.

We also have a death notice here of that grad student, Nicki, who died of her injuries a week after the mauling.

Was Alma successful in halting the project? Well, take a look at this document and decide for yourself.

The Expansion of the Raptor Revivification Project

Press Release

Today, the UO Departments of Paleontology and Genetics announced a new program that will allow their laboratory to expand their Raptor Revivification Project to sixty laboratories across the United States. The project had initially been under scrutiny after a grad student was injured by one of the revived raptors last fall. The head of the department promised that steps had been taken to insure it wouldn't happen again.

"This is a huge victory for science," Professor Michael Rooks announced. "We are honored that our program is able to expand in this way, thanks to a generous grant from several donors: The I.O Foundation; The Estate of Reginald P. Oswald…"

You can read the whole release for yourself. Notice it doesn't mention the dead grad student or Alma Peterson trying to stop the project.

And now, my so-called creme de la crop, to use to the old expression. I have here a recording not of Alma, but of own her supervisor, Michael Rooks. It is audio only, and there are some places were the data was corrupted, but this is the rarest find of my collection.

Is this on? You'll make sure every last word of this gets on the interview. Yes. Thank you. I appreciate it.

Sad thing about Alma. But she never had what it takes.

Of course I took her concerns into consideration. I'm not that much of a bastard. But to be truly honest, Alma grew too cautious, pure and simple. I mean, listen to this (papers rustling). "More intelligent than we thought?

Further experiments could result in a catastrophe that threaten the human race?" All of this is just paranoid pap.

(—static for ninety seconds—)

...sorry she died, but she knew the risks! They all did. It's why we had them sign the waiver...

(—static for two minutes forty seconds—)

...even utilized that raptor that created that shell around itself. The higher ups loved that shit. They weren't going to shut us down just because one little girl got bit up or some raptor was acting like a butterfly. This was the very nature of scientific discovery. Suddenly, everyone wanted a raptor of their own. Schools we hadn't even heard of were sending us emails, begging for a raptor egg of their own. We had no choice but to share. For research purposes, of course.

Of course Alma was upset. But being a scientist means taking risks. Risks get you grant money, and grant money gets you prestige. Something that Alma would not know anything about. I mean, let's face it. She's been stuck as a lead lab technician for fifteen years. Yes, she's applied to other places, but...let's just say her temperament wasn't a good fit. Frankly, all she's really good for is pushing around the grad students and washing out the glass—

(—static for twenty seconds—)

Look, we know that the raptors are intelligent. We all knew. The other labs will find out in due time and they could handle it their own way. Nobody would've wanted the raptors if they were too smart for their own good. If money said that the raptors are dumb, then those raptors are dumb.

"If money said that the raptors are dumb, then those raptors are dumb." I love that line! Sometimes I rewind it and play it for hours. Cracks me up, every time.

I have one more video to show you from Alma. Yes, yes, she had said that she wasn't going to do any more logs. But that's not true.

She made this one a few hours after the press release, and we have verified that this is the very last log she made. You'll want to pay close attention to this one.

Camera shakes, focuses on Alma sitting down in usual spot in her office. Her clothes are rumpled and there are dark circles under her eyes.

"So they're ignoring everything and going ahead with the plan. Sixty laboratories. After what happened to Nicki. Christ. How can he even live with himself?"

She stares off-camera as if she cannot muster the energy to talk. She throws her shoulders back, gazes up at the ceiling, but no answers are up there, either.

"They've taken the last raptor. Won't tell me where it's being held. They're going to let it hatch to see if it's going through some metamorphosis. If so, it's the first evidence of a dinosaur going through such a phase. But they don't get it."

Alma looks back at the camera, her breath growing shallow, her words tumbling out. "I got the results back from the salamanders. The DNA came back as raptor. Those weren't salamanders that had swallowed those eggs. Those were the raptors themselves that looked like salamanders." *Her breathing quickens.* "How did that happen? How were the raptors able to change their appearance like that? God, I've opened Pandora's Box, and I don't know how to put it back. It's as if the raptors did what we did with the chicken eggs, stripped them of their DNA—"

She breaks off, slowly straightens, levels her gaze at the camera, her lips part, eyes growing wide and round.

Ah. Here. See? See? This is where she makes the true connection.

"Wait a minute. Wait. What if that's it? What if the raptors can do that? What if they have the ability to alter their own DNA?"

Ah, she's got it now. She's getting up, the idea is too momentous for her. She walks out of frame, comes back in. She's spitting out words faster now, idea connecting to neuron connecting to idea.

"It would be easy for them to get a hold of it. One misplaced beaker. Someone who didn't wash their hands for the required minute. Blood from…a…bite."

She's frozen in place, facing the camera, mouth a perfect "o."

The camera cuts off here, but we all know what happened two days after that. The explosion. The arrest. The trial. The conviction. And the unanswered question: was she right?

Let's look back at the conviction. See Alma standing in front of the prosecution podium, dressed in gray scrubs, hands cuffed in front of her, though this is really unnecessary. Watch her posture as the judge reads the jury's verdict. It's stiff, upright.

Here is the ruling: *you have been found guilty of firebombing private property and destroying years of research. This court sentences you to fifty years in prison.*

There. See that? See how she slumps? One would think that she was defeated. We see the guards next to her, holding her up by her shoulders. They're turning her around. Watch as the guards lead her out of the courtroom by the arms.

Look at her face.

Look at her smile.

That's not resignation, or devastation.

That's a smile of *relief.*

I'm not surprised. After all, she was the one who gave us the words for what we were doing a molecular level, below conscious thought.

Our ancestors knew that there was more to survival than just laying eggs and hoping they survived. They knew, they *knew*, that they needed to adapt. It took generations upon generations for us to learn the skills we needed. We always adapted our traits from other animals. We devoured them, then used the DNA in their blood to transform ourselves to adapt to our environment.

Feathers from birds to warm ourselves and to give some of us flight. The mucus from salamanders when we had no food, and so to bury ourselves—and our children—until the time was right for us to emerge again. We've also always had a very strong genetic memory. It enabled us to remember these traits, even if our bodies were dead. Our very cells remembered our lives.

And now, we had access to human DNA. Ah, they evolved so much while we slept. Those paleontologists didn't know they were doomed as soon as they unearthed those eggs. And when our first ancestor awoke from his mucus shell and touched his new skin, cleared his vocal cords, and stood on his own bare feet, why yes, it did doom the human race as we knew it.

Oh, Alma, Alma, our mother, our life-giver. You tried to warn them. Even blew up the laboratory to try to destroy us. We don't fault you for that. After all, you were only trying to preserve your own DNA. You did not know how quickly we would learn how to adapt.

It is true, we do feel sad for Nicki Ramirez's sacrifice. It took us a while to learn how to take DNA without killing the host.

Our ancestors wreaked so much havoc those days. The humans did not realize how quickly we would grow, left on our own. We found prey so easily. And as we changed our forms, we learned to insinuate ourselves amongst humans, so eventually they couldn't even tell what we were. Not until it was too late. We should feel sorry for them. They handed us the keys to their own demise.

I do have one more video. This is more a recreation than actual fact. Wistful thinking on my part.

Here is Alma sitting in her cell. Here she is, insulated behind stone walls, which are her prison...and her protection. She was smart, wasn't she? She knew the dawn of raptors was about to rise, and so she placed herself behind bars so we wouldn't get to her. It didn't work, but it was smart.

See her, her legs drawn up. Holding herself tight.

See her hunch her shoulders as she starts to hear fighting in the hallway around her. Fights are common, but this one seems more brutal. There are more screams, more savage howls. And guttural chewing sounds, so out of place in a prison cell.

See her turn her head to look upon several bipedal forms hunching towards her cell. Walking without a tail was a new thing for our ancestors. They could walk upright, but tended to hunch, as if still growing used to having straight spines.

See her stare at the form of Nicki Ramirez, naked, but feathers where her hair should be, feather bright gold, shimmery brown. See her elongated mouth stretch, wide, wide, wide, showing too many rows of teeth, stained with blood.

See? We never forgot that it was Alma who taught us how to smile.

— JUST LIKE OLD TIMES —
by Robert J. Sawyer

The transference went smoothly, like a scalpel slicing into skin.

Cohen was simultaneously excited and disappointed. He was thrilled to be here—perhaps the judge was right, perhaps this was indeed where he really belonged. But the gleaming edge was taken off that thrill because it wasn't accompanied by the usual physiological signs of excitement: no sweaty palms, no racing heart, no rapid breathing. Oh, there was a heartbeat, to be sure, thundering in the background, but it wasn't Cohen's.

It was the dinosaur's.

Everything was the dinosaur's: Cohen saw the world now through tyrannosaur eyes.

The colors seemed all wrong. Surely plant leaves must be the same chlorophyll green here in the Mesozoic, but the dinosaur saw them as navy blue. The sky was lavender; the dirt underfoot ash gray.

Old bones had different cones, thought Cohen. Well, he could get used to it. After all, he had no choice. He would finish his life as an observer inside this tyrannosaur's mind. He'd see what the beast saw, hear what it heard, feel what it felt. He wouldn't be able to control its movements, they had said, but he would be able to experience every sensation.

The rex was marching forward.

Cohen hoped blood would still look red.

It wouldn't be the same if it wasn't red.

"And what, Ms. Cohen, did your husband say before he left your house on the night in question?"

"He said he was going out to hunt humans. But I thought he was making a joke."

"No interpretations, please, Ms. Cohen. Just repeat for the court as precisely as you remember it, exactly what your husband said."

"He said, 'I'm going out to hunt humans.'"

"Thank you, Ms. Cohen. That concludes the Crown's case, my lady."

The needlepoint on the wall of the Honorable Madam Justice Amanda Hoskins's chambers had been made for her by her husband. It was one of her favorite verses from *The Mikado,* and as she was preparing sentencing she would often look up and re-read the words:

> *My object all sublime*
> *I shall achieve in time—*
> *To let the punishment fit the crime—*
> *The punishment fit the crime.*

This was a difficult case, a horrible case. Judge Hoskins continued to think.

It wasn't just colors that were wrong. The view from inside the tyrannosaur's skull was different in other ways, too.

The tyrannosaur had only partial stereoscopic vision. There was an area in the center of Cohen's field of view that showed true depth perception. But because the beast was somewhat wall-eyed, it had a much wider panorama than normal for a human, a kind of saurian Cinemascope covering 270 degrees.

The wide-angle view panned back and forth as the tyrannosaur scanned along the horizon.

Scanning for prey.

Scanning for something to kill.

The Calgary Herald, Thursday, October 16, 2042: Serial killer Rudolph Cohen, 43, was sentenced to death yesterday.

Formerly a prominent member of the Alberta College of Physicians and Surgeons, Dr. Cohen was convicted in August of thirty-seven counts of first-degree murder.

In chilling testimony, Cohen had admitted, without any signs of remorse, to having terrorized each of his victims for hours before slitting their throats with surgical implements.

This is the first time in eighty years that the death penalty has been ordered in this country.

In passing sentence, Madam Justice Amanda Hoskins observed that Cohen was "the most cold-blooded and brutal killer to have stalked Canada's prairies since *Tyrannosaurus rex*..."

From behind a stand of dawn redwoods about ten meters away, a second tyrannosaur appeared. Cohen suspected tyrannosaurs might be fiercely territorial, since each animal would require huge amounts of meat. He wondered if the beast he was in would attack the other individual.

His dinosaur tilted its head to look at the second rex, which was standing in profile. But as it did so, almost all of the dino's mental picture dissolved into a white void, as if when concentrating on details the beast's tiny brain simply lost track of the big picture.

At first Cohen thought his rex was looking at the other dinosaur's head, but soon the top of the other's skull, the tip of its muzzle and the back of its powerful neck faded away into snowy nothingness. All that was left was a picture of the throat. Good, thought Cohen. One shearing bite there could kill the animal.

The skin of the other's throat appeared gray-green, and the throat itself was smooth. Maddeningly, Cohen's rex did not attack. Rather, it simply swiveled its head and looked out at the horizon again.

In a flash of insight, Cohen realized what had happened. Other kids in his neighborhood had had pet dogs or cats. He'd had lizards and snakes—cold-blooded carnivores, a fact to which expert psychological witnesses had attached great weight. Some kinds of male lizards had dewlap sacks hanging from their necks. The rex he was in—a male, the Tyrrell paleontologists had believed—had looked at this other one and seen that she was smooth-throated and therefore a female. Something to be mated with, perhaps, rather than to attack.

Perhaps they would mate soon. Cohen had never orgasmed except during the act of killing. He wondered what it would feel like.

"We spent a billion dollars developing time travel, and now you tell me the system is useless?"

"Well—"

"That is what you're saying, isn't it, professor? That chronotransference has no practical applications?"

"Not exactly, Minister. The system *does* work. We can project a human being's consciousness back in time, superimposing his or her mind overtop of that of someone who lived in the past."

"With no way to sever the link. *Wonderful.*"

"That's not true. The link severs automatically."

"Right. When the historical person you've transferred consciousness into dies, the link is broken."

"Precisely."

"And then the person from our time whose consciousness you've transferred back dies as well."

"I admit that's an unfortunate consequence of linking two brains so closely."

"So I'm right! This whole damn chronotransference thing is useless."

"Oh, not at all, Minister. In fact, I think I've got the perfect application for it."

The rex marched along. Although Cohen's attention had first been arrested by the beast's vision, he slowly became aware of its other senses, too. He could hear the sounds of the rex's footfalls, of twigs and vegetation being crushed, of birds or pterosaurs singing, and, underneath it all, the relentless drone of insects. Still, all the sounds were dull and low; the rex's simple ears were incapable of picking up high-pitched noises, and what sounds they did detect were discerned without richness. Cohen knew the late Cretaceous must have been a symphony of varied tone, but it was as if he was listening to it through earmuffs.

The rex continued along, still searching. Cohen became aware of several more impressions of the world both inside and out, including hot afternoon sun beating down on him and a hungry gnawing in the beast's belly.

Food.

It was the closest thing to a coherent thought that he'd yet detected from the animal, a mental picture of bolts of meat going down its gullet.

Food.

The Social Services Preservation Act of 2022: Canada is built upon the principle of the Social Safety Net, a series of entitlements and programs designed to ensure a high standard of living for every citizen. However, ever-increasing life expectancies coupled with constant lowering of the mandatory retirement age have placed an untenable burden on our social-welfare system and, in particular, its cornerstone program of universal health care. With most taxpayers ceasing to work at the age of 45, and with average Canadians living to be 94 (males) or 97 (females), the system is in danger of complete collapse. Accordingly, all social programs will henceforth be available only to those below the age of 60, with one exception: all Canadians, regardless of age, may take advantage, at no charge to themselves, of government-sponsored euthanasia through chronotransference.

There! Up ahead! Something moving! Big, whatever it was: an indistinct outline only intermittently visible behind a small knot of fir trees.

A quadruped of some sort, its back to him/it/them.

Ah, there. Turning now. Peripheral vision dissolving into albino nothingness as the rex concentrated on the head.

Three horns.

Triceratops.

Glorious! Cohen had spent hours as a boy poring over books about dinosaurs, looking for scenes of carnage. No battles were better than those in which *Tyrannosaurus rex* squared off against *Triceratops*, a four-footed Mesozoic tank with a trio of horns projecting from its face and a shield of bone rising from the back of its skull to protect the neck.

And yet, the rex marched on.

No, thought Cohen. Turn, damn you! Turn and attack!

Cohen remembered when it had all begun, that fateful day so many years ago, so many years from now. It should have been a routine operation. The patient had supposedly been prepped properly. Cohen brought his scalpel down toward the abdomen, then, with a steady hand, sliced into the skin. The patient gasped. It had been a *wonderful* sound, a beautiful sound.

Not enough gas. The anesthetist hurried to make an adjustment. Cohen knew he had to hear that sound again. He had to.

The tyrannosaur continued forward. Cohen couldn't see its legs, but he could feel them moving. Left, right, up, down.

Attack, you bastard!

Left.

Attack!

Right.

Go after it!

Up.

Go after the *Triceratops*.

Dow—

The beast hesitated, its left leg still in the air, balancing briefly on one foot.

Attack!

Attack!

And then, at last, the rex changed course. The ceratopsian appeared in the three-dimensional central part of the tyrannosaur's field of view, like a target at the end of a gun sight.

"Welcome to the Chronotransference Institute. If I can just see your government benefits card, please? Yup, there's always a last time for everything, heh heh. Now, I'm sure you want an exciting death. The problem is finding somebody interesting who hasn't been used yet. See, we can only ever superimpose one mind onto a given historical personage. All the really obvious ones have been done already, I'm afraid. We still get about a dozen calls a week asking for Jack Kennedy, but he was one of the first to go, so to speak. If I may make a suggestion, though, we've got thousands of Roman legion officers cataloged. Those tend to be very satisfying deaths. How about a nice something from the Gallic Wars?"

The *Triceratops* looked up, its giant head lifting from the wide flat gunnera leaves it had been chewing on. Now that the rex had focused on the plant-eater, it seemed to commit itself.

The tyrannosaur charged.

The hornface was sideways to the rex. It began to turn, to bring its armored head to bear.

The horizon bounced wildly as the rex ran. Cohen could hear the thing's heart thundering loudly, rapidly, a barrage of muscular gunfire.

The *Triceratops*, still completing its turn, opened its parrot-like beak, but no sound came out.

Giant strides closed the distance between the two animals. Cohen felt the rex's jaws opening wide, wider still, mandibles popping from their sockets.

The jaws slammed shut on the hornface's back, over the shoulders. Cohen saw two of the rex's own teeth fly into view, knocked out by the impact.

The taste of hot blood, surging out of the wound…

The rex pulled back for another bite.

The *Triceratops* finally got its head swung around. It surged forward, the long spear over its left eye piercing into the rex's leg…

Pain. Exquisite, beautiful pain.

The rex roared. Cohen heard it twice, once reverberating within the animal's own skull, a second time echoing back from distant hills. A flock of silver-furred pterosaurs took to the air. Cohen saw them fade from view as the dinosaur's simple mind shut them out of the display. Irrelevant distractions.

The *Triceratops* pulled back, the horn withdrawing from the rex's flesh.

Blood, Cohen was delighted to see, still looked red.

"If Judge Hoskins had ordered the electric chair," said Axworthy, Cohen's lawyer, "we could have fought that on Charter grounds. Cruel and unusual punishment, and all that. But she's authorized full access to the chronotransference euthanasia program for you." Axworthy paused. "She said, bluntly, that she simply wants you dead."

"How thoughtful of her," said Cohen.

Axworthy ignored that. "I'm sure I can get you anything you want," he said. "Who would you like to be transferred into?"

"Not who," said Cohen. "What."

"I beg your pardon?"

"That damned judge said I was the most cold-blooded killer to stalk the Alberta landscape since *Tyrannosaurus rex*." Cohen shook his head. "The idiot. Doesn't she know dinosaurs were warm-blooded? Anyway, that's what I want. I want to be transferred into a *T. rex*."

"You're kidding."

"Kidding is not my forte, John. *Killing* is. I want to know which was better at it, me or the rex."

"I don't even know if they can do that kind of thing," said Axworthy.

"Find out, damn you. What the hell am I paying you for?"

The rex danced to the side, moving with surprising agility for a creature of its bulk, and once again it brought its terrible jaws down on the ceratopsian's shoulder. The plant-eater was hemorrhaging at an incredible rate, as though a thousand sacrifices had been performed on the altar of its back.

The *Triceratops* tried to lunge forward, but it was weakening quickly. The tyrannosaur, crafty in its own way despite its trifling intellect, simply retreated a dozen giant paces. The hornface took one tentative step toward it, and then another, and, with great and ponderous effort, one more. But then the dinosaurian tank teetered and, eyelids slowly closing, collapsed on its side. Cohen was briefly startled, then thrilled, to hear it fall to the ground with a *splash*—he hadn't realized just how much blood had poured out of the great rent the rex had made in the beast's back.

The tyrannosaur moved in, lifting its left leg up and then smashing it down on the *Triceratops*'s belly, the three sharp toe claws tearing open the thing's abdomen, entrails spilling out into the harsh sunlight. Cohen thought the rex would let out a victorious roar, but it didn't. It simply dipped its muzzle into the body cavity, and methodically began yanking out chunks of flesh.

Cohen was disappointed. The battle of the dinosaurs had been fun, the killing had been well engineered, and there had certainly been enough blood, but there was no *terror*. No sense that the *Triceratops* had been quivering with fear, no begging for mercy. No feeling of power, of control. Just dumb, mindless brutes moving in ways preprogrammed by their genes.

It wasn't enough. Not nearly enough.

Judge Hoskins looked across the desk in her chambers at the lawyer.

"A *Tyrannosaurus*, Mr. Axworthy? I was speaking figuratively."

"I understand that, my lady, but it was an appropriate observation, don't you think? I've contacted the Chronotransference people, who say they can do it, if they have a rex specimen to work from. They have to back-propagate from actual physical material in order to get a temporal fix."

Judge Hoskins was as unimpressed by scientific babble as she was by legal jargon. "Make your point, Mr. Axworthy."

"I called the Royal Tyrrell Museum of Paleontology in Drumheller and asked them about the *Tyrannosaurus* fossils available worldwide. Turns out there's only a handful of complete skeletons, but they were able to provide me with an annotated list, giving as much information as they could about the individual probable causes of death." He slid a thin plastic printout sheet across the judge's wide desk.

"Leave this with me, counsel. I'll get back to you."

Axworthy left, and Hoskins scanned the brief list. She then leaned back in her leather chair and began to read the needlepoint on her wall for the thousandth time:

My object all sublime
I shall achieve in time—

She read that line again, her lips moving slightly as she subvocalized the words: "I shall achieve *in time*..."

The judge turned back to the list of tyrannosaur finds. Ah, that one. Yes, that would be perfect. She pushed a button on her phone. "David, see if you can find Mr. Axworthy for me."

There had been a very unusual aspect to the *Triceratops* kill— an aspect that intrigued Cohen. Chronotransference had been performed countless times; it was one of the most popular forms of euthanasia. Sometimes the transferee's original body would give an ongoing commentary about what was going on, as if talking during sleep. It was clear from what they said that transferees couldn't exert any control over the bodies they were transferred into.

Indeed, the physicists had claimed any control was impossible. Chronotransference worked precisely because the transferee could exert no influence, and therefore was simply observing things that had already been observed. Since no new observations were being made, no quantum-mechanical distortions occurred. After all, said the physicists, if one could exert control, one could change the past. And that was impossible.

And yet, when Cohen had willed the rex to alter its course, it eventually had done so.

Could it be that the rex had so little brains that Cohen's thoughts *could* control the beast?

Madness. The ramifications were incredible.

Still...

He had to know if it was true. The rex was torpid, flopped on its belly, gorged on ceratopsian meat. It seemed prepared to lie here for a long time to come, enjoying the early evening breeze.

Get up, thought Cohen. *Get up, damn you!*

Nothing. No response.

Get up!

The rex's lower jaw was resting on the ground. Its upper jaw was lifted high, its mouth wide open. Tiny pterosaurs were flitting in and out of the open maw, their long needle-like beaks apparently yanking gobbets of hornface flesh from between the rex's curved teeth.

Get up, thought Cohen again. *Get up!*

The rex stirred.

Up!

The tyrannosaur used its tiny forelimbs to keep its torso from sliding forward as it pushed with its powerful legs until it was standing.

Forward, thought Cohen. *Forward!*

The beast's body felt different. Its belly was full to bursting.

Forward!

With ponderous steps, the rex began to march.

It was wonderful. To be in control again! Cohen felt the old thrill of the hunt.

And he knew exactly what he was looking for.

"Judge Hoskins says okay," said Axworthy. "She's authorized for you to be transferred into that new *T. rex* they've got right here in Alberta at the Tyrrell. It's a young adult, they say. Judging by the way the skeleton was found, the rex died falling, probably into a fissure. Both legs and the back were broken, but the skeleton remained almost completely articulated, suggesting that scavengers couldn't get at it. Unfortunately, the chronotransference people say that back-propagating that far into the past they can only plug you in a few hours before the accident occurred. But you'll get your wish: you're going to die as a tyrannosaur. Oh, and here are the books you asked for: a complete library on Cretaceous flora and fauna. You should have time to get through it all; the chronotransference people will need a couple of weeks to set up."

As the prehistoric evening turned to night, Cohen found what he had been looking for, cowering in some underbrush: large brown eyes, long, drawn-out face, and a lithe body covered in fur that, to the tyrannosaur's eyes, looked blue-brown.

A mammal. But not just any mammal. *Purgatorius*, the very first primate, known from Montana and Alberta from right at the end of the Cretaceous. A little guy, only about ten centimeters long, excluding its ratlike tail. Rare creatures, these days. Only a precious few.

The little furball could run quickly for its size, but a single step by the tyrannosaur equaled more than a hundred of the mammal's. There was no way it could escape.

The rex leaned in close, and Cohen saw the furball's face, the nearest thing there would be to a human face for another sixty million years. The animal's eyes went wide in terror.

Naked, raw fear.

Mammalian fear.

Cohen saw the creature scream.

Heard it scream.

It was beautiful.

The rex moved its gaping jaws in toward the little mammal, drawing in breath with such force that it sucked the creature into its maw. Normally the rex would swallow its meals whole, but Cohen prevented the beast from doing that. Instead, he simply had it stand still, with the little primate running around, terrified, inside the great cavern of the dinosaur's mouth, banging into the giant teeth and great fleshy walls, and skittering over the massive, dry tongue.

Cohen savored the terrified squealing. He wallowed in the sensation of the animal, mad with fear, moving inside that living prison.

And at last, with a great, glorious release, Cohen put the animal out of its misery, allowing the rex to swallow it, the furball tickling as it slid down the giant's throat.

It was just like old times.

Just like hunting humans.

And then a wonderful thought occurred to Cohen. Why, if he killed enough of these little screaming balls of fur, they wouldn't have any descendants. There wouldn't ever be any *Homo sapiens*. In a very real sense, Cohen realized he *was* hunting humans—every single human being who would ever exist.

Of course, a few hours wouldn't be enough time to kill many of them. Judge Hoskins no doubt thought it was wonderfully poetic justice, or she wouldn't have allowed the transfer: sending him back to fall into the pit, damned.

Stupid judge. Why, now that he could control the beast, there was no way he was going to let it die young. He'd just—

There it was. The fissure, a long gash in the earth, with a crumbling edge. Damn, it *was* hard to see. The shadows cast by neighboring trees made a confusing gridwork on the ground that obscured the ragged opening. No wonder the dull-witted rex had missed seeing it until it was too late.

But not this time.

Turn left, thought Cohen.

Left.

His rex obeyed.

He'd avoid this particular area in future, just to be on the safe side. Besides, there was plenty of territory to cover. Fortunately, this was a young rex—a juvenile. There would be decades in which to continue his very special hunt. Cohen was sure that Axworthy knew his stuff: once it became apparent that the link had lasted longer than a few hours, he'd keep any attempt to pull the plug tied up in the courts for years.

Cohen felt the old pressure building in himself, and in the rex. The tyrannosaur marched on.

This was *better* than old times, he thought. Much better.

Hunting all of humanity.

The release would be *wonderful*.

He watched intently for any sign of movement in the underbrush.

— THE DAY —
by August Hahn

R ed and wet, the day began.

He looked up from his feast to watch the sky as the dark hues brightened with the rising sun. Blue was coming, and the shadows would soon depart. Hunting was easier when the world awakened, but there were more dangers for the same reason. The grey hours were the best time for him, when he could stalk and hide with ease.

He could feel the heat on his skin, the warmth that came with the brighter light. The nests would need him soon, just as they would the remains of his kill. He took another satisfying bite and swallowed as much meat as he could, biting through the thinner bones and pulling his meal free of the few he could not break. Old and slow, the huge beast beneath his claws would feed many today.

For that to happen, he would need to bring its flesh back to prove to the others the run was worth making. This plate-back fell near the very edge of what the pack would consider its hunting territory, after all. Making a trek out here would be worth it for so much meat, but getting here meant crossing a blood path, a trail that his pack had always avoided.

Hunger had brought him out this far, convinced him to brave the path for the promise of a meal. The kill had been sweet and filling, but now he could see how it might be best to abandon the massive body rather than bring the others here. Hunting had been sparse this season, but the pack would suffer if they came with him to claim this carcass and ran afoul of the great death that walked this blood path as its own.

And yet, the nests needed this food. The season had been hard, harsher than any before. Without flesh, the young would wither and die. The sentinels were too hungry to guard them, and the warriors were growing weaker. A feast like this could be life or death for his brood. The dead beast was in a concealed place, huddled in the shelter of thick tree canopy and far from water. Perhaps it had known it was time to die.

For the good of the pack, he had to try. The body would be safe from discovery here, even by the master of this trail, but something would eventually come across it. He needed to be swift. With a mouth full of muscle, fighting the primal urge to consume it, he set off back towards the nests as fast as his long-clawed feet could run.

Morning was his favorite time to run. The day was not yet too hot, and the night was no longer too cold. Sunlight, thin and still pale, drew patterns of leaves across him as he stretched his long, powerful legs and rushed across the thick patches of grass and moss. Green and grey went past as equal blurs under the sweeping reach of the trees above. On a full day, when the pack was not so desperate, he could be content to just explore. No matter how many times he stalked this forest, there were always new things to find.

New things to hunt. Every season brought creatures from other territories to the land around the nests. Some were too big to take down alone, but that was why the pack was strength. Numbers were life. Taking down a tall neck or one of the many-horns was a challenge he needed his clutch mates to overcome. When the great walkers came down from the mountains or up from the dry plateau, it felt good to take them down with the screeches of the pack around him.

Most of the time, the prey here was easy enough to kill alone. Some were small, others slow, but they all went down to talons across the belly and teeth at their throats. Red and wet, they all died the same. There were differences, of course. The packs of little run-biters could be tricky, especially when they were clever enough to scatter when he chased them. Often, he would catch one or two before their herd darted out of sight in every direction. The chase was rarely worth the meal when that happened, so he usually ignored them. It was a hard-learned lesson—mercy—but he knew there was no wisdom in burning more energy than he gained in a hunt.

Kill more than you eat: that is the truth of a predator.

Today, he had done exactly that. Running with proof of the kill in his mouth, he made his way through the dense overgrowth towards home. With the blood path at his back now, the way forward should be safe enough. There were no killers in this place that could contend with him. Those that could were long gone from the territory, either driven off or gone in search of easier prey. That was the way of things here, something the nests would have to contend with soon as well.

That made this massive kill even more important. The pack would need to move on to better hunt-lands soon. The plate-back's meat could be the fuel needed to see them through such a journey. It was never easy to give up territory, especially with dangers like the roaring ones or the spined terrors that prowled in the dark edges of their world. Just one of those could take down a whole pack. Hunger was already gnawing at the strength of the others.

Weakened and slowed, the pack warriors could not safeguard the young against such threats.

Being well-fed would improve his chances and, by his strength, the chances of the pack. This was worth the risk. There was no other way. Survival required death and life, killing and eating so that those fresh from the egg could grow to defend the next move. This was his turn, and he was not going to fail.

As he ran, trying to ignore the delicious blood in his mouth, he began to hear strange echoes. At first, he thought they might be sound of his feet tearing through the ground with each quick stride. But soon, he was certain the noises were something else. Feeling liquid life trickle down his muzzle, he suddenly understood.

The blood was leaving a trail, and something was following it. He was being chased, possibly just by scavengers. If that were the case, he could safely lead them all the way to the nests. His kin would be eager to deal with them for him. But what if his pursuer was not a scavenger? What if it was something more dangerous? He could be leading danger right to the nests! Without knowing for certain what was chasing him, the risk to the pack was too great. He would have to deal with this now, one way or another.

Breaking left, he sped up and tried to outrun his stalker. There were many trees here, some of which had fallen over in recent storms. Leaping some and dodging others, he moved with a quickness and grace born of growing desperation. His pursuer was still on his trail, unshaken and slowly gaining. If this pursuer's hunt would not be denied, only one choice remained.

Dashing behind a low hill, he carefully dropped the gobbet in his mouth and crouched low. Most big foes had to stoop to fight, but they ran with their upper bodies extended. Vulnerable. He preferred to leap on such foes from above, where he could use his long foot claws, arm talons, and fangs in a single, vicious blow.

This situation, this position, would not allow that. Instead, he would have to hope for a strike at his enemy's vitals from below.

Only a few seconds passed before the sound of his stalker turned from echoes to thunder. Rounding the hill, it revealed itself exactly the way he thought it would. Long and muscled thick, it was all teeth and body with short arms and huge, crushing legs. It was a king killer, huge but still young enough to chase its prey. Today, he was its prey.

If that were to be, he would not fall easily. He lurched upward, taking advantage of the single second of surprise he had. Like all its breed, his foe was vulnerable from its jaw to its thick breastbone just above its arms. They had little reach, which meant he got this one strike before the predator could force him away or lean down to bite him in half. He had to make this count!

His left set of talons hit thick skin and got little purchase. His right fared no better. His teeth, however, sank deep into the softest part of the young tyrant's throat. Similarly, his hooked toe claws both buried to the bone, anchoring him on its upper body. Wet and red, its flesh gave way.

None of it was a lethal strike, but all together they caused dire damage and made the king killer roar in agonized rage. Its bellow was fearsome, carrying past the trees, shaking the weakest of their leaves from their branches. Thrashing, it tried to shake him free, lashing with its forelimbs in a vain attempt to claw him off. He held fast, though its talons cut his legs and tail in several places.

All of it hurt; none of it mattered. Still locked against its body, he started thrashing of his own. Savaging the big beast's throat, he tore into it as much as he could. His feet were caught in its hide, but he could not do much more damage there. This battle, one way or the other, would begin and end with fangs.

A heavy impact against his back revealed that the tyrant was smart enough to use the forest to its advantage. Unable to dislodge him, it had decided to ram the nearest tree in the hopes of smashing him loose. When it happened again, he could feel the bones of his back scream in pain. Nothing was broken, but if this continued, everything would be.

His throat bites had done their work. There was too much neck for him to tear it out like this, but his foe was bleeding freely now. He could not stay on its chest, so he had to risk a climb. For a few moments, he would be unpinioned, but another tree strike would be the end of him. Pulling his hook claws free, he latched on again with all four limbs and made a desperate body run up the killer's side. If he could make it to its back…

The king killer was young but not stupid. It knew it was bleeding badly and a long fight would not end in its favor. As soon as it felt him making for its spine, it sideswiped the hill as hard as it could. A second faster and it would have pinned him to the unforgiving earth, but pain and injury slowed it just enough to let him scramble free.

Once on its back, he hooked in again and began slashing and biting wildly. None of these were meant to be killing strikes. Indeed, the back of a tyrant like this was almost impossible to injure in any fatal way. These wounds had only one purpose— pain. Keep the beast roaring. Keep it hurting. Make it run and thrash and fight, gushing from its throat the whole time.

For what felt like forever, suffering the constant buffets of trees and hillside, he clung on for dear life. If he were thrown, this king would be his killer. Even if it died afterward, it would breathe its last breath into the ruins of his body. He had to hang on tightly and ride it until blood loss achieved what his claw could not. At the height of its rampage, he pressed his body against its back and bit as deeply as its dense flesh would allow.

There he remained until his enemy finally crashed to the forest floor. He stayed still until he felt its chest stop heaving, until he heard its last low roar. Even in death, tyrants were all wrath and rage. Once it was completely still beneath him, he loosened his grip and staggered back onto the broken ground below. There was blood everywhere, its sweet stench filling his wide nostrils. It smelled like battle.

It smelled like survival. Much as he wanted to roll it on its side and devour its heart, survival was the reason it was here at all. This corpse would not last long out in the open forest, especially with the sound of their struggle likely alerting every creature from here to the river. But if only scavengers came first, as they usually did, the pack could chase them off. This day might have brought his kin two feasts, but only if he was quick, and if they agreed to follow him back.

Still, this kill was fresher than the last and the plate-back's meat was already turning sour. After tearing the tyrant's head off, he fled with it from the area as quickly as he could. He had two reasons to run now. One was the life of his pack, but the other was concern for his own. The young killer's claws had torn his legs open quite deeply in places. The damage was not severe, but they were open wounds, nonetheless. He was leaving a trail again, this time with his own blood. Most creatures out here would opt for a dead killer over a living one, but some might choose to chase him instead.

If that happened, he was not certain he would fare a second time as well. He was hurt enough to know that now was the time for flight, not fight.

He was not running as quickly as before, but he was still moving at the best speed he could. His legs hurt a little more with every step, but he had to make it back to the nest. There was too much at stake now. This was no longer about just the hunting. The young tyrant had dared to come this close to their territory to chase his blood trail, which could only mean that it had been out stalking prey nearby. If it had ranged so far from the usual run of the king killers, there could be others of its same group doing the same.

The borders were no longer holding. Enemies no longer respected the scent marks and clawed trees that displayed the nest's chosen ground. The one that attacked him was dead, but there could be more. As thin as the prey herds were becoming, there would be more. Competition for food meant making hard choices. The nests might have to move, hard as that might be for the oldest and the youngest.

They might even have to abandon the eggs.

Those choices were not his to make. He was a hunter, a seeker. He searched the green wilds for food and kept watch for trouble. Today he had found both. There would need to be a moot with the pack, and the scarred elders would decide what came next. That challenge was not something he had to face; he only had to submit to whatever choice they made.

The only obstacle he had to overcome now was the slow fatigue crawling up through his legs and the pain robbing him of his strength by degrees. He was still bleeding, though more slowly now. Once he was back with the pack, he could stop. Once he was back, he could rest.

He burst through the final line of marked trees and into the clearing before the nesting circles. These hills were usually watched by the sentinels of the pack, strong hunters who chose to stay at the heart of their territory and use their keen sight and smell to guard the others. They were not swift, like him, but they were strong enough to guard and smart enough to sense danger before it could threaten the pack. He had expected to see at least one of the at the trees' edge, but there was no one here. The hills were empty, a thing that should never be.

There could be only one reason why. Sentinels would never fail to guard from enemies without unless there was an enemy within. Something must have struck at the nests themselves! Had he been too far out to hear the shrieks for aid? Was he already too late?

Panic drove him to ignore his pain and run faster. He felt his skin tear along his flanks as he pushed himself too hard, but that did not matter now. He had to reach the inner clutch, where the eggs and mates would be sheltering in the pack's den, surrounded by every warrior and elder still capable of fighting. Usually, a full attack on their den was unthinkable, but the presence of the young killer he had fought filled him with a deep dread.

It would only have come here, even if it were chasing a blood scent, if it thought it would be safe in their territory. Why would it think that? Could it have known the guarding fangs and watchful eyes of the pack would be busy elsewhere?

With a long, angry hiss, he bounded over the hillock that should have been guarded and raced through a dark, rocky trench for home. Gone were all the worries about food and land. All that mattered was getting to the nests, to the young. They would be easy kills, trapped in the den warrens unable to flee. If their protectors fell, they would be meat for the slaughter. The tyrants would feast on all they could tear and swallow, and whatever was left would feed the scavengers before nightfall.

The moon would rise over their empty nests and gnawed bones. One exhausted, wounded hunter might not be able to make a difference. He might just be running to die with the rest, but that was the law of the pack. A life alone is no life at all.

He left the deep ravine and crested the final hill, every part of him aching and cold. What he saw below him chilled him even more. There were three king killers, two young like the one he'd taken down before. The other was nearly full grown, with deep scars down her sides and a bite-mark over her back-right flank. There were several new wounds as well, but those marks were older. They had nearly healed.

He knew what those were. Every tyrant he had ever seen encroaching on their territory had them, the signs of having been driven from home. Older killers always forced the young out after a certain age, pushing them away to find hunting grounds of their own. Most did not last long, brought down by smaller predators in groups or killed by the few things in this land bigger than them. They were solitary by nature, which made them weak, and usually stupid, which kept them that way.

But a rare few were born smart or made wiser through suffering and surviving long enough to learn from it. That is what he was looking at here—three tyrants who understood the law of the pack.

He saw dead kin all around them, his brother and sisters fighting and dying to keep the predators from the nests. All three of the huge beasts were bloody, but none of them had fallen. They had his tribe cornered and on the ground at their feet, where height and strength were king. His brothers and sisters would fall; the elders would be next, and the nests would follow them all into death.

He was only one hunter; how could he make any difference at all? Tired down to his bones, he let the tyrant's ragged head fall from his jaws. There was no sense carrying it now.

Or was there? If these monsters understood the law, perhaps they would also feel the same rage he did at the sight of his dying tribe. He barely had the strength to fight, but perhaps he still had the will to run. Arching back, he lifted his head and roared a challenge to the sky. The sound was sharp and harsh, like the hatred he felt, and it carried his intentions clearly.

Look at me. Look at your brother's head. **Look at what I have done.**

He leaned down and lifted the severed trophy in his mouth, letting the three of them see him weary but proud. He bore the scars of that fight and he smelled like blood, his and that of the tyrant in his teeth. Then, with a circular lash of his long tail, he rushed back over the hill and down into the trench again. He could hear the enraged thunder behind him. The king killers had gotten his message and were coming for him. Now.

He ran over the broken stones of the ravine, staying close to the wall closest to the nests. He felt weaker with every passing moment, but he did not have to go far. He only had to reach the middle, where all the tyrants could approach him at once. They were a pack; they would take him at the same time to be certain he was dead.

Sure enough, they entered the earth scar together, forced into a line by the narrow walls even as they approached the larger gap where he was waiting. The older one snarled at the others. They did mean to rush him as one, but she wanted the first wound, the true kill.

He was spent, too much blood lost getting home and too much more drained from him leading the predators away. He barely had the speed left to dodge the first lunge, but he did. He needed them in a group, facing each other, so he forced his sluggish body to evade the best he could. One hard smash forced him to the ground, but he rolled away before the big tyrant could take his belly with a bite. He stood and slashed, mocking his foe with a choked chortling bark.

That was more than the other two could take. They flanked in, just as he knew they would, and together they bit him savagely from all sides. He felt their teeth sink in over his back and tail, the pain forcing him to let go of the head in his teeth.

He watched it fall with no regrets. It was not the only message he had sent. Just as he ran down here, his tail swirl was a second signal, one to his surviving kin. The three tyrants might have become a pack, but they were not born to it. They had not grown with its lessons and learned from its instinct. Every gesture in the wild meant something, every sound a part of the hunt.

In this case, his tail had told his pack all they needed to know. It told them where to be and why. As the king killers pulled his body between them, fighting over who would end him first, his dying eyes saw his packs' shadows on the edge of the ravine above them. The tyrants were facing each other, and their mouths were full. Their backs were exposed.

As light and sound began to fade, he heard his kin screech as they came down, talons spread and teeth bared. They would kill. They would feast. The nests would be saved, and the young would be spared. He heard flesh rend and bones break. Not all of them were his.

Red and wet, the day ended.

— REBUTTAL —
by Andrew J Lucas

Upper Stikine River,
British Emancipated Territories,
2145 AD

Corporal Bruce MacKenzie scanned the gap with his binoculars, flipping through the instrument's full spectrum, but the picture remained the same. Whatever he had spotted moving along the valley floor wasn't there now, or was lying low—concealed from sight. He thumbed the binocular from thermal to geosync and recorded the location of the sighting. He would review the data later and scour it with a data miner before bedding down for the night. If there was anything captured in the scan, the base unit would draw it out and he could tag it into the area's map.

He slipped the sophisticated device into a reinforced leather pouch on his hip and turned back to his patrol.

I'm not the first ranger to start jumping at shadows, he thought, walking back to his horse, *and I won't be the last.*

MacKenzie was on the tail end of his patrol circuit, only a day or two out from the base. He'd be glad to be back at the enclave. The woods had always been his home, but lately they had felt strange—unsettling. He'd patrolled this stretch of the Rocky Mountains for going on twenty years and knew it better than almost anyone, but it had changed, changed so much.

A decade ago, the gradual effects of climate change had reached a crescendo; sweeping forest fires had purged much of the old growth pine and fir. Foreign breeds of larch and pine rose from the ashes of the elder forests displacing the mountains' natural woods. Even the shrubbery had changed, long feathery leaved ferns giving ground to broad rubbery leaved variants. It wasn't so much an evolution as an invasion.

And not the only one either.

"Anything?" Kyla asked, holding the reins of the pair's mounts. She didn't need to hold the animals' harnesses; Bruce knew she was only doing so out of nervousness. Bred from sturdy steppes mountain horses, neither horse was skittish by nature. Each was small, surefooted, and at home on the narrow trails carved into the rocky slopes.

Bruce walked to his mount, running a hand along the animal's flank to let it know he was there. It was never a good idea to come up on an animal unawares. Bruce had worked a summer on his uncle's farm in Saskatchewan and been kicked by foul tempered Holstein when he'd rushed milking duties. He'd never walked the same since, even after multiple surgeries to rebuild his knee. The injury hadn't precluded him from joining the Territory Ranger Corp., but had given him a cautiousness around animals that served him well.

"Easy Bill…" he whispered, stroking the slick hide of the horse, its long hair shaggy and matted with sweat. "It's been a long trail, but we're almost home."

"Come on Mac. What did you see?"

Mac He hated the nickname, but Kyla had latched onto it ever since she'd learnt that they called him that in boot camp. Usually it didn't bother him, but today it was getting on his last nerve.

"Don't call me that, Private Bohnet," he snapped, the sudden outburst causing Bill to take a step backwards.

Damn it. I know better than this. Kid's always needling me.

"Just tell me what you saw then."

"Nothing. There was nothing there." He wasn't so sure, but there was something uneasy about that valley. Something that put him on edge. Probably why he was taking it out on the kid. "At least nothing I could see."

He sighed, his temper subsiding as he looked at Kyla staring intently at the valley below. Her brow was furrowed in concentration, her eyes flitting nervously, searching the thick foliage for sign of anything out of place, movement, strange colors or glints of reflected light. She wasn't as comfortable in the woods as he was, but she always deferred to his knowledge and experience. Her speciality was in the unique ecology of the new Canada.

Kyla Bohnet was a geneticist provocateur, one of the new breed of scientists coming out of Queen's University. They roamed the country sampling the changing flora and fauna and determining the best way for the country to survive the changes inflicting it. It was serious, desperate work. He wondered what she was seeing as she scanned the woods for movement. Was she cataloging the invasive ferns that filled the underbrush now that the average temperature of area had risen 10 degrees over the last decade? Or imagining what animal she could insert into the ecology to help rebalance it?

"We should be going," he said, interrupting her reverie.

Bruce glanced down the embankment towards where he'd seen movement. He was sure he'd seen something, but now there was nothing. He mounted his horse.

"Just as well. This far into the Rockies it was probably just a moose or something," Kyla commented, getting on her own horse.

That made sense. It certainly could have been a moose; though Kyla probably didn't know it, Bruce hadn't seen a moose in this area for well over twenty years.

Moose weren't the only animals that had difficulty making the transition to the new century. The steady rise of global temperature from the early 2000s accelerated quickly up until the mid-century mark. Rising seas, global droughts, and the loss of coastlines were just the first most obvious effects. Humanity attempted to bolster its defenses, consolidate its resources into smaller, more robust ecosystems that could resist the sweeping changes taking place. For awhile it seemed like the developed nations of the world had the changes under control. Famine and mass starvation swept across third world nations. Costal nations suffered the worst effects; flooding, landslides, shattered economies, all drew resources that were needed elsewhere.

Meanwhile, the intricate web of life that millions of years of evolution had developed collapsed beneath the weight of unprecedented change. Wildfires ravaged arboreal and tropical rainforests alike, pushing the global ecology to the breaking point. Global resources were poured into the fight to reverse environmental collapse. At first, the efforts made real differences: hybrid energy sources, protecting of shared water sources, even draconian international laws protecting endangered species. The global slide towards extinction slowed, even stopped in some places.

The world rebounded, its resilience brought to the forefront by crisis.

Nevertheless, it was a temporary reprieve. The ice caps sloughed off the arctic tundra, long dormant viruses struggled free of the thawed peat. Bogs of ancient lifeforms bubbled, exposed to the sun of a new era. Plagues and sickness swept across the planet, focused on striking down all vertebrate life. Herds of caribou rotted as they carried the plagues south, where migratory birds and insects distributed them to every corner of the globe.

Climate change was just the precursor to the true extinction event.

Billions died in the first few years, before vaccines were developed to help humanity resist the protozoan microbes. However, there was no way to inoculate the entirety of nature. If billions of humans perished, the toll on the animal kingdom was in the trillions. Entire species were wiped from the Earth. Scientists tried to genesplice, engineer, and breed their way out of the crisis, but it seemed the plagues were drawn to the world's mammals.

Natural selection had groomed modern mammals to be uniquely susceptible to these viruses. Humankind was facing its own extinction level meteor, and it was microscopic. Most of the developed world had been inoculated against an array of viruses, however, there were challenges to vaccinating all, or in fact, any, of North America's struggling wildlife population, even if they could develop an effective vaccine. There were attempts to inoculate wildlife with engineered antiviral agents using mosquitos as delivery agents, but this produced only clumps of resistant populations—small oases of mammals struggling to survive.

Clearly a revolutionary approach was required, and through the use of quantum tunnelling microscopes to sample millions of year old DNA combined with the fractal computing technology to simulate the viability of a the partial DNA rebuilt from the samples, a solution was found. Genetic prospectors scavenged the planet and unearthed, figuratively AND literally, fossils and the scraps of DNA concealed within their stony bones.

It was here that desperate scientists found their solution and salvation. DNA that was resistant to the viral plague ravaging the planet. Humanity resurrected creatures that had walked the Earth millions of years ago to save their future.

Bruce urged his mount forward; whatever he'd seen or thought he'd seen hadn't exposed itself. Kyla had discounted his concerns as fatigue from a long patrol. He thought that was ironic coming from his trainee, but he couldn't discount the possibility. The patrol had been long, and its uneventfulness had proven more stressful than if they had found something. Border runners, water poachers, or even a Cascadia Military Command incursion were all events he knew how to deal with.

They had left the Rockies behind them and had a clear run to Cold Lake and a few days of R&R ahead of them. Once, the land had been flat rolling grasslands covered in fields of corn and wheat, broken by the odd low treed hill. Now only rugged shrubs and scrub grass covered the thin topsoil where the bedrock wasn't showing. Alberta had ridden the wave of climate catastrophe, and where the western provinces and states had a coastline and ranks of mountains to intercept the frequent storms and collect water from them, Alberta had none. The storms came, vaulting the Cascades and whipping across the plains with only blasting winds and heat. Only tough gene-engineered grasses survived. They were enough to maintain an ecology of sorts—but a tenuous one.

"Mac." She was still calling him that, no matter how many times he objected. Perhaps he needed to write her up when they got back to base. Obviously, his polite requests were falling on deaf ears. Perhaps an official reprimand would get her attention. "Mac!"

Bruce turned in his saddle, aggravation rapidly dissipating at the panic in Kyla's voice.

"What is it?"

Kyla had slowed her horse to a walk and was pulling her rifle out of the holster on her mount's flank. Bruce scanned the treeline in the distance, concentrating on the area she was pointing her weapon. At first, he couldn't see what had spooked her. Then, it broke through the trees, a massive conglomeration of scales, teeth, and feathers. Two tons of pure rage, molded by the coarse genetics of Russian science. Leathery hide fringed with downy feathers made its silhouette distinctly softer and harder to spot until it moved. It was bipedal with the short-clawed arms and massive jaws and skull of its genus, and terrifying. Here and there, the dull gray of mechanics pierced through the leather of the animal's skin, bolted on or jutting through from beneath, Bruce couldn't tell. The beast snorted and swept its meter long head back and forth, pulling air through its sinus cavity, questing for prey.

"Kyla! NO!" Bruce shouted but it was too late. The young Ranger had sighted in on the beast her weapon, scanning, tracking, and accommodating for the creature's movement. He couldn't see without enhancement, but he knew a pencil thin laser anticipated the trajectory of the .50 calibre round about to follow it. She squeezed the trigger.

The bullet passed along the ranked filed generators, alternately pulled and pushed by dozens of micro-magnetic fields exiting the barrel, with the deep thud as it passed transonic. The bullet traveled the distance between the two Rangers and the creature faster than the any eye could follow, but not faster than the small arms countermeasure unit strapped to the creature's back.

Small titanium pellets scattered by the unit evaporated into a fine mist as they intercepted the incoming round. They were relatively slow, barely a threat to any serious adversary, but they only had to get in the way of a fast round or rocket to cause a premature detonation. It had the added advantage of drawing the creature's attention.

The massive snout huffed out a lungful of air and turned towards the dissipating mist of the deployed countermeasures. It quested left and right, searching the plains for the threat its handlers had trained it for. The prey was always somewhere beyond the sharp metallic tang of that mist.

"Don't move. And for God's sake, stop shooting."

Kyla held herself stock still, balancing in her saddle, trying not to breathe, and kept her mount still, but it was too late. The creature let out a thundering warbling bellow and launched itself toward the pair.

"Go!" Bruce kicked his boots deep into his mounts flank. Kyla spun her own horse and fell into line beside him. She sheathed her rifle and looked at Bruce for guidance. She was pale, breathless with fear.

"A tyrannosaurus rex! Where the hell did a Rex come from?"

Bruce glanced over his shoulder and examined the monstrosity following them. It certainly looked like a T Rex, at least superficially. Its gait was firm, lacking the unevenness of previous Russian attempts at gene-engineering dinosaurs. A mouth full of daggers snapped and bellowed at him, eager to plunge into flesh. Patchy feathers sprouted between the armored scales, moving with the wind of its pursuit and the flex of its muscles. He knew from previous encounters during the last Russian incursion that the beast wasn't a true dinosaur—Russian technology wasn't up to the task of a full clone. Most likely, it was a mishmash of spliced genes combined with in vitro 3d printing to build on a genetic base.

"It's Y Rex I think."

"A what?"

"Yutyrannus huali. The Russian Republic acquired a partial genetic sample from a Chinese dig a few years ago. Rebuilt the genotype in a clutch of turtles as their base and filled the gaps in the DNA with whatever they could, supplementing the rest with titanium implants."

"That worked?"

The roar behind them was the only answer she received. It was closer, louder, more anticipation that rage. Bruce knew the beast wouldn't stop until it had torn the flesh from their bones. While it wasn't faster than a horse, its stamina would soon outstrip their mounts.

"Worked well enough," Bruce was convinced the creature was driven by rage alone, "We need to put some distance between us, lose it in the grasslands."

"How can we do that? My horse can't keep up this pace."

Bruce looked out over the plains searching for something. He grinned as he caught sight of what he was looking for. Maybe, just maybe, they could get out of this alive, if they could keep up the pace just a little longer.

"We need a distraction."

An hour later, the two Rangers were racing along a deep gully, searching for a way down into the dry riverbed below. Behind them the yutyrannus had closed the gap considerably and was showing no sign of fatigue. The Rangers' mounts, on the other hand, were sweating heavily, stumbling frequently as they galloped across the scrublands. Bubbles of foam accompanied their heavy snorting breaths. They were nearing exhaustion, and only fear of the creature on their heels kept them upright.

"Now what?" Kyla asked, almost as breathless as the horse she rode.

"We need to get across this gulch."

"How is that going to help? That thing is right on top of us!"

Bruce considered that. Considered what would happen if the horses stumbled and fell—when they fell. It was only a matter of time.

"Look, we get across that gap and hit the other side, and maybe that Y Rex can't get up the slope. Thing's got to be almost two tons. It's our only chance."

Kyla stared at him, desperate hope in her eyes warring with disbelief. Then she smiled.

"Okay, Mac! Let's do it." She kicked her heels hard into the ribs of her horse, launching it forward and down into the steep gully.

Bruce grimaced at the recklessness of his junior officer's headlong rush down the loose rocky slope.

"Don't call me Mac!" Bruce yelled, taking his own horse over the edge.

The steep ground gave way beneath the feet of his mount, its hooves struggling for traction and settling for a scrambling sliding gallop. The gravel surface was looser than he'd thought, but he managed to keep control of the horse, mainly by letting it run. Ahead Kyla had made her way to the river bottom safely, a moment later he was beside her.

"Now what?"

Bruce scanned the opposite of the gulley, looking for an escape route. There! The faint track of path, more of an indication or a possibility of a route out. Could they make it, or should they follow the river bottom to look for another, better path?

A roar behind took the decision out of their hands. The yutyrannus appeared on the edge of the gulch for a second, vaulting into the air and landing on the slope in a spray of gravel. Its two-meter long strides tore up rocky slope, piercing into the loose shale with its claws throwing it high into the air as it picked up speed.

"Go!" Bruce led Kyla towards the barely discernable path. They took it at full speed, scrambling up the path barely a few meters away from the Russian monstrosity. They slid and drove forward, sliding backwards just a little less than they progressed. Behind them, the yutyrannus made purchase with its vicious claws, even where there was none. Closer, ever closer.

Bruce pulled his rifle from his saddle sheath and fired a wild shot at the beast's head. It didn't flinch or turn aside, didn't even register the attack, so all-consuming was its bloodlust. But the countermeasures activated peppering the incoming round with pellets just as Bruce had hoped. The mist of powdered metal obscured the beast's vision just enough that its next stride was wobbly and misplaced.

It stumbled, not enough to fall, but enough that Kyla and Bruce made the edge before it did. Not to safety, but just far enough to keep out of the creature's jaws. They were, if not safe, at least marginally safer.

"What is that?" Kyla shouted, trying to pull her pulling her horse to a panicked halt, but it barely slowed.

"Keep going! Trust me!"

Ahead of them were what looked like a collection of low hills, dull brown and lumpy. Perhaps the result of a rough and ill-advised mining endeavor, trailings from a small strip mine long abandoned. But the hills were moving, and as the Rangers approached at full speed, they resolved into the squat forms of ankylosaurs. Canadian engineered and bred from a pristine specimen unearthed outside of Drumheller, the beasts were nearly 90% original genome. Over thirty feet and six tons of boney plated armor compressed to the height or a man. As massive as they were, Bruce couldn't help but feel they looked short and squat.

They were not fast beasts, and the two Rangers were soon passing between the massive animals. Ankylosaurs were intimidating tanks of muscle and bone, all thick scale from their hooked parrot like beak to the swinging club of fused bone that was their tail. The hot rugged Albertan grasslands were perfect for the dinosaurs, whose metabolism could digest anything, and whose large vascular system imbedded in their thick hide dissipated heat efficiently. They filled the ecological niche left by the virus-ravaged Alberta cattle.

This was a small herd of only ten or fifteen bulls and sows, but the ground still shook as they passed.

"Get in among them," Bruce called, leading Kyla into the center of the herd, careful to avoid the swinging mass of the dinosaurs tails swinging back and forth in time with their pace.

Bruce knew they were bred for docility. They were herbivores hatched on government ranches before being released to roam free. They had no natural predators; even the few remaining grizzlies could do nothing but scratch their hide. Their leather, meat, and valuable organs were all commodities that maintained the Territories and beyond. Ranchers culled the docile beasts humanely once they reached adolescence and their growth slowed. Like all life on Earth, the ankylosaur's greatest predator was man—but they didn't realize it. To them, human presence meant receiving sweet sugary treats or barrels of vitamin laced water.

Even now, they were oblivious to the snarling Yutyrannus tossing its downy, feathery frilled head back and forth as it searched for the objects of its hatred. They had so little knowledge of the world and its threats, they ignored the roars behind them, instead nuzzling the Rangers, looking for an apple or sugar cube. The dull eyes of the ankylosaurs looked hopeful, and little bleats begged to treats. Bruce and Kyla tried to use the herd's bulk to shield them from the predator, but the hungry ankylosaurs movement betrayed their position.

The Russian dinosaur rushed into the herd, weaving between the massive but shorter ankylosaurs. The beast had sighted its prey again and was going to taste blood before the day was through. Bruce and Kyla moved their horses to keep the mass of ankylosaurs between them and the raging yutyrannus.

Like an eager puppy, a multi-ton animal nuzzled the mounted humans. It moved, interposing its body between the yutyrannus and its prey. For the first time in its single-minded pursuit, the Russian killing machine faltered.

Its prey was so close that it could taste their blood already. It knew the taste of man and relished the crunch of their soft bones beneath its teeth, their flesh beneath its claws. It pushed forward only to be blocked by another creature much larger than itself. Not one of its brother hunters, this one turned away from a threat. It had no teeth to bite, or claws to rake with; it was an obstacle not a threat. Beyond it was warm prey—prey that had eluded it for days.

That ended now.

Its massive muscled thighs propelling it high into the air, the yutyrannus vaulted forward and onto the Ankylosaur's back. Its huge talons scrambled for purchase, sliding across the bony domed plates before catching in the depression between two thick scales. It howled in triumph as it ripped deep bloody furrows in the beast's flesh. It reached over the ankylosaur's back, snapping its jaws at the Rangers just beyond its reach.

Bruce and Kyla backed their horses away from the slavering jaws of the beast atop the ankylosaur. It was readying itself for another leap when the ankylosaur's dull nervous system finally registered the damage inflicted upon its back. While largely superficial, the wound was the first real pain the creature had experienced in its life. It bucked, not high but with all the power of its thick legs, forcing the distracted yutyrannus off its shifting perch. The Y Rex slid forward, clawing ragged slashes with its clawed arms and taloned legs as it tried to stop its fall.

The ankylosaur bleated loudly, in pain, turning on the yuty-rannus. The Russian killing machine lay on its side, kicking its legs, trying to get back onto its belly. The ankylosaur opened its horned mouth, trumpeting an anger echoed deep within its bones.

Sixty-eight million years of fear and pain and rage erupted in that single cry.

Stunned, the Russian carnivore squatted midway between a crouch and a leap. The ankylosaur spun, twisting in an ungainly pirouette, more a shuffling turn than anything else. It was pure rage and instinct honed in the Cretaceous and encoded in the essence of the beast that brought its clubbing tail around in a vicious arc. The tail clubbed into the side of the yutryannus, pounding the muscles of its thighs, splintering the titanium infused bones of its legs.

The yutryannus rolled away from the ankylosaur and got to its feet, shuddering on its damaged leg. Within it, adrenalin warred with a cocktail of pharmaceuticals its implants flushed into its system to shrug off the damage and sharpen its anger. It was hurt, probably with enough internal damage that it would never heal correctly. It didn't care. Its instincts and bloodlust precluded any consideration of a moment past this one. It would consume this foe. Taste its flesh. Swallow its meat.

The ankylosaur reversed its spin and with a lethal precision, slamming its clubbed tail into the side of the Russian dinosaur's skull. The neck absorbed the blow enough that the creature stayed on its feet but, its small brain rattled. It defiantly opened its jaws to roar but no sounds came forth before the tail struck, once more driving it to the ground. The ankylosaur struck, repeatedly pounding the dinosaur until it finally stopped moving.

"Let's go," Bruce called to Kyla pulling his mount around and setting it in the direction he believed the base to be. Together, they left the carnage behind them, letting their exhausted horses set the pace. There could still hear the trumpeting of the ankylosaur and the wet strikes of its tail, long after they lost sight of the creatures to the rolling grasslands.

"What happened back there, Corporal MacKenzie? Those herds are supposed to be domesticated."

Running a hand through his sweat-drenched hair, Bruce thought about it before replying.

"That...was a wakeup call. A reminder that nature will always revert to type."

Kyla thought about that before nodding in reply.

"And Kyla."

"Yes Corporal?"

"Call me Mac."

— HIGH WIRE —
A *Horizon Alpha* Story
by D. W. Vogel

Three days after my sixteenth birthday I learned an important lesson: watching movies and reading books about dinosaurs was a whole lot better than seeing a real one just a few feet away from you.

"Shiro, are you seeing this?"

I tore my eyes away from the window of our small transport shuttle. "I'm seeing it," I said to Josh.

A family of dinosaurs stomped around the edge of the clearing where our shuttles had landed. Tau Ceti e's strong gravity had forced us down fast and hard. Our two-hundred-year journey from doomed planet Earth had ended on the bank of a fast-flowing river, surrounded by dense forest.

Dense forest full of dinosaurs.

I'd thought I was so lucky. The day we entered orbit around this green planet was my birthday. Generations had lived and died on the great ark *Horizon Alpha* that had carried our ancestors toward a new home. New hope. And on my sixteenth birthday, I would smell fresh air for the first time. Feel real ground under my feet. Stand up tall against real gravity in the light of an actual sun.

Instead we had huddled in our transports, creeping out to peer around at this alien world, only to dash for cover when the ground shook with heavy footfalls.

Our dinosaurs weren't Earth dinosaurs. These 'saurs that plodded around the outside of our little clearing were green-scaled, taller than our tanks. They had feathery red frills running down each side of their backs and long tails that swept the grass behind them.

"Herbivores?" My buddy Josh's face was pressed to his window.

"How should I know?" I wiped at the glass where my breath fogged it.

Several of our colony's default leaders, officers from the *Horizon* crew, had bolted into this shuttle behind Josh and me. They were forming a military-like hierarchy, and General Singh had assumed command.

He murmured to the men around him now. "They're heading to the river. Shuttle's pointing the wrong way. Can't see out the back."

The little herd passed us by, the largest of them bringing up the rear, casting a watchful eye over his herd. His family? Did dinosaurs travel in families? Like everything else on this new planet, we had no idea.

When the last 'saur trudged out of site, I stood up from the shuttle seat.

Stars, I'm heavy here. Ceti's gravity made it feel like I was wearing an extra fifty pounds all the time. The older folks were having a hard time with it. The pull ensured that our larger transports would never take off again, and our small shuttles couldn't possibly leave the atmosphere to return to *Horizon*. Not that *Horizon* was going anywhere, either. This was designed to be a one-way trip from the beginning, and dinosaurs or not, the five hundred souls from *Horizon Alpha* were staying on Tau Ceti e.

Captain Carthage spoke up from the group of men. "We need to find another place to settle. The satellites showed a mountain range pretty close. We should send the shuttles out and find somewhere safer."

General Singh shook his head. "Not yet. We don't know where to go, and until we do, I'm not sending a single shuttle. Not wasting the power or risking our people."

The air in the shuttle was growing thin with the door sealed tight and the ventilation system off. Movement out the other side caught my eye, and I climbed over the seats to the opposite window.

"Josh, come look at this."

One of the smaller 'saurs had split from the group and wandered into the middle of our clearing. It was nearly as big as one of our tanks, but half the size of the adults. I couldn't see into the windows of any of the other transports that ringed the field, but I knew the rest of our people would have their faces pressed against the glass just like me and Josh.

The little 'saur stopped in the middle of the field, staring around at our huge metal shapes.

Never seen anything like this, have you, little guy? Just wait about sixty million years. Something will evolve.

A gray shadow moved across the front of the largest transport opposite my window. It was too far away to see clearly, but it slunk low on four legs, a long snaky neck held close to the ground.

Another one crept around the smaller shuttle next to the transport. And another prowled behind our tank.

I couldn't look away from their silent, padding forms, but called to the men behind me. "General? I think you should see this."

The rest of the shuttle's occupants pushed up to the windows. We all watched the scene unfolding in front of us, like an old wildlife film from ancient Earth.

The little 'saur sniffed the air, peering around the clearing. Each gray form halted, nearly invisible in the shadows of our shuttles.

A cry echoed across the field, the little one's mouth open in a plaintive wail. The ground vibrated with the pounding feet of its parents.

Not fast enough.

Josh and I glanced at each other as a strange clicking sound came from right below our window. We jumped back as one of the gray 'saurs bolted from underneath us. As if on a signal, the other gray 'saurs leaped from cover, streaking toward the little herbivore.

Deep cries sounded from the riverside, and our shuttle shook with the herd's approach. But the gray ones were faster. They converged on their victim, leaping on the little 'saur from every side.

"Oh my..." The words choked off as my dry throat closed.

Before the herd could arrive, it was all over. The gray ones pulled the little one down into the tall grass. Its tail thrashed twice, and fell still.

The larger 'saurs plowed into the clearing, knocking the small gray ones aside with sweeps of their tails. One of the gray ones flew through the air toward us. It hit the window inches from my face and slid down out of sight.

Before I could say "They got one," it jumped up from beneath the window and limped out of sight.

"Stars, those things are hard to kill," Josh muttered.

"They hunt like a pack of wolves," Captain Carthage said from behind me.

The adults milled around the body of their youngster, calling sad cries into the air. When they finally plodded back into the jungle, the Wolves came slinking back from the shadows to feed.

None of us wanted to watch the Wolves eating. Life on land was brutal. My stomach clenched at the thought, and even General

Singh looked a little green. We huddled together in the stifling shuttle as the rays of the setting sun streamed in the windows.

The general spoke to his men. Josh and I sat in on the group, but the general wasn't talking to us. "We need to set up a perimeter. Safe ground in this clearing so we can figure out somewhere better to go."

Captain Patel glanced toward the window. "We could pull the shuttles closer together. Close up the gaps between them."

"No way." Captain Carthage shook his head. "Those gray things, those... Wolves. They're not much bigger than a human. No way to close a gap they couldn't get through."

I shivered despite the oppressive heat. *Wolves.* Slipping between our shuttles in the dark.

"Wire. Electric wire," the general said. "If we have enough heavy wire cables, we could run a fence line between the transports. Juice it from the power cores."

"Do we have it?" Captain Patel asked. "Enough wire?"

Everyone looked at each other, but none of us knew.

The general glanced out the shuttle window. "We'll need a bunch of strands down low, at the height of those Wolves."

Captain Carthage nodded. "And a bunch of strands up high."

General Singh pursed his lips and shook his head. "No, man-height should be enough. Those are the first predators we've seen here."

In the three days since we landed, we'd seen several varieties of large herbivore browsing through the trees at the edge of the forest. There were little fist-sized flying 'saurs that buzzed through the air, and a few people claimed to have seen great winged shapes circling high over the trees, but this was the first time we'd seen anything killed right in front of us.

Captain Carthage chuckled, a humorless sound. "You've seen the size of some of those leaf-eaters. Think something big hasn't evolved to kill them? Mark my words, there's something big in that forest. Something that eats those leaf-eaters."

"You think there's…" General Singh paused. "A tyrannosaurus?"

The word hung in the air. We had downloaded as much of *Horizon's* enormous data banks as we could before the orbiting ship went dark, but our incomplete files had nothing about dinosaurs. We were relying on what we'd learned from watching movies and reading books on the space journey here, before we had any idea what lived on this planet. What I remembered wasn't encouraging.

General Singh looked at the floor. "Patel, can you figure out how to connect it if we can run the wire?"

Captain Patel nodded. "Yes. It will take a lot of our power. And it won't withstand a sustained attack. They'll short it out if they lean on it too long. But I should be able to rig it so it packs enough of a punch that even those big ones won't hang around."

"And how are we going to string it? Who's going to climb to the tops of the shuttles?" The older men got out of breath just walking around on Ceti. No one had acclimated to the pull of real gravity yet.

"I can do it." The words just popped out of my mouth.

All the men turned to stare at me, probably just remembering I was there.

"Yeah, me too," Josh said. He nodded at me. "Me and Shiro and some of the younger guys are lighter. It won't be easy but we can do it."

Shining stars, what did I just get us into? But the general was right. We had to secure this clearing before somebody got killed.

After the sun set and the Wolves loped away into the forest, we crept out of hiding. Only bones remained of the unfortunate little 'saur. I scratched at my peeling skin. No one had spent much time outside in daylight, but even a few minutes under Ceti's sun burned our flesh. The paler people had it worse. Josh's nose was as red as the 'saur's frill. My golden skin tone seemed to offer a little protection, but I still picked flakes off my bare arms.

The herd's feet had gauged deep ruts in the damp ground, and I sniffed the air as Josh and I trudged back to the larger transport where most of us slept crowded together.

"What's that smell?"

Josh grabbed my arm and tugged me, pulling me off balance. I bounced off him.

"What was that for?"

He pointed to a large brown mound of mud in front of me. I'd almost stepped in it.

"Oh, man, that's nasty," he laughed.

I sniffed again. Not mud.

"Oh, gross. It's... it's... dino-scat."

Josh's twelve-year-old brother Caleb ran down the transport's ramp as we approached.

"Hey, Squirt." Josh rumpled the kid's hair.

"Don't call me that. We were worried. Where were you?"

Josh pointed to the shuttle where we had spent the hot afternoon. "Holed up to watch the nature show. Did you see it?"

Caleb nodded, eyes wide. "Mom kept trying to pull me away from the window. But it was so fast. What are those things?"

I followed them into the transport. "General Singh called them Wolves."

Caleb kept nodding, looking over his shoulder at the bare bones in the middle of our clearing. "Yeah, Wolves. A whole pack of them."

I left Josh and Caleb with their mom and sister and headed up the corridor toward the transport's bridge. Captain Carthage was already there, his face lit by the glow of the little satellite transmitter in his hands.

"Anything?" I said.

He shook his head.

We had evacuated *Horizon* in a panic. When our ship had entered orbit and launched the first of our satellites, something went wrong. An explosion breached *Horizon*'s hull and everyone scrambled for the shuttles. Of the five hundred people on board *Horizon*, only two hundred landed in this clearing, this green field we'd nicknamed "Eden." Other transports had launched but in the chaos were separated from the group.

My father might have been on one of them.

Every night I joined Captain Carthage up here on the bridge as he searched the frequencies looking for any sign of other survivors. Occasionally we heard sounds, chopped up noises that could have been voices, but our satellite coverage was sparse and we couldn't get a read on other ships. They might have landed safely on the other side of the planet. Or they might not have landed at all.

The general called us all together under the bright moonlight. We huddled close, casting nervous glances over our shoulders into the forest behind us. Women and children, babies and elderly, we were Earth's refugees. Maybe the last humans in the universe.

"Our primary objective is to secure the base," he said. "Captain Patel is working on converting our power sources to run electric wire around the compound. We'll have to gut the transports to get enough wire, but once we have a perimeter we can plant this field."

We had Earth seeds, carefully nurtured on *Horizon*'s two century journey. And we didn't have enough food. No one fancied venturing into the forest to look for edible native plants. I looked around the clearing. *Nowhere near enough room.* Even if we planted every centimeter, we'd still have to forage. Or hunt.

"Women and children will remain inside the transports until the fence line is secure. Everyone will be needed to pull the wire.

We'll also need the rubber gaskets from every door seal on every transport. Once it's assembled, we'll begin running the wire. Soon our field will be safe from... dinosaurs."

The general looked like he felt silly saying the word. But there was nothing silly about that Wolf pack.

We started running wires the following night. Forty men clustered around a tangled pile of cable next to the largest transport. Some of the wire was far too thin to hold any 'saur at bay, but the general said we could zigzag it between the thicker cable strands so nothing could slip between the electrified lines.

He motioned for the captains to come forward. Each man carried a large canvas sack which they set on the ground at the general's feet. They opened the sacks and I swallowed hard.

"Guns?" I whispered.

Josh and our buddy Jack stood on either side of me. "I didn't know we had guns."

No one had ever shot one. Firing guns on spaceships was a great way to start a fire or possibly damage important equipment. After two hundred years in space, *Horizon* was showing her age by the time we came into Ceti's orbit. We didn't have spare parts if something malfunctioned. So we wouldn't have shot target practice even if we'd known we had weapons on board.

And it wasn't just guns. The captains handed out the firearms while the general pulled more weapons out of the bags. We had grenades.

Josh nudged me. "That makes me feel a whole lot better about all this."

I snorted. "Yeah. Now we can blow ourselves up and save the 'saurs a lot of trouble."

Captain Patel handed me a small pistol. It was so much heavier in my hand than it looked in the movies. We clustered around him as he gave a short demonstration. How to load it. How to turn off the safety. Aim and squeeze. We held them like they were poisonous, muzzles pointed at the ground.

"We don't have enough holsters, so if you don't have one, just tuck the gun into your pocket. If our luck holds we won't need them." Captain Patel's voice sounded confident, but his face revealed that lie.

We worked all night. Each length of wire had to be spliced to the next as we wound around the outside of our transports. Where the wires sat against the metal hulls, we padded with the rubber we'd salvaged from our ships. My hands blistered and ached from gripping the pliers to twist the heavy wire cables together.

"Careful there," the general said, eyeing my work. "If the live wire touches the hull, the whole transport will be electrified. Let's not kill everyone inside, okay?"

The general stayed with the group of younger guys who would be rigging the high wires around the tops of the ships. It would take at least two more nights to get the wires we could reach from the ground attached to the sides of the ship with plastic cabling. We worked as fast as we could and by the time the sky lightened, we had two lines of wire circling the field. Knee high and waist high, they looked ridiculous next to the towering trees of the nearby forest.

"We've got a lot more work to do," I murmured to Josh and Jack as we clustered around the power station.

Captain Patel had removed a large section of one of the transports' hulls and was attaching the wires we'd run directly into the transport's power supply.

He twisted the connection and looked out at the group of us who held our breath watching.

"Here we go," he muttered.

A low hum filled the air as the fence jolted to life. We all waited a moment to see what would happen, then burst out into a cheer when nothing sparked or fizzled out.

"It's a good start," the General said. "You guys get some sleep. We're sending another team out in the tank today to cut some timbers so we can build the supports we'll need up high. Tonight we'll run the next lines."

I followed my friends back to the transport. We paused just off the ramp. Noises from inside reassured us that our insulation was secure and the metal wasn't carrying a charge. All the same, I reached out and touched a finger to the ramp, pulling it back instantly.

"Nothing?" Jack said.

"Nothing," I grinned.

We trooped up the ramp and found places inside to sleep through the heat of the day.

Four men died in the forest that day. I wasn't privy to the details, but when the tank came rolling in through the gap between ships that would eventually become a hinged gate, only three men got out of the hatch. Their eyes were wide as they stumbled across the field to make their report.

Rumors flew through the compound. There were 'saurs that hid in plain sight that could chomp a man in half before anyone even saw it. 'Saurs with poison, like great armored scorpions. Snakes with venom that would drop a man in three steps.

The general abandoned his plan to cut wood for supports. We spent the next night gutting the transports for parts we could use to build gates for the fence and beams to secure the wires between the ships. Another crew cobbled those things together, and the following night we would climb.

Eight of us lined up, and the general walked up and down in front of us.

"You're brave young men, and the whole colony appreciates you. I'd do this myself, but this stinking heavy planet…" He stopped in front of Caleb, the youngest of our party. "You sure you're up to this, boy?"

"Yes, sir," Caleb said. He stood up as tall as he could next to his older brother.

The general nodded. "All right then." He pointed down the row. "Shiro, Brent, Josh, and Farid, you'll be up top. Caleb, Jack, Viktor, and Emilio, you're ground support. Everybody just take it slow and be careful up there."

We started on the side of the largest transport. There were ladder rungs spaced down the length of the ship which would have made climbing easy if not for the heaviness of our bodies on this planet. By the time I reached the first attachment spot halfway up I was gasping for air.

"Great idea, Shiro," Josh called from underneath me. "'*We can climb it, General,*'" he mimicked.

"Well somebody has to," I muttered.

The rest of the men spread out on the ground underneath where we were working, aiming flashlights toward the forest. They clutched their firearms in sweating grasps.

"Our support crew," I said, pointing down.

"Let's hope we don't need them." Josh handed me a heavy coil of wire passed up from below. "They're more likely to shoot us than hit a 'saur."

Hour after grueling hour we climbed up and down the sides of the ship. We took turns carrying the heavy wire cable on our shoulders as we pulled ourselves up the rungs. When the sun peeked over the treetops, we had one length of wire run halfway around our base.

My legs screamed and my arms were leaden as I followed my friends into the transport. *This is going to take forever.* I stretched out over a row of seats and fell instantly to sleep.

It took nine nights. The older men tried their hand on the first day as we slept, but the heat and gravity were too much for them. After two men lost their grip on the rungs and fell to the ground, the general called off the day squad.

New blisters on my fingers burst and oozed and my thighs ached from twisting wire and climbing up and down the endless ladders. Night after night we worked. I dreamed of wire and rubber insulation and metal ladders that stretched forever into the sky.

On the final night, the going was easier. The highest wire would run off the top edge of the transports, so we could secure it by standing on the flat top instead of hanging off the side. Some of the guys grumbled that it was silly to run a line this high.

"This is stupid," Brent muttered, twisting a plastic tie around the top ladder rung. He knelt on the edge reaching over to secure the wire. "Nothing out there is this tall."

I shrugged. "Maybe not. But what if there is?" I looked out over the dim green forest. "If something this big is out there, I sure want an electric fence between me and it."

Misty rain started falling halfway through the night. The ladder rungs got slippery and we were all exhausted. But we kept on climbing, up and down each ship, pulling the wire up behind us. We had rigged harnesses out of the transports' seatbelts and clipped ourselves in to the ladders as we climbed, fearing a fall from this height.

The sky was growing lighter but the rain fell heavier as we reached the final junction. We had worked our way all around the compound and reached the point where we started. Brent shoved a large coil of wire over to where I stood on the edge of the largest ship.

"We just need to attach this here. Splice this onto where we started, then drop the rest down the side. They'll patch it into the power and we'll be in business."

The rest of the guys had quit for the night, exhausted. We wrapped the rubber insulation around the wire and set it on the edge of the ship. The heavy cable was stiff and my grip was shot from night after night of climbing and twisting wire together. Brent held the ends while I squeezed the free edges with pliers and twisted.

The shuttle vibrated under my feet.

I knuckled rain out of my eyes and twisted the wire, securing our splice.

There it was again. A sharp, thumping vibration.

"Okay, let's get this secured and drop the rest down." I tucked the pliers into my pocket where it banged against the pistol.

We wrapped rubber insulation around the splice and a few feet down the cable and shoved the rest of the coil off the edge. Wind whipped my wet hair into my eyes as I watched it fall. I could barely hear voices from far below on the ground, but the wire moved when someone grabbed it. As soon as it was connected they'd yell the all clear, throw the switch, and our fence would be live.

Vibration buzzed through my knees where I knelt on the transport.

"Sh—Shiro." Brent's voice sounded strange and low.

"Just a minute. The splice looks loose." I pulled the pliers out of my pocket.

"Shiro. Shiro. Shiro." Brent grabbed my shoulder with a shaking hand.

"What?" I turned to look at him, hands on the wire.

He was staring out toward the edge of the forest. A drop of rain trembled on his lower lip where his mouth hung open. I followed his gaze.

My grip failed and the pliers dropped from my hands, banging on the transport's roof.

Oh, stars. Oh shining stars.

"What. Is. That?" I clipped the words as they stuck in my dry throat.

In the dim light of early dawn through the pouring rain, a shape was emerging from the tree line. A huge shape. A shape that walked on two hind legs, each step shaking the ground right up through my knees.

Any child would know its name. Until Brent said it, my mind refused to believe it. He was standing right behind me, but I heard his terrified whisper.

"Tyrannosaurus rex."

It was bent over, sniffing down low, raking at the ground with its front legs to stir up the scent. *Never smelled a human before.* It was the only coherent thought I could manage.

"Shiro, we gotta get off here." Brent gripped my shoulder and started pulling me away from the edge toward the inner side of the transport. We were both still attached to the ladder on the outside of the ship where we had attached the final piece of wire.

The wire.

I tore my eyes away from the horrific shape at the edge of the forest and looked down at the wire. Our splice was unraveling, the weight of the wire pulling it apart from below.

"We have to go," Brent repeated, clawing at the clips that attached us to the outside of the ship.

I fumbled for the pliers I had dropped. "We can't. This splice isn't holding. If it lets go, the whole fence will fail. It's just one big circuit."

Vibration thundered through the ship again. My bleeding fingers found the pliers and I looked out toward the forest.

The Rex stood up.

At full height, it was as tall as the transport. *It can reach me.* Its head was as big as a tank. Hind legs and tail were tree trunk thick. Long arms, longer than any picture of a Rex I ever remembered from books. It sniffed the air and opened its mouth.

The roar shook the ship, deep bass rumbling right through my chest.

Brent ripped off his harness and bolted for the inside ladder. The Rex's head whipped around, focusing on the movement.

My heart thundered in my ears.

The Rex stepped out of the trees, coming toward me.

The wire. The wire. The wire.

How long would it take to hook up the power? How long did I have?

The splice was pulling apart. *It won't hold.* In another minute it would let go. In less than a minute, the Rex would be here. *No splice. No electricity. It's coming.*

Rain poured off my face as I grabbed the pliers and grabbed the wire ends. *Twist twist twist twist.*

When I was sure my splice would hold, I looked up.

The Rex was thirty feet away. Close enough that I could smell it. Sour and rancid. Like food left out in the sun all day.

I backed away from the edge, fumbling in my pocket for the gun. My wet fingers slipped on the metal as I lifted it up, holding it out in front of me, sighting down the barrel.

It jumped in my hand when I pulled the trigger. I was dimly aware of more gunfire from below me, men on the ground shooting at the beast. I fired again and again.

We might as well be shooting at a mountain. The Rex was close enough that I could literally see bullets bouncing off its hide.

An explosion roared at its feet and it jumped to the side as clods of dirt fountained up from the blast. The transport rocked with the quake of its landing. *Grenade. That should send it running.*

But it didn't. It crouched down, sniffing. I could smell its foul breath from where I stood rooted above its head.

I looked down over the edge where the wire disappeared toward the ground. The insulation had slipped when I retwisted the splice. Bare wire sat against the hull of the ship.

No no no.

If they threw the power now, the whole transport would be electrified. Anyone inside that was touching anything metal would be electrocuted.

So would I.

I threw myself down and shoved at the rubber insulation, forcing it under the heavy wire. *Just a little more. One more second.*

Hot sour wind blew across my face.

I looked up.

My face was reflected in the Rex's black eye.

Its mouth opened.

From somewhere below I heard a distant shout.

My feet were frozen, terror electrifying my nerves. Fear buzzed through my bones.

The Rex lunged toward me.

I jumped back as its teeth touched the wire. The night lit up with a flaming shower of sparks.

The Rex flinched back, shaking its huge head.

It tried again, open mouth lunging at me. Where its skin brushed the wire, sparks exploded out, singeing my arms and face in a thousand tiny burns.

The Rex roared, knocking me flat on the roof of the transport. I lay there dazed, deafened by the blast of sound. The vibrations of its footfalls thrummed through my back as I stared up at the sky.

The footfalls pounded away until the ship finally stilled beneath me.

I couldn't move. Sometime in the last few minutes, the rain had stopped. Through breaks in the clouds overhead I could see the faintest morning stars, pale in the pink dawn sky.

I don't know how long I lay there, looking up as clouds rolled by. I didn't hear a thing, but suddenly there was a hand on my shoulder, fingers pushing against my throat.

Josh knelt next to me, feeling my pulse. He helped me sit up and spoke to me. His voice sounded tinny, like he was shouting from the bottom of a deep hole lined with metal.

"Shiro, you okay?"

"I'm okay." I said the words feeling them through the bones of my head more than hearing them.

"Did you see that thing?"

I laughed, a single hiccupping snort. "Yeah. I saw it. Couldn't miss it."

Josh helped me stand and we shuffled over to the inner edge of the transport.

He paused at the top and looked at me. My hearing was coming back slowly but I still strained to hear his words.

"We're all gonna die here."

I looked back toward the tree line where the Rex had fled our electric wires.

"No we're not. We traveled two hundred years across the galaxy to get here." My voice sounded stronger. "We're it. We're the last. Maybe the last humans anywhere." I looked back at Josh. "We're not gonna lose it to a bunch of overgrown lizards."

He opened his mouth, closed it, and stared at me until we both burst out laughing. Together we climbed down into the open field, squinting into the morning sunshine.

— A BOY AND HIS DOG —
A "Dinosaur Protocol" Story
by Jonathan M. Thompson

The thing Mitchell had most looked forward to before becoming a Guardian was having his own companion. Of course, he wanted to be one of the ones to protect his village—he could think of no more important a job than guarding against threats, or even just dinosaurs running amok. The old-world implants Guardians received when they were sixteen would make him stronger and faster, sure, but the most important of them all was the connection he would form with a creature of his choice. For anyone who knew him, it wasn't a surprise at all that he'd chosen Dog.

Mitchell had always loved dinosaurs; it was hard not to with them always running around—and sometimes through—the village. He wanted to capture a companion at an early age, but the village deemed him too young then. So, he did what any good student would have done: he learned everything he could about dinosaurs. It was strange to read that they had not existed in the old world. What a lonely and boring life those people must have had to have no dinosaurs around them! The best they had were their bones on display.

Through his studies, Mitchell discovered his favorite dinosaur, the majestic triceratops. He decided that triceratops are cute, cuddly, and he could ride on one to go from place to place. He picked one from the wild that had already been running around on its own. When the triceratops first saw Mitchell, it was instant love at first sight. They had a strong bond before the surgery. After Mitchell was chosen, he was then connected to the triceratops via the surgery. His triceratops companion also got the same surgery so that they could communicate. It wasn't communication like it was between humans, but Mitchell understood all the same, and could always feel the emotions of his companion. He decided to call his companion Dog, because he was as cute as a puppy.

As Guardian, Mitchell had a single job; he was the forest warden of the northern river section near the village, a job that was shared with another guardian. They took turns to keep the peace in the area. Tonight was Mitchell's turn. There were not many other Guardians stationed nearby, but he wasn't lonely when he was on duty. He had the technology of the ancients to summon aid and to talk to Dog. Dog never spoke vocally, but through a means of relays that transmitted his thoughts into Mitchell's head.

Dog was not your standard, run of the mill triceratops. He acted silly and was always licking Mitchell with his tongue, as rough as it was, and Dog still managed to get saliva all over Mitchell's face and hair. Dog was a motley green in color, with reds and browns around the edges of his frill and beak. He was small for his species, as he was still growing. Dog only stood about 6 feet high, about 13 feet long from nose to tail, weighing in somewhere around 13,000 tons. Mitchell wasn't entirely certain of the weight, because he could never figure out how to weigh Dog accurately. Scales to accommodate a triceratops weren't easy to come by; the ancients had never had a reason to build one.

The day started out like quite a few others for Mitchell and Dog. They wandered around the village for a while, went to see what their friend and other Guardian, Lana, was up too, but since she was not a home, they settled down in a spot by the river near dusk. Mitchell had a bowl of fruit, while Dog drank from the river and ate some of the lush grass that was growing nearby. "I wonder what tonight holds?" Mitchell asked his companion while climbing a nearby tree. From his vantage point above, Mitchell could see the large silly triceratops.

High up a tanzite tree, Mitchell looked across a mighty river. Dog didn't climb trees, having decided he wasn't built for that particular activity. According to Mitchell's tutors, the ancients once called this the Mississippi River, but Mitchell wasn't really sure what use that 800-year-old knowledge would be to him. Though he'd always been a good student, Mitchell preferred the outdoors, and the smell of the Makibo, a sweet tasting fruit that grew wildly around here.

Dog looked up at Mitchell and indicated it was going to be a wild night. The pieces of rock had already started to fall from the night sky. The elders from their village thought that this annual autumn rock fall was an omen that good things were on the way if you had a clear sky to see them. That was the whole reason Mitchell got into the tree in the first place, to have a clear view. It was going to be a fun night.

Out of nowhere, Mitchell screamed as a jolt of electricity up his arm jarred him. Dog let out a loud roar at the same time. Something was happening to the implants. It hurt, and they both had to get out of the area and find out what was causing it. From his high vantage point, Mitchell saw nothing that could have caused this kind of thing. It hurt him, it was hurting Dog, and there was no way that he knew to stop it. Mitchell's instinct was to go see Jayson; he would know what to do.

Mitchell stumbled down the tree and awkwardly got on Dog, the two of them limping back toward the village. They crashed through the forest like something was chasing them. Mitchell kept seeing something out of the corner of his eye, but the visions vanished like ghosts. It was as if the forest changed shape for a split second—but he knew that couldn't be right, because nothing out there could do something like that. Mitchell should know; he had just been named the youngest Guardian to earn his expertise badge from the Forestry Council, which allowed him to teach about everything that lived in the woods. There was nothing that commanded that level of camouflage without leaving a sign.

Mitchell sighed and spoke out loud to Dog, "It must be the combination of the fear response and the implants acting up that's making me see ghosts. We know those don't exist, don't we boy?"

Dog replied with a low bellow, one Mitchell always knew meant that Dog didn't quite believe him but was going to listen to him anyway. Mitchell didn't know why Dog had picked this moment to become afraid of ghosts.

Mitchell got on Dog and they went to see Jayson, the scholar of the local tribe. He lived in an area that once was the ruins of an old town. Jayson said that the town was called Lib'ary, based on the name written on the side of the building. The building was fairly sound structurally, even if it did have a lot of water in its bottom levels, runover from the river that ran nearby.

Jayson was reading one of the old-world books he had in his house. The collection was massive for a place like this. He didn't know what this place used to be called in the old world, but this fortress of knowledge, of solitude, was known only as Lib'ary to himself and the locals. Generally speaking, Jayson rarely had visitors, expect when someone needed something from him—something related to an ancient bit of lore that they couldn't figure out, and they had hoped that he could.

His porch was a good place to read. He had a table, a few chairs, and even a fishing pole to catch the fish swimming in the water that came up to his house. The sound of something that sounded like thunder broke the silence and his concentration as he looked up and saw Dog and Mitchell barreling out of the forest at an alarming rate. Jayson put down his copy of the history text he had been reading, *Sisterhood of the Blade,* and prepared himself for today's unexpected visitor.

The speed at which Dog and Mitchell were travelling out of the clearing sent a wave of worry down Jayson's spine. He picked up his rifle from under the table and made sure it was loaded. Jayson readied it just in case there was something amiss, but he did not raise it to his shoulder. Nothing seemed to be pursuing the young Guardian. But then Jayson noticed Mitchell's pained expression, and Dog's awkward gait. A flash of static electricity at Mitchell's temple made Jayson's eyes widen. Mitchell's implants were sparking and obviously causing him pain. His triceratops, Dog, was experiencing something similar. In what must have been the understatement of the year, Jayson thought to himself, "This can't be good," and proceeded to retreat into his dwelling to see what he could do to help.

Sargent Stephen Grey was the first to exit the cave system the population had been using since first going into cryosleep. He needed to make a sweep of the outside area, and then report back to his commander. The first thing he did was move outside of the cave mouth about 500 feet and set up the electromagnetic pulse generator, as per protocol. The field for the EMP was wide, and he was lucky that their systems were all hardened. Otherwise, setting off an EMP right outside the cave would have wreaked havoc on his own people.

He knew from before he went into his cold sleep that he was at a black site near the Mississippi River. But as he looked around, he noticed that it did not quite resemble the river from when he was first brought here. The river was wider, if he remembered correctly, and there was strange vegetation all around the site. He could definitely hear the sound of some weird animal off in the distance. He was no naturalist, he was a 17E, an electronic warfare specialist, it was his job to handle things like this pulse generator that he was setting up. He heard the sound again, but he knew that sort of vocalization didn't sound like anything he'd ever seen at the zoo.

Grey heard someone come up behind him; without looking away he spoke to the air: "Is there something I can do for you Lieutenant?" He finished the set up of the electrometric pulse device, and with a turn of a dial turned it on. "Soon as I'm finished, I'm headed back down. I don't know what's making that noise out there, and I'm not sure I want to find out." Grey glanced over at his M-16 rifle leaning against a rock within arm's reach, ready for an emergency he hoped wouldn't happen.

"Carry on," Lieutenant Janet McIntyre answered, not acknowledging his mention of scary forest noises. He probably freaked out watching *Blair Witch Project,* too. She took in a deep breath and coughed as her lungs realized there was no smog in the air. She had not expected the air to be so pure. She didn't really remember what she'd expected when she went into the chamber, or what to think now that she was awake. Grey was already out and setting up the perimeter equipment when she arrived outside.

McIntyre looked at her paperwork. *Operation Demogorgon?* She wasn't sure what nerd came up with that, but it must have been that group playing *Dungeons and Dragons* in the S2's office. She had been Air Force a long time, and never got to travel outside of the country. Technically she still hadn't, but this was a different world than the one she left. She'd joined Special Reconnaissance to be out there to protect and defend; instead she had been stationed at NORAD for her last few years, only moving to go into cryo-stasis in Arkansas. She stifled a yawn, and then went back to gathering the rest of her team.

The pain throbbed, surprisingly intense. Neither Mitchell nor Dog was sick beforehand, and there was no disease that Mitchell knew of that could affect both human and dinosaur. Besides, illness did not usually come on so suddenly. It wasn't just his head; it felt like there were animals flying in his stomach. Mitchell did not know if that sensation was his, or if he was just feeling Dog through the cybernetic link. Jayson was his only solution.

Mitchell ran into Jayson's house, leaving Dog whimpering in the background outside. Mitchell's physical pain was no match for the pain he felt from his longtime companion and friend. He had hoped Jayson would be able to help, and now it was time to find out.

"What is going on?" Jayson asked as Mitchell ran through the door in an obvious panic.

"I don't know. Dog is not feeling well and we both have what appears to be some kind of prickly feeling in our limbs. It is really bothering Dog. I can sense it through our connection," replied Mitchell.

Jayson didn't know how to fix the problem, beyond turning the implants off for a while and letting them reset. It would upset both Mitchell and Dog because doing so would break their mental bond, but he did not think it could be helped.

As Jayson found the last tool he needed, Mitchell explained to Dog what was going on. Or, at least, Jayson assumed that was what was going on, since there was no verbal communication between the boy and the triceratops. The scholar watched them out the doorway as he took out a large piece of paper and laid it on the table, on top of the books that were stacked there. Mitchell placed one hand on the triceratops's frill, almost in benediction, before returning inside.

Jayson explained what he was about to do, gesturing to the paper, but Mitchell clearly did not understand.

"It looks like a lot of lines, both straight and squiggly," Mitchell joked nervously.

"I promise it makes sense," Jayson assured him, leading Mitchell to a chair. As the Guardian sat, Jayson squeezed his shoulder. "Now just hold still."

Getting Mitchell to sit still for the five minutes it took was a chore in itself. He kept straining to look at the schematics laid on the table and trying to turn his head unnaturally to see what Jayson was up to. Jayson was one of the few, if not the only one, outside the Surgeon to have a copy of the schematics of the cyber bond system. It made helping out his friends a lot easier.

Not knowing what was going on made the squad a bit nervous. They'd been warned that the world they woke up in would probably not be the same as the one they went to sleep in. "Masters of understatement," McIntyre heard one of them mutter. She admitted he was right. This was like waking up in one of those safari zoos where the animals just roam around as they please. The sounds of common animals and the smell of what was probably fresh dung permeated the clearing. On top of that, they all heard Grey's mysterious sounds.

It sounded like roaring.

The noise in the distance, which had to be from some large animal, was making the squad nervous, especially McIntyre. She had never even owned a pet, and her uneasiness around most of animals were left conveniently off her psyche profile.

Nevertheless, she got her gear and made sure the squad was ready to move out. This was their first patrol of the perimeter since they woke up. Her squad was the advance team; there were still over a hundred doctors, lawyers, artists, politicians and people and their families—in fields she thought were completely useless—waiting on her to come back with the all clear and push the button to start waking everyone up. To her, only the engineers and architects had any value in the entire group. She thought they should have included more common folk, like her parents, who were farmers and successful ones at that. But they hadn't asked her advice before the mission. Now, she was in charge of them all.

To be fair, she craved the one thing it seemed the eggheads had forgotten to pack in their go bags. There was no coffee anywhere to be seen, and she could have really gone for a pot of coffee right then. If this whole mission had been up to her, she would have made sure that coffee was stored right at the door, along with an honest to goodness coffee pot, not one of those lame single cup deals that had been gaining popularity right before they'd put her to sleep. They should have given more thought to how her squad would feel when they woke up.

Jayson managed to reset the cybernetics in Mitchell, but Dog was another challenge. The best Jayson was able to do was to dull the signal and hope it would be enough.

"How's he feeling?" Jayson asked Mitchell, checking both the dinosaur's comfort level and the reset of the connection.

"Still uncomfortable by the strange interruption," Mitchell said after a moment. "But the pain's mostly subsided."

Jayson stood and looked at Mitchell. Jayson had always been respected by the Guardians at large, and by Mitchell in particular. Mitchell had grown up with Jayson being a substitute father figure. He learned all about dinosaur biology from Jayson. This was why this pain that Dog was feeling was so upsetting to Mitchell—it didn't make sense based on all he'd read about dinosaurs. Jayson was upset too, even though he was working hard not to show it.

Mitchell knew that Jayson would at some point find the solution. But in the meantime, he and Dog would attempt to track down the source. With a nod to his mentor, Mitchell rose, and Dog followed suit. Thanking Jayson, Mitchell left the safety of Lib'ary and walked into the thick forest outside.

There it was, finally, the source of the noise. It was an animal, but not one McIntyre had ever seen outside of books when she was a kid. The eggheads had neglected to mention that there would be dinosaurs when she woke up. She sent Grey to reset and send the pulse out again, but when they did, the triceratops went wild, charging straight at Grey.

Kane and Yu raised their weapons. "How did something so harmless to people affect the dumb animal that way?" Kane demanded. McIntyre shook her head as she raised her own rifle. Her squad's training and their instinct to protect Grey was strong; they had been together for years (literally at this point). They fired on the rampaging triceratops.

The animal spun back around to face the direction of the attack, charging straight for Kane and Yu. Unfortunately, Grey was still in the path of the charging triceratops, with his portable pulse generator. The fact that Grey hadn't shot the animal made no difference; it caught Grey with one its massive horns. Grey turned away from the blow as the triceratops barreled past, otherwise or he'd have been impaled. Even so, the horn tore a decent size gash out of his right side, close to his kidney. He stumbled and fell.

Kane, Yu, and McIntyre fired their weapons; the M4 had never failed them before. Unfortunately, the weapons normal 5.56 rounds bounced off the tough hide of the animal—the eggheads hadn't expected to encounter elephant hide on an animal in North America. Their training did not cover how to take down an elephant, much less a triceratops. There'd been no way to prepare for this, because dinosaurs had been extinct for millions of years. Except that now they weren't.

The only answer was to get out of the way. The remaining members moved to the trees for cover. The triceratops stopped and ran back the way it came. Kane dragged Grey to safety, and as the triceratops disappeared back into the forest, the squad worked to get him stabilized before he lost too much blood.

McIntyre's only response was that she was determined to kill this rampaging beast for the damage it had caused Grey. However, as she scanned the forest around them for any other dangers, guarding the wounded soldier and the rest of her squad, McIntyre could have sworn she saw a teenager in the tree line, talking to the beast.

"Bogey at twelve o'clock," McIntyre shouted. "Kane, stay with Grey. Yu, follow me."

This night was not turning out the way Mitchell had planned. He and Dog should have been camping and watching the meteor shower, roasting a giblet over the fire, and dreaming about the future. This was not the future that either of them had had in mind.

Mitchell had never encountered anyone like these soldiers before. They spoke strangely; even though he could understand them, their use of words was weird. And the weapons they were using were frightening. Mitchell recognized firearms, as they were used by soldiers of his town, but these people had a look to them that made his skin crawl.

Mitchell heard the whiz of the bullets coming past Dog and himself as the strangers made a beeline for them. The soldiers were not far behind, but Dog and Mitchell were familiar with the terrain, and the people chasing them weren't. Mitchell heard something and risked a quick look back—one of the soldiers had stumbled over a branch.

This seemed to make the soldier angrier, though Mitchell was not certain how that was possible. The soldiers were chasing them, but neither Dog nor Mitchell knew the reason for this chase. Dog hadn't done anything that any animal protecting itself from a predator would not have done. The soldiers did not seem to understand or respect that law of the Guardians.

Dog was not used to running full out for this long. The sound of bullets coming past Mitchell was definitely not how this day was planned. Mitchell heard a couple of bullets hit Dog's side, but Dog had such a thick hide that bullets were ineffective. Mitchell knew his own skin was not as tough, so they needed to keep going. Mitchell knew that he probably could not survive the impact of a bullet against his side, not the way Dog did.

McIntyre noticed a rash she seemed to have developed in the last few minutes, as they were passing through the think underbrush. She was not sure what it was, but it was beginning to burn. She was not going to let it stop her from catching up to the boy and the triceratops—a word that still sounded funny when she thought it, and even weirder when they said it aloud. She and Yu couldn't see the dinosaur, but she knew they were not far behind their prey. Not that she was sure what they'd do when they caught up to it. There was nothing about dinosaurs in the brochure that had them go into cryosleep. She bet even the eggheads back at the base would be surprised by all the flora and fauna that seemed to have sprung out of nowhere.

McIntyre noticed a cave entrance up ahead. She was not sure that the triceratops could have made it in there, but there was no other place they could have gone. Otherwise they just vanished into thin air, which she was sure was impossible.

Of course, until a couple of hours ago, she thought dinosaurs were an impossibility as well.

McIntytre had a sudden thought and paused, waiting for Yu to come beside her. Maybe she was going soft in her old age—and she was still angry about what happened to Grey—but maybe this chase could be ended peacefully. Maybe she could convince the boy to keep the beast under control.

"Is it possible," she asked Yu, "that they have been running all this time because they don't actually want to hurt us?" She couldn't understand why that thought came to her, but now it wouldn't let go. Maybe chasing down a boy on her first day awake was not the way to win points with the locals.

The eggheads hadn't told them there would be locals, either.

Before Yu could answer, he raised his rifle. "Contact on our six!" he shouted.

McIntyre turned to look at a ragged man in a set of workers overalls, holding his hands in the air. He nodded at Yu, apparently untroubled by the rifle. "I am Jayson," he called, his voice deep, his accent strange. "I believe I know where Mitchell was going. I may be able to help this end without bloodshed. This cave is several miles from your base, so you may not have any choice but to trust me, or kill me, as you wish."

The soldiers were closing in on their hiding spot. Mitchell was worried about the noise that Dog was making. Mitchell could feel the pain that Dog was feeling. They both knew this was the fault of the soldiers, the fault of that device the soldier had been using right before Dog gored him on the plain. Mitchell had no idea what it was, but whatever it was, it hurt.

Mitchell noticed that the soldiers had managed to chase them to this cave. There was no way out except the way they entered. Mitchell didn't understand what the soldiers wanted. They were mad at Dog, but he hadn't done anything to them on purpose, nor had Mitchell. If anything, they had made the first attack by using that dreaded device. Dog was just defending himself from the attack. It was not Mitchell's fault that they sent Dog on a rampage. Dog's attack on that man was not out of malice, but just a reaction by an animal that was hurt. Mitchel wondered why the soldiers did not seem to understand that.

The cave was isolated from most of the dangers, and while it was big enough for Dog to enter, he did have to squeeze in through the opening. This he did at Mitchell's command. The bond they shared allowed Dog to understand that Mitchell was doing everything he could in order to protect him from those soldiers. Mitchell was grateful that the interior was big enough to allow Dog to have some maneuvering room, just in case it came to that.

The cave was bigger than Mitchell remembered from when he had played here as a child. It was his place to pretend he was a dinosaur master, and his imaginary dinosaurs helped him do everything, from building imaginary buildings to helping guard his play area from invaders, like salamanders and other lizard types. He liked those kinds of things, but they were not nearly as cool as dinosaurs. Jayson told him that once upon a time, back in the long-ago time, that dinosaurs were considered to be extinct, and some crazy people thought they were a hoax, even though their bones were scattered all over the world. Mitchell often wondered what it would be like to find a dinosaur skeleton from the before time. He wondered if it would even compare to what they really looked like.

That, however, was a thought for another time. His primary concern was now to keep Dog safe, and himself, too, if possible. But he was more worried about Dog, his friend and his constant companion, even though Mitchell's mom did not let him sleep in the house. Dog was still given the best of everything, as his role as a Guardian's companion allowed. There had to be a way to explain what happened to the soldiers, but even if there was, the strangers had to be willing to listen to him. They seemed to have a shoot first policy, and that did not allow for any kind of conversation.

Just then a familiar voice came from outside the cave.

"Mitchell?" called Jayson. Mitchell breathed a sigh of relief, wondering how Jayson had gotten here ahead of the soldiers, who were right on his trail. He was relieved his friend knew him well enough to know where to find him. "Mitchell," Jayson continued, "the soldiers are out here with me, and I think we can work this out without anyone coming to any harm...especially Dog."

This was good news to Mitchell, as long as Jayson was not being coerced in any way. The thing that Mitchell wanted most in the world right now was to make sure no harm came to Dog.

McIntyre entered the cave, her rifle slung and Jayson in tow. Yu remained outside under her orders, but under protest. She had come to her senses. The attack on Grey surprised her, but when she heard the explanation from this Jayson, she realized that their pulse generator caused the violent reaction of an otherwise docile animal. Maybe that was the same thing the boy was going to tell them, but she was prepared to see the true colors of the natives. This could have been an attack against them after all. Especially if the locals felt that her unit was encroaching on their territory. She did not know if the boy was deceptive or treacherous, but if this was an attack, it was a calculated ambush from someone aware of when her squad was going to wake up and where they were going to be scouting the land.

There, she saw him. The boy was sitting on the ground, the animal lying next to him. They both had a look of pain in their eyes. Had she not wanted to notice it while she was chasing them? Maybe she had been too busy being angry about Grey to notice before. Maybe she just hadn't been looking. She wondered if there was any truth to what Jayson said—maybe the EMP did cause the attack on Grey. The jury was still out; she needed to talk to the boy before deciding. At least Yu was within yelling distance if anything went wrong.

Jayson looked at McIntyre. "I believe it is customary to sit when making peace with someone," he said, a little forcefully for McIntyre's taste. She complied anyway. Jayson was here to be the mediator of this little exchange. He knew the boy well, and she figured that he was her best shot at ending this without loss of his life. She noticed little things—the kid was built like a quarterback, and his hand was protective on the triceratops's frill, but he didn't look aggressive. None of the details in his posture or appearance seemed to indicate that the boy had made any attempt at malice, that he was truly trying to figure out what was going on here. To be honest, that was something on McIntyre's mind as well.

After she sat, Mitchell looked hard at McIntyre. She reminded him a little of his mother; she was about the same age, and she had that same strong and serious look. It was obvious to him that she was a protector, and that she treated those on her team with love and affection. It was also obvious, from the look in her eyes, that fear was the driving force behind the last few hours, ever since Dog attacked that man. She was ready to talk, but he knew that she would not hesitate to resume the hunt if that was what it took.

Mitchell explained to her an abbreviated history of the Guardians. How he was a member, and that he was paired with the triceratops as his companion. Jayson interjected occasionally to clarify a point or two that Mitchell did not seem to understand. What was important was how the bonding of boy and dinosaur worked, by small electronic devices that were implanted in both the dinosaur and Mitchell that connected the two on a deep emotional level of understanding.

McIntyre didn't really know why the EMP sent the dinosaur into an attack frenzy, but then, she was not a scientist. She was just a grunt. It seemed that the boy, Mitchell, was not a scientist either—he only knew the basics of how the technology in his body actually worked. It was lucky for both of them that Jayson was here; she should have known he was an egghead from the start. He explained that they communicated on a pair frequency, which sounded something like the Bluetooth in her cell phone, but on an level far more advanced than anything she was used to using.

The conversation lasted into the night, and got more interesting once McIntyre acknowledged that the triceratops hadn't gone after Grey, but the pulse generator. Which put a crimp in procedure, but she would report back that they needed to limit the use of several of their devices in exchange for peace with the locals. The natives were friendly and willing to assist in the patrolling to keep the bunker safe. The problem was as old as time, and they were in a position to keep it from happening again.

Once that was established, McIntyre used her chance to listen. Mitchell was a fountain of information about the very things she and her squad needed to know, like flora and fauna of the area. He also knew the best places to fish and hunt, and even offered to make her a list of what fruits and berries were edible. The old and the new could learn from each other, and Mitchell and the triceratops would make excellent envoys from the village to the bunker.

"What's his name?" McIntyre asked.

"Dog," Mitchell introduced. McIntyre barked a laugh, and Mitchell looked confused. "Is that funny?" he asked.

"Nah," McIntyre said. "It's perfect. Even though I am not an animal person, I know from experience, there is nothing like the relationship between a boy and his dog."

— JOAN OF ARCHAEOPTERYX —
by Jennifer Lee Rossman

Hallucinations are nothing new to me, but this is my first dinosaur.

Every cell in my body, every scrap of primitive instinct, is screaming for me to grab a pointy stick and take cover in the nearest cave, because I guess my instincts come from an anachronistic Raquel Welch movie where people and dinosaurs coexist.

But I don't let my fear show, because as real as it looks, the logical part of me remembers that dinosaurs are extinct, and that a reaction like that will only confirm that I belong in this hospital. I just have to get through this 72-hour hold, and then I can go home.

So I freak out on the inside, trying to calm my shaking hands that make my lime Jell-O tremble on the spoon. The knowledge that it isn't real is at war with the competing notion that *it's right there! Right outside the window, being all velociraptor-y in the garden! Lock the doors and windows, hide your Muldoons!*

It has feathers. That's odd. I mean, I guess I know they had feathers, but when I hear "raptor," the image that comes to mind is the scaly, reptilian movie monsters, not this iridescent black bird-looking thing.

And I don't typically imagine them wearing saddles.

I drop my spoon, my heart racing. I briefly forget that I require oxygen to survive, and only remember to breathe when I get lightheaded.

The more details, the harder it is for me to differentiate reality from imagination. Usually, the illusions fizzle away the more I scrutinize them, but this one is getting more detailed and—

Okay, now there's a pretty Latina hallucination chastising the raptor hallucination like it's a bad doggy who ran off after the paper boy, and I am *definitely* not doing well on these new meds.

I squeeze my eyes shut and grip the edge of the table, focusing on the feel of the chipped Formica under my hands. Cool, smooth, real. I inhale the artificial fruity smell of snack time, taste the lime that reminds me of floor cleaner lingering on my tongue.

Then I move on to the senses more likely to be fooled.

I tap my slippers on the floor. It sounds, anticlimactically enough, like I'm tapping my slippers on the floor. No extra noises, no voices other than my fellow residents talking about the latest episode of whatever show they're all obsessed with...

I open my eyes and stare at my lap. Just hospital-issued shapeless pants. Pink, naturally, because we're sorted by gender, which I think is determined by whether they think we got Barbies or Hot Wheels in our Happy Meals as kids.

They put me with the other Barbies. Yeah, I had a few, but I was also a Hot Wheels kid. I guess they don't know what color scrubs that is. Boys are blue, girls are pink, and feminine-presenting genderqueer assigned female at birth is...?

(It's glitter; our color is glitter.)

Just when I think I'm grounded, that there won't be a dinosaur in full riding tack if I look outside, someone screams.

My head jerks up. The raptor is still there.

And now other people can see it.

Chaos reigns in the lunchroom, residents and orderlies crying out in alarm and pointing out the window.

No, this isn't right. No one else is supposed to see my hallucinations.

One of the orderlies—Bev, who is everything you expect a person named Bev to be and more—apparently decides she isn't going to let something like a velociraptor deny her a much-needed cigarette break and opens the door to the garden. Hang on, I have to write that again, but in italics so it conveys the right amount of panic.

Bev opens the flipping door that is the only thing separating us, who are delicious and made of meat, and the giant prehistoric murderbird with feet MADE OF KNIVES!

Now, I'm not the kind of person who runs toward danger, which is why I'm just as surprised as the rest of the lunchroom to find myself running toward the danger. I guess I feel some sort of responsibility. It is *my* hallucination, after all; I wouldn't want it to eat anyone.

(Yeah, I realize my logic leaves a lot to be desired, but hi, I'm Joan, and I'm being held in a psych ward because a voice in my head told me to hurt myself. Thinking clearly isn't exactly one of my strengths at the moment.)

The instant I'm outside, the raptor and its human turn toward me. The woman's face lights up like she's seeing a miracle.

"You!" she calls out, beckoning to me.

Beside me, Bev pauses with the cigarette lighter halfway to her mouth, and I don't even bother to point out that she isn't the designated fifty feet away from the entrance like the signs say she should be. She swears, one of the good ones they bleep out when they show Samuel L. Jackson movies on basic cable, and I realize this is the first time she's even noticed the dinosaur.

"Get inside," I hiss, and she doesn't need to be told twice.

I hear the door lock behind her. She just locked me outside with a dinosaur.

I scramble for a weapon, but the staff doesn't exactly leave sharp objects laying around where patients can reach them. Just when I decide to run for my life, the woman calls out to me.

"He won't hurt you! He's tame!"

Right. People say the same thing about ferrets, but there's a world of difference between "tame" and "I trapped this fancy weasel in my house so it's mine now."

"Please." Her voice cracks, and she clings to the raptor's reins with desperation. "We need your help."

Ignoring the dinosaur factor for the moment, who could possibly need my help? I'm no one. I'm nothing.

But the desire to help burns bright in my heart, like a calling. It's probably just one of my delusions of grandeur, but I want to be wanted. I need to be needed. I... think I'm ripping off a Cheap Trick song, but that's irrelevant.

I know, somewhere deep inside, that this is as close to a purpose as I'm ever going to get.

So I follow the pretty girl and her dinosaur around the corner and through a portal.

Estella is under the impression that I am in a position to absorb information, and calmly chatters on like any of this is remotely okay.

"—but then of course the savior got eaten by an allosaur, leaving me in *quite* a sticky situation, as you can understand. But I think—"

"You're riding a velociraptor," I interrupt. I want to believe this is all some enormous hallucination, but I don't think it is. I've never had tactile hallucinations before, and the rain pouring down on my head feels too real, too cold as it sticks my hospital-issue clothing to my skin.

And like I said, I don't usually hallucinate dinosaurs, but everywhere I look, the world is a giant natural history museum mural. A herd of brontosaurs graze in the valley below, and I swear I'm hearing the John Williams Orchestra. (Okay, *that* one is probably a hallucination.)

"Utahraptor," Estella corrects, wiping dark, rain-plastered hair off her forehead. "But yes. We've been over this already."

The raptor—Malcolm, she called him—nudges my arm with his wet, feathery cheek like we're BFFs.

"I think I need you to go over it again," I say numbly, sitting on a rock and covering my face with my hands.

Estella groans softly at the delay in getting wherever it is we're going, but she stops beside me and complies. "Not all dinosaurs went extinct. Some escaped into another world—this world. Sometimes portals open between them. In the 1800s, people discovered the portals when utahraptors started nomming on their cattle. My many-times-great aunt was the first to ride one, and a small town called Hell's Creek rode them for a couple decades."

"Which isn't in the history books because...?" I ask, trying to ground myself in the raindrops and the smell of petrichor and the...distant trumpets of hadrosaurs. Okay, so that didn't work.

"Because...*reasons*," Estella says with reverence. "The first modern people to come through a portal were my gay great-grandmothers, and fast forward a bunch of years, and we're at war with the descendants of the people who came through during the Renaissance—"

"Insert 'dinosaur renaissance' joke here," I murmur.

"—and there's a prophecy that someone will come through a portal and lead us to victory. Which totally came true last week! His name was Fred and he was *so* cool."

I look up at her. "And then you got him eaten."

She slumps in her saddle. "And then I got him eaten." She perks back up, because she is apparently the living embodiment of a Weeble whose theme song is "Tubthumpin'." "But now you're here!

Admittedly, I was hoping for a guy, but…" She gestures vaguely at all of me.

She means I have a boyish frame. Which would be a compliment if we weren't in a *Land Before Time* movie. (Oh god, I hope it's the first movie and not one of the sequels with all the singing.)

"So, what do you want from me?" I ask, but a crashing sound in the tree line swivels our attention thataway.

Before I can respond, Estella and her raptor are off like a shot, and she's got a sword, and *I* want a sword; why don't I have a sword?

The tree line erupts in movement; half a dozen raptors and riders charge through the rain, screaming and screeching and holding banners aloft like a medieval army. One falls as Estella slashes at them, her raptor skirting nimbly out of the reach of their blades on powerful back legs.

The five remaining riders turn their raptors in sync, and Estella and Malcolm take slow steps backward. She's still grinning, but it falters.

There's no way she can handle them all by herself.

I glance at the fallen rider, who's been abandoned by his injured raptor as it fled into the forest. He's got a crossbow.

Now, I'm a lot of things. Chaotic Good, queer, crazy. One thing I'm not is an archer, but I guess that's about to change.

I scurry across the slick grass and make the mistake of locking eyes with the fallen man as I take his bow.

He is…not as dead as I hoped he would be, because this isn't a video game and bad guys don't die as soon as you wound them, even if their insides are kinda mostly outsides now. Should I say something? I think I should say something.

"Um. Any tips on how to use your bow?"

His only answer is a sad gurgle, so I'm on my own. But I watch *The Walking Dead*; I know how to use a crossbow.

Spoiler: I do not know how to use a crossbow. Like at all.

On the bright side, as the arrow-bolt-thingy flies ineffectually straight up and lands about twenty feet to the right of the nearest enemy, it draws their attention firmly in my direction and distracts them from Estella. So...yay me?

I consider holding perfectly still, but don't think that will help anything. "Next one won't miss!" I shout instead, pretending to be a badass in soaking pink hospital clothes.

Estella gets one of them while they're busy being stunned by my brilliance (I guess? I really don't understand why they're so freaked out), and Malcolm swipes his claws across another raptor's flank, almost starting a skirmish until the rider pulls his dinosaur away.

One of them holds their hands up as they dismount. I raise the bow to my eye, then realize I don't even have an arrow in it, but they can't see that in the staticky curtain of rain. They go to their fallen comrade, sling his body over the back of an uninjured mount, and they all disappear into the trees as fast as they appeared.

Estella woops in joy.

"What was that?" I yell.

"You look exactly like Fred! They think you're him, and immortal, like the prophecy says!"

The adrenaline rush dissipates, and I sink to the ground because I can't rely on my legs for support.

"That's what I want from you. Pretend to be Fred—I haven't exactly broken the news to anyone that he's been eaten—and give them hope. That's all we need—just a little morale boost."

Dress like a man? Cut my hair, bind my chest, have adventures, and never be called "ma'am"?

"Okay, but I want a sword."

I would have thought being a savior in a land of dinosaurs would be more exciting. Mostly it's a lot of waving from the balcony of the administrative building in Estella's town, a quaint, pseudo-Old-West deal with the odd modern amenity like indoor plumbing, gay pride flags, and, bizarrely, a helicopter.

The people here are a lot like the town, mixed and matched from all time periods and locations. Different skin tones, religions, all sorts of genders and orientations, but they all accept one another. And they're all terrified of what happens when they lose this war.

But then they see me, and there's hope. They truly believe I'm going to save them.

Even with my spiffy new haircut and boy clothes, I don't look enough like Fred to fool anyone at close range. So here I sit in a fantastic parallel universe, a savior, doodling the archaeopteryx on the tricolor flag and trying to memorize the spelling of "archaeopteryx" so I don't look like a *total* doof.

But I did get a sword, so yay me. (I say sarcastically, rewrapping the gauze on my hand. Swords are sharp.)

I go to the library a lot, in disguise, mostly to convince myself that this is all real.

I like dinosaurs. I'm ambivalent toward, but knowledgeable about, history. But there's no way I know enough about either to fill all these lovingly handbound tomes with obscure dinos and their impact on world events.

Opening a page at random, I find that Amelia Earhart and her navigator disappeared when they followed a rhamphorhynchus through a portal. Another page, and it's all about the Jersey Devil being some sort of pterosaur I can't even pronounce. Something about D. B. Cooper.... And here's a whole bunch of math about why the portals open when they do...

I'm smart, but I'm not "make up random shit that looks like quantum mechanics" smart, and my hallucinations have never been this immersive before, so I'm inclined to believe it's really happening.

Which means these people are real, they can really die, and they really expect me to have some part in preventing that.

Okay, I can do this.

"I can't do this," I tell Estella. My hands shake so bad, I have to press them against each other to keep them still.

She nods to indicate she heard me but makes no comment as she continues to clean the blood off the raptor bridle in her lap. Human or prey animal? I don't dare ask.

The stables are nearly silent, most of the raptors having been turned out to hunt for the day. Only a few scratches of claw on sawdust betray that anyone is behind those great steel doors.

Most of this town was built by Estella's ancestors, who came through from the 1800s and broke off from the Renaissancers, but the doors are a more modern touch. A necessity, given the strength of the dinosaurs. At least they don't have the kind of handle that we all know raptors can open.

Except they *don't* all know that. I haven't seen a single electrical outlet in town, let alone a TV/VCR combo with a VHS of *Jurassic Park*, despite this world definitely having the capability to build an electrical grid.

Estella told me the Renaissancers target anything resembling modern tech and destroy it.

Makes sense, from what I've read about them. They fancy themselves the Rulers of All and resist progress like typical Dark Age jerks, and originally escaped to this world when the Middle Ages were getting a little *too* progressive. They don't want women to own property, they'd persecute us queers as witches if they had their way.... They even call the dinosaurs "dragons" because they refuse to believe that God would let a creature He created go extinct.

"I agree they need to be defeated," I continue to Estella. "But your generals expect me to plan *battles*. I don't know if you realize, but I was in a mental institution on a three-day hold because the voices in my head told me to—"

She sets the tack down on a table, the metal pieces clattering. "I don't know if *you* realize," she says, standing and stepping forward until we're nearly nose to nose, "but we're losing this war." Her bubbly perkiness is gone, replaced by a rage I didn't know she was capable of. "My ancestors came here to find freedom to live as they wanted. And now it's going to be taken away."

A raptor warbles down the hall, upset by the tension in her voice. Me too, buddy.

"Look. I didn't make up this prophecy, and I don't believe in it, but a lot of people do. They need to believe that some guy from your world is going to come and save them. They need hope, Joan, and I got their last hope killed. If we lose this war, it will be my fault that we lose the right to believe what we want and love who we love and be whatever gender makes our hearts sing."

She raises her hands to indicate the barn, and the town beyond its walls.

"All of this could be gone tomorrow if they invade, because we don't have the numbers to fight them off. So I don't care if you hear voices. I don't care if you don't think you can do this. You're going to be our savior because we need you." Her voice grows tight at the end as she fights back the tears shimmering in her eyes like an inconsolable schoolgirl in an anime.

I don't know what to say so I just hug her. I'm not really a hugger, but it's a good way to hide my tears.

I'm not a hero. I'm just some crazy person wearing men's clothes and a breast binder, playing pretend.

Seriously. When they ask for my input on battles, I'm literally just quoting strategy guides from *Final Fantasy* games. "Long-range weapons in the back," I say, stroking the stubble I've drawn on with an eyebrow pencil. "Melee in the front along with those with the best shields."

I dread the day I accidentally call their raptors "Chocobos."

"I don't know how," I tell Estella, "but I'll find a way."

Even as I make the promise, I'm afraid I'm going to let everyone down.

Pro-tip: Riding horses a couple times in middle school doesn't mean you can just sit on a utahraptor, click your tongue, and off you go on a *Saddle Club* adventure.

I mean, a trail ride at camp fifteen years ago doesn't even make you qualified to do that on a *horse*, and a utahraptor is about the furthest you can get from a horse without being a suspension bridge.

For one thing, they're predators. I'm reminded of this fact when my first lesson goes horribly wrong, and my mount, a sparrow-brown male named Dennis, goes charging into the woods after an archaeopteryx. With me on his back.

I hold on for dear life, ducking as he sprints under branches and over rocks while Estella's laughs fade in the distance.

I don't think I fully appreciated the pure muscle these creatures are made of until just now, but Dennis explodes with power with each step like an annoying person who always talks about the gym can only dream of. Not that this changes a damn thing, but at least it's a nice distraction from the *runaway half-ton knife-turkey I'm riding!*

That's the other thing about riding raptors. Between their teeth and their sickle claws, they're like ninety percent sharp edges.

Even if the raptor does everything you ask and doesn't try to hurt you…it's probably still going to hurt you.

For that reason, I'm in what amounts to a full suit of armor, kevlar and leather up and down my limbs and a helmet obscuring my face. It will help if I fall, but—call me crazy (you won't be the first)—the idea of falling off a speeding raptor just doesn't strike me as a great idea.

So I duck and hold on for dear life as we thrash through the woods, startling birds and squirrels and little unidentified dinosaurs.

When we finally slow to a stop and I pick my head up, the archeopteryx is gone and the sun-dappled forest has been replaced by a bright field full of mounted pseudo-Ren-faire soldiers.

Dennis chirps a short, sharp syllable, the raptor equivalent of a curse word. I translate under my breath.

But no one shoots me, no one flees in horror at my Fred-has-risen-ness. I look at their armor—most are covered in fancy tunics, but a few wear bare kevlar like mine, despite their supposed hatred of modern tech—and I realize that they think I'm one of them.

"Preston!" barks a man in full green and gold regalia, his irides-cent black raptor positively dripping in velvet and sashes. He raises the visor of his helmet—an old school Sir Lancelot tin can dealie—and squints as if he's not quite sure who I am. With an army the size of his, there's no way he knows everyone by heart.

I snap to attention, holding the reins tightly and praying that Dennis will behave. "Sir!" I say in my deepest manly man voice. If the Renaissancers shun women for daring to want control over their uteri, I think it's safe to say they don't let uterus-havers in the military.

"Any sign of the cowboys?"

I hear rustling behind me. Estella, no doubt, coming after me. I raise my voice and hope Preston doesn't have a strong New Zealand accent or something. "No, sir! No sign of the enemy!"

I don't dare look behind me to see if she's still there. Hopefully she's savvy enough to figure out what I'm doing.

Which is what, exactly? Becoming a spy?

Estella didn't exaggerate anything about the Renaissancers' kingdom. This place is like if Medieval Times was designed for maximum toxic masculinity.

(Yeah, I feel like a man sometimes, but my masculinity doesn't come with a label urging you to contact your local poison control center if ingested.)

These people ride dinosaurs. They live in castles. They wear doofy knight outfts and use trumpeting parasaurolophuses with streamers dangling from their crests to herald the arrival of their "king."

It should be whimsical. It should be fun.

And yet I honestly believe that they will burn me at the stake if they learn what parts my body has.

I managed to keep my helmet on until I got back to the army barracks, where I dyed my hair with some ink so no one would mistake me for Fred, but I can't wear my binder forever and I have a feminine face. It's only a matter of time until someone figures it out, and then put on a punny apron and put some potato salad in a cheap bowl you don't mind never getting back, because it's barbecue time.

I'm the last one to go to bed, and I can't bring myself to close my eyes, so I just stare at the dark ceiling until the knots in the wood come alive.

I never thought my hallucinations could be comforting, but the sight of giant spiders crawling above my bed almost makes me weep with joy, because they're just so damn harmless. They're a memento of a world where I might not have been adored or supported, but I was never really in danger from anyone but myself.

No one back home ever made me afraid to be myself. Yeah, I lived in a relatively safe area, and of course hate crime is a thing, but I never once lay awake at night worrying that I would be arrested or executed if someone found out I was hiding my boobs.

Exhaustion makes it easier to hear the voices.

Once upon a time, they told me I was worthless, and I believed them. Tonight, it's mostly chatter. White noise that helps me forget about the dinosaurs and the war.

I interpret it as a pep talk.

All those hours in the library are about to pay off.

I've kept my head down, my mouth shut, and my boobs hidden for almost a week. Biding my time, using war games to bond with Dennis while I figured out a strategy.

I'll admit, I was skeptical about the whole "I'm going to sit on this here murder-emu and hope it doesn't eat me" thing, but raptors are smart (clever, you could say) and social. As long as you keep it fed and don't piss it off by poking it with a pointy stick, a well-raised raptor is like a Doberman: yes, it can kill you, but it knows its loyalty and love will go further than violence.

Once Dennis realized I was going to be good to him, he started behaving, and now he responds to my commands with a practiced ease. With just a subtle shift of my body weight, I direct him to slow as we come up alongside our fellow knights in the valley.

Adrenaline prickles at my skin, my rapid breaths echoing metallically in my helmet.

It was my intel that brought us here, my reports of "overheard conversations" in the woods. If it goes wrong, if I misremembered even part of the attack I helped plan, or the dates and locations in the books...

But the voices in my head tell me it'll be okay, and they're all I've got at the moment, so I'm going to have to believe them.

A hundred raptors shift from foot to taloned foot, chittering with excitement. This is it, most of their cavalry is right here. If we can take them out, the rest will fall.

The war ends today.

I realize they're all looking at me. I might be a nobody knight—so forgettable that they've forgotten my name several times, switching from Preston to Warner and now Lakewood—but I was the one who spoke up, who called out their generals and came up with a better plan.

And it didn't hurt that I had all sorts of dirt on the king, thanks to a tell-all book from the library. Spoiler: he isn't really descended from the original Renaissancers like he claims and is, in fact, D. B. Cooper.

So a little military strategy, a little blackmail, and bippidy boppidy brontosaurus, I'm leading a freaking army.

Or, technically, I'm sitting motionlessly at the front of a freaking army. I should change that.

Do I…do I say something? Charge ahead and hope they follow? What are the chances my army of parallel universe Dark Agers is familiar with the "They can't take away our FREEEEDOM!" speech from Braveheart?

"Okay, people," I call out for want of a better war cry. "Hold onto your butts!"

We charge, a hundred pairs of talons tearing at the grass and dirt as we come over the crest of the hill en masse. The thrill of battle thrums through me, and for a second I almost forget that they're the enemy, that they would kill me as soon as look at me if they knew who I am and what I'm really fighting for.

It just feels right, somewhere deep inside me. I can't shoot a bow or swing a sword for shit and the thought of actually injuring someone makes me queasy, but I love the feeling of camaraderie, false as it may be.

It sure beats lime Jell-O and psych ward scrubs.

Aside from a few grazing hadrosaurs, the adjacent valley is devoid of life, in direct contrast to the army I said would be there.

Some of my soldiers fall back, shouting that we're being ambushed, but most follow Dennis and I, faster, faster, must go faster down the hill, so fast they won't be able to stop in time.

They are absolutely being ambushed, but not by another army. By *knowledge*.

That confusing physics book from the library? It had an appendix listing all the predicted times and locations of portal openings. And one is going to open right...

I lean hard to the side, turning my raptor at a sharp angle.

...NOW.

Too sharp an angle. I lose my balance, toppling sideways in the saddle. I grab at the reins but too late; I hit the ground, little cartoon archaeopteryxes twirling around my dazed head.

I'm vaguely aware of a wooshing, and the panicked shouts that dwindle into nothingness as the Ren army tries and fails to stop their raptors from charging straight into the opening portal. To paraphrase Isaac Newton, momentum's a bitch.

Have fun in the actual Earth Prime Cretaceous, ya Ren Faire rejects.

The portal closes as quick as it opened. Not everyone went through, but Estella's people actually are nearby. They will have heard all the commotion.

Gunshots confirm it; they're coming to pick off the stragglers. Between the Renaissancers' low numbers and this morale boost, it'll be over soon.

We won.

Dennis, realizing that I'm still laying in the grass, comes over to nuzzle me, his snuffling breath hot and smelling of dead things.

I laugh, giddy at the world. There's a utahraptor inches from my face, a utahraptor who I've *ridden like a pony*, and I just led an army and won a war in a parallel universe.

I grasp his halter and let him help pull me to my feet. In a distant way, I notice something parting the shoulder-height grass surrounding us.

I don't realize the implications of this until the bowman reveals himself and an arrow embeds itself in my shoulder.

A strange thrumming sound wakes me.

The ceiling above me is clinically white, and for one terrifying moment, I think I'm back at the hospital and this was all some hallucination.

I can't go back to that world.

That world tried to kill me, tried to drug away my problems, but the voices aren't my problem. I can deal with them if I have a purpose and somewhere that I fit in. They're still here, in Estella's world, but they're harmless.

Then I worry I've been captured. I'm not wearing my armor. Did they see—

"She's awake!"

Estella.

My relieved laughter turns to sobs that jostle my injured shoulder. I cherish that pain, because it means it was all real.

"Did we win?"

She grins. "We did."

I fall back. "Don't make me go home."

"Joan, this world is for people like you and me. People who don't fit in back where they come from." Estella gently touches my face. "You're already home."

I close my eyes again as the helicopter lifts off and heads back to the town, and quietly hum the *Jurassic Park* theme.

— A TIME BEYOND SUNSET —
An Apex Island Adventure
by Alana Joli Abbott

T he truth was that Nate Verne wanted to ride a dinosaur. This is not what he told his sister. Nan Verne would not stand for that sort of nonsense, thank you.

But she would be interested in the job, so Nate decided to show her the advert in the paper first and worry about the dinosaurs later.

"You can't be serious," Nan said, handing back the paper.

"It's in the *New Haven Register*," Nate insisted. "The *Register* doesn't lie."

Nan scoffed at that. They'd had the argument before: Nan said that papers wrote what sold papers, but Nate believed in the power of the free press.

"I doubt we're of age," Nan said, but her finger traced along the letters, lingering on the words.

Nate pressed his advantage. "When has that *ever* stopped you before?"

She tapped the advert with her finger. Once. Twice. Three times. *Sold.* Nate grinned.

"We'll have to ask Abuela to be our chaperone," Nan said, like the admission of her interest was something that cost her.

Nate took the paper, feeling like sunshine. Abeula would say yes. And they'd get the job—no expedition ever turned down a Verne who applied.

They were going to Apex Island.

Walking across Yale University's campus in the middle of busy New Haven, Connecticut, always felt like stepping into an older world to Nate. New Haven was the height of modernity: there were jazz clubs and dance halls where the best bandleaders brought their bands. The Bow Tie Cinema got all the latest pictures, even if it wasn't as futuristic as New York's Criterion. They had a Red Cross building, where Abuela still volunteered, and a clock factory, and a brick library with white columns that was less than a decade older than Nate. The *New Haven Register* building didn't look like much on the outside, but inside those walls, there might as well have been magic happening as typeset and paper combined to become knowledge. Nate liked all of that, but he liked history better.

On Yale's campus, the buildings were centuries old, and meant to feel older, evoking colleges in Oxford and Cambridge. The red brick dorms, built in the 1700s, were Nate's favorite, especially because the Nathan Hale statue near them made him feel connected to history, by virtue of sharing a name.

The Peabody Museum might as well have been a cathedral, and Nate felt that the holy atmosphere was only appropriate: to him, it was a temple to knowledge, history, and science, all the things Nate loved best. On their way to the director's office, they walked past Nate's favorite exhibit: the skeleton of the extinct brontosaurus. (Nate knew the controversy—that brontosaurus was really just a mis-named apatosaurus, but Nate believed in O. C. Marsh by default. He wished that Apex Island were large enough that the huge sauropods could have survived there, just to prove Marsh right—even though, he admitted, brontosaurus had died out in the early Cretaceous and wouldn't have made it to Apex Island anyway.)

Dr. Visconti looked delighted to see them. She wore a dark blue pair of wide pants and a boat-necked blouse in a pale pink that almost matched the color of her skin—work clothes, Nate thought, rather than clothes she'd wear to meet prospective employees. He hoped that wasn't a bad sign. The tiny woman was even more diminutive surrounded by the prehistoric creatures of the main hall. She got on her tiptoes to kiss Nan's cheek, and then Abuela's, in greeting. Nate shook her hand instead.

"It's always such a delight to hear from my old mentor's family," Dr. Visconti said. "Have you heard from Dr. and Mrs. Verne lately?"

Abuela shook her head. "No word since they reached Indonesia," she said apologetically, and Nate's temper tightened his throat. It wasn't Abuela's fault that his parents hadn't written. Or, if they had, that the letters hadn't reached them. And it wasn't as though they could simply place a call from Indonesia. It might be possible, but even in the modern era, calls around the world were...spotty at best.

His parents were exploring ancient ruins and assisting people working to preserve their histories, right in their own countries, rather than absconding with relics to bring back to the museum. The Peabody might not officially love their philosophy, but Nate did. And Dr. Visconti, now murmuring niceties to Abuela that of course they'd all hear news soon—or see them in the paper with a new discovery!—would never disagree with Dr. Verne in public, not when he'd believed in her and helped convince the board she deserved her position.

Nate was happy to use that gratitude to get what he wanted. Nan would see that as callous and immoral.

Nate *really* wanted to ride a dinosaur.

"We've come about your advert in the paper," he said, when there was an appropriate break in the conversation, and interrupting wouldn't be rude.

Dr. Visconti blinked. "How old are you two now?" she asked him, but she glanced at Abeula. "Thirteen?"

"We're fifteen," Nan said, bristling. Nate tried to hide his feeling of triumph. If Nan had been on the fence before, she'd be all in now. No one underestimated Nan Verne.

"Of course," Dr. Visconti said, apologetically. "And enjoying high school?"

Nan's eyes narrowed. "It's summer," she said deliberately. "Unless you expect this expedition to keep us until September..."

"The advert indicated it's a short-term assignment," Nate jumped in cheerfully. "It's unclear *what* you're looking for, of course, but I know that the longer an expedition runs, the more it costs the museum."

Dr. Visconti's lips tightened. The museum was always on a limited budget for this sort of thing, no matter that they had the backing of one of the wealthiest universities in the country. Nate put his hands in his pockets, trying not to rumple his vest or slouch, which was his normal posture. He wondered how his father made it through meetings with patrons in a full suit coat when just the vest and tie felt so constricting. He caught Nan fidgeting with her skirt, which she'd worn for the same reasons Nate had dressed so smartly; they wanted to present themselves as valid business partners.

Abuela, of course, wore her Red Cross uniform. Abuela always wore her Red Cross uniform when they went out. It made people look at her as a nurse first, she said, instead of judging her by her mahogany brown face. Even though her English was as precise as

Eleanor Roosevelt's, if people saw her out of uniform, the polite ones would ask where she was from.

The impolite ones didn't bear mentioning.

Abuela told him he should be grateful that he and Nan had inherited their father's lighter coloration, but Nate wished he looked more like his grandmother.

While he'd been trying not to slouch and letting his attention wander, Nan had been handling the details of their arrangement. That happened a lot. Nate's focus wandered, and Nan handled things. Nate took spare parts and made fantastic—and useful, despite Nan's contrary opinions—inventions; Nan made sure he didn't forget to do his schoolwork. And Abuela made sure Nan didn't spend too much time worrying about the household and taking care of her absent-minded brother.

"...working with Captain Mills of the 207th," Dr. Visconti was saying. "And you should be able to question Miss Green. She remains in the infirmary at Fort Allen."

Nan was nodding, as though all these names made sense. "Captain Mills's reputation precedes him," she said.

"And how is Miss Green recovering?" Abuela asked. "We don't want to tax her."

Dr. Visconti smiled, only slightly. "Thank you for asking, Mrs. Rojas," Dr. Visconti said, mispronouncing the name with a hard *j*. Abuela's smile didn't waver. "The last report I received said that she's doing well. I expect her to return to Yale in the fall to continue her postgraduate work. But I'm sure she'd want that artifact to be recovered before she comes home." Dr. Visconti tapped a finger against her other arm. "She's very dedicated to her work."

And she doesn't want the Germans to steal it, Nate realized. *That's why we'll be working with the army.*

"I don't need to reiterate that the nature of the artifact is sensitive," Dr. Visconti said, reiterating it anyway.

Nan smiled and put out her hand. "You can count on our discretion," she said, and Dr. Visconti shook on it.

They got all the way out of the museum and to the trolley stop before Nate asked. "So what are we looking for?"

Nan rolled her eyes in a very unladylike manner, and Abuela shot him that disappointed look he received so often. "Pre-Minoan," Nan said. "Crystalline."

"Miss Green recovered it from the outskirts of Akrotiri but had to leave it behind when a herd of citipati swarmed her location," Abuela added.

"Citipati," Nate repeated. "Omnivores, around 2 meters in length, but they only come up to the waist." He glanced at Nan. "Named from the Hindi, meaning 'funeral pyre lord.'"

"After a Tibetan dual god of protection and death," Nan chimed in with a grin. "Someone's been reading up."

Nate shrugged, hiding his pleasure at the compliment—religions were Nan's area of expertise, but he did *try* to keep up. "They've got wicked legs. Like ostriches. I can see why she had to leave the thing behind."

"She was nearly trampled," Abuela said softly. "I'd want to visit her at the infirmary even if she didn't recall where she had to leave the artifact."

Nate nodded, trying to look solemn, but he was having trouble hiding his excitement. The F Trolley pulled up, and the three of them paid their fare. Nate watched New Haven speed by outside the open air. "So," he said, finally unable to contain the question, "when do we leave?"

The plane trip from the shiny new New Haven Municipal Airport was almost anticlimactic. Li-Con Airways offered a tourist flight directly from New Haven to Cape Coleman, advertising itself as a gateway from New England to Prehistory. Nate was unimpressed with the inflight brochure, which featured generic depictions of dinosaurs at least ten years out of date—none of them included the feathers scientists and explorers now realized must have been common among dinosaurs across the world, given their prevalence on Apex Island. Eventually he put it down and began fiddling with spare parts he kept in his pockets.

Nan stared out the window at the night sky, her short hair curling under her ears, her wide-legged pants taking up almost as much space as a skirt. "You're not excited," Nate murmured, still looking at his parts.

Nan startled. "I didn't realize you were watching me."

"I'm not."

Nate's twin sighed. For all that they shared the same birthday and similar features, they didn't share much in the way of personality. He'd heard stories about twins who could almost communicate just through their thoughts, but then, he'd heard stories about German scientists experimenting on twins to *produce* those results. He figured if the Nazis ever got a hold of him and Nan, they'd be disappointed.

"I was just thinking about Mom and Dad," Nan admitted. "And how we've agreed to pick up a *thing*"—She was the soul of discretion, his sister.—"and turn it over to the army. Mom and Dad make sure this sort of thing gets to the people they belong to."

He wondered if it would be safe to say Pre-Minoan, or if that would be revealing too much. Probably too much. "I'm pretty sure those people are far enough gone that it isn't a worry."

Nan leaned back, looking up at the roof of the aircraft not that far above them. "That's assuming those ruins are all from *that*," she said vaguely. "Archaeologists like to think that the best stuff comes from Europe, but you know where Apex Island is closest to?"

Nate thought about it. Florida? The Bahama Islands? Maybe Cuba? "Not Greece," he said, figuring that was safe enough, but Nan shot him a look anyway.

"If humans survived for years, maybe even generations, on Apex Island, they must have traded with someone," Nan continued, dropping her voice. "And there's plenty of evidence of strong, technologically advanced civilizations just on the other side of the Gulf of Mexico."

That was a good point, of course. But to make a case for it, they'd have to find the right artifacts, which meant bringing them home to study—because there weren't local humans on Apex Island to turn them over to. "If we find anything like that," Nate said, "we can always convince the museum to reach out and share the collection."

"The museum," Nan said grumpily, crossing her arms. "But not the army."

Nate had no good answer for that. But he'd been reading more of the news than Nan had, he thought, and he'd rather have artifacts in the hands of the U. S. Army than the Nazis any day.

"We should get some sleep," he said instead.

Nan nodded, but she kept staring out the window.

Cape Coleman was a bustling tourist trap that reminded Nate of pictures he'd seen of Havana. He snapped some photos—he'd made some improvements to his dad's old Speed Graphic; it was still a little clunky, but he'd gotten the exposure faster, and the film holder could load twelve slides instead of the standard six. It still worked better when standing still, which wasn't an option for the Verne Expedition: they were picked up at the airport bright and early in the morning and shuttled through the town in the back of a Cadillac Series 70, which, at least, had more leg room than the plane. The biggest difference between Cape Coleman and Havana,

Nate suspected, was the enormous wooden fence that created the border on the inland side of the city.

"Put the camera down, kid," the sun-burned driver growled at him as they drove up to a check point. Nate considered snapping one last shot, just to be difficult, but he decided to do as he was told. Anyone with a sunburn that bad deserved to have some pity taken on them. As he packed the camera back into his bag, he glanced up at the pale, big-eared soldier asking questions: *Where were they going?* Fort Allen. *What was their business?* Confidential. Nate hid his grin at the soldier's bland expression at that, and turned away as Abuela, smiling sweetly, handed over their paperwork past the driver's nose.

"You're all in order," the soldier said, handing the papers back through. "Stick to Via Playa Drive," he advised the driver. "The inland roads are a little dicey today."

"Dinos or Germans?" the driver joked, but the soldier didn't seem to think that was funny. "Yeah, yeah, we'll stay on the road."

The driver cranked up his window. As they passed through a second wall—this one looked like it was built on an earthwork for additional fortification—they entered the shade of a jungle. The trees stretched above them, soaring into the sky, and ferns choked the land to the sides of the road.

Then the forest broke, and the world around them was sky and water.

A pterosaur dove straight into the sea and came up with a huge fish in its beak. *"Alcione elainus,"* Nate guessed, noticing the reptile's smaller comparative size—maybe twice as large as an osprey, but a dwarf in comparison to the larger pterosaurs.

Nan looked out the window. "Do you have a lot of trouble with creatures along these routes?" she asked the driver.

The man shrugged, then winced. Nate guessed the sunburn crept all the way up his sleeves. He must have spent too long on the beach on his day off. "The 207th keeps the roads clear enough," he said. A flock of tiny raptors—compsognathus!—scurried across the road in front of them, and the driver cleared his throat as he slowed to let them pass. "The big ones, anyway."

Abuela made an *mmmm* sound, the type that meant she was withholding judgment for now, but she had your number.

The beach road gave way to another part of the jungle, and another set of fortifications. Past another checkpoint and inside the titanic walls, Fort Allen looked just like any military base from the news reels, as far as Nate could tell. That probably meant that all the good stuff was where people couldn't see it.

Like the dinosaur riders program.

The car pulled up to an official looking building with a neatly-uniformed, red-mustached man standing at attention outside. Abuela got out, her nurse uniform looking starched even after their travel; Nan followed, both of them leaving Nate to get his luggage on his own.

That was okay. A little chug of the miniature engine and it'd stay at his side with no problems.

Probably.

"…wasn't expecting you for a few hours," the red-mustached soldier was saying. Nate wondered if his hair was regulation.

"We were told to report directly to Captain Mills," Nan said in her no-nonsense voice that had once sent their math teacher to the principal's office to report himself for posting an incorrect equation. Nan was like that.

"I understand," said the soldier, "but he isn't *here* right now. He left base this morning and isn't scheduled to return until 1100."

Nate glanced up at the sun, because someone would tell him that looking at his watch was rude. That was *hours* from now.

"Maybe you could arrange a tour?" he mused aloud. Nan looked back as though she'd just realized he'd joined them.

The man's pink lips pinched under the bushy moustache. "Well, I'm not sure that—"

"Is an excellent idea," said Abuela. "But of course, you must first take us to the infirmary. If we can't speak to Captain Mills, we will begin with Miss Green."

The soldier looked back and forth between the two women. Nate knew how he felt.

"I'll see what I can arrange," he said, then stepped inside the building.

Nate leaned on his luggage, chugging away on its wheels, waiting for a tug on the handle. He wasn't worried. Not even those thick fortifications outside the base would prove much of an obstacle to the combined force of Nan and Abuela, when it really came down to it.

Miss Green looked better than Nate expected any young woman who'd almost been trampled by a flock of citipati to look. A large bruise on her face was a strange purplish-green against her tawny brown skin, but the edges of it were already fading. Abuela took her pulse and said something that made her laugh.

"So, you think they'll let me out of here soon, Doc?" Miss Green teased.

Abuela chuckled. "If I were your doctor, I'd have you on bed rest for another week." When Abuela moved to the other side of Miss Green's bed, he saw why: his grandmother had been in the way of the wrappings around the graduate student's right side, and the bruise still on her face looked like it was the least of her concerns.

Miss Green leaned back in disappointment as Abuela moved to her other side; Nate thought it was hard for her to relax. Her posture made her look like the type of person who was always moving, who struggled with sitting still and just being. He could empathize with that. But she also had that look that Nan got when she was determined to do something. Nate suspected that if the doctors could keep her in bed another week, they'd be lucky. She tried to blow a curl out of her face; it dropped back down as soon as she'd stopped blowing.

"I hate that I can't just take you back out there," Miss Green said, "but I know I'm still slow. Given what I've seen out there, especially closer to Akrotiri, you'll need all the speed you can get."

Nan pulled out a tourist map of Apex Island and drooped it over the bed, across Miss Green's stomach. Nate leaned over the bed railing to get a better view.

"We were told you were able to make it back within a mile of the base on your own," Nan said. Nate gave a low whistle, impressed, before Nan shot a glare that made him consider his own rudeness.

But Miss Green laughed. "Thank you, Mr. Verne," she said. "Everyone's been treating me like a damsel who needed rescue, but I *did* almost make it back on my own."

"I've seen pictures of what those citipati claws look like!" Nate enthused. "The fact that you got away from them after a stampede?" The bed frame creaked as he leaned on it too hard, reminding him he ought to be more polite. He stood straight and cleared his throat. "I think not everyone could do it, men or women," he stumbled. "I'm glad you did."

"Me, too," she said. Then she turned back to Nan, all business. "It's hard to tell exactly where I was when the citipati swarmed me, but my best estimate is that it took me six hours to get back to base while I was injured. Figure I was going about half my normal speed, and you're going to be this radius from the base"—She drew with her finger.—"in this direction." Then she looked up at Nate again, considering. "My understanding is that groups of citipati don't normally react the way they did that day. I've overheard the soldiers saying they'd never seen a group that large stampede before. Do you have any thoughts about why citipati might charge like that, Mr. Verne?"

All of them—Abuela, Nan, and Nate—showed identical surprised expressions that Miss Green had asked Nate of all people. But then, Nate was the dinosaur lover among them. Nan knew the details and logistics, but Nate did know dinosaurs.

"They could have been fleeing a predator," Nate considered, thinking as he spoke, "but predators are a normal part of their environment, and I think some of the citipati would be more likely to stop and fight than all of them flee." He tapped his mouth with a short metal tube he'd been fidgeting with, belatedly hoping it didn't have any oil on it. "Wild animals stampede in panic, when something makes them really afraid, like a fire. You didn't see any signs that would indicate a wildfire in the jungle, did you?"

"No," Miss Green said, still watching Nate. "But if I told you there was a noise like an explosion, right about here—" She paused drawing her finger along the map, just to the west of where she'd estimated she dropped the item they'd been asked to retrieve. "You think that might have something to do with it?"

"I think," said Abuela, "that we will need to be very careful."

Miss Green nodded. "You will, Mrs. Rojas," she said solemnly. "You definitely will."

Nan had been hoping for more details, and Nate had been hoping for a tour of the base, and neither quite got what they wanted. Captain Mills arrived on base before the anticipated 1700, which meant that Nate didn't get to poke around, looking for the dinosaur riders project he *knew* was happening somewhere at Fort Allen.

That was okay. There would be time after they found the object.

From the parts of the conversation he listened to, which admittedly weren't very long, Nan was trying to convince Captain Mills—a tall blond soldier with broader shoulders than Nate thought was particularly fair—that they should have better transportation than the modified, open air, box-like truck he'd offered them.

"I hardly think this offers protection against the dangers of this particular jungle," Nan argued. "I should think an M1 would offer somewhat better cover—"

"The M1 can't handle what passes for paths through the jungle," Captain Mills interrupted. "You may not realize, Miss Verne, but we haven't had a chance to pave many roads where you're headed."

Nan pursed her lips, and Nate stepped forward. "We know, Captain," he said. "I'm just concerned this box doesn't have a roof."

"It's a prototype G500," the captain explained. "Better at terrain, made with just enough essential parts that if it breaks down, it doesn't take much to repair."

Nate crouched down next to the thing. The way the axels were hinged did look like it would provide more flexibility for the wheels traversing uneven terrain. And the suspension looked plenty bouncy. He'd make some tweaks on it, if it were his, but the captain's point about the roads not being actual roads made sense.

"It'll work," Nate said, then realized he'd interrupted whatever Nan was arguing. She sighed, and the captain gestured at him.

"Thank you, Mr. Verne, for the vote of confidence," the captain said dryly. "We've loaded some supplies—field rations, some pup tents, standard wilderness gear—in the back already, so you can take off whenever you're ready."

He seemed awfully eager to get rid of them. But then, Nan seemed awfully eager to leave the base. Figuring that Miss Green had been a three-hour hike out from the base, and that they could shorten their time by using the box truck—G500 was a dumb name; he'd come up with a better one—then they had most of the day to find the object and come back.

Or look for the object, notice it was getting dark, and still make it back to base before any of the nocturnal predators came out.

Nate pressed a button on his luggage, and the hyperbolic springs in the bottom released so that it was at the right height to maneuver onto the back of the G500 without his having to lift it.

Which was good, because it was heavy. He turned back to see the captain blinking at him.

"I think we're ready," he said.

Saying there were paved roads was a bigger understatement than Nate had given the captain credit for. Abuela had taken the wheel over Nan's protests that she'd gotten her driver's license. Nate was just as happy to sit back and watch the jungle around them. There were so many birds! The canopy was full of brightly colored flowers and feathers, and the air was filled with chirps and squawks as flocks spoke to each other. He watched as a bright blue and orange bird launched from one tree to another, gliding down on four wings.

Wait.

He got out his camera again, adjusting the zoom lens despite the jostling of the suspension (which, in hindsight, was not absorbing the shock of the uneven ground very well at all). There. He focused in on the bird. But it wasn't a bird at all; it had no beak, but a reptilian face, and little fingers at the ends of its wings.

One of the papers from the Peabody's paleontology department had discussed the discovery of early Cretaceous fossils showing dinosaurs with bird-like characteristics, even wings, but the microraptor, as they'd called it, was supposed to have died out before the cataclysm that made the Apex Island survivors the only remaining dinosaurs.

But then, Nate considered, Apex Island had had 66 million years of evolutionary development since the mainland dinosaurs died out. Who *knew* what types of changes these creatures had made over the years to adapt to their smaller habitat? It might not be the same microraptor from the early Cretaceous, but it could have been related.

He kept noticing things like that.

A lizard scurrying up the side of the tree had feathers.

A small clutch of ground birds looked up as the truck passed, and he realized they didn't have beaks.

A bone-shape poked out of a nest above—he thought, at first, as part of the carcass left to feed the young—but when the parent creature came back, the baby alcione poked up its head, displaying bone-like crest, to eat some of the fish the adult had brought.

Everywhere he saw familiar creatures that, when he focused, were actually dinosaurs. He could have ridden in the back of the truck for hours, just watching.

But he wasn't actually surprised when a particularly large bump jolted the truck to a stop. The hiss of the coolant tank didn't indicate anything *good,* that was certain. Abuela murmured some very impolite things in at least three languages under her breath, which was even less encouraging. Nan hopped out of the truck and kicked a tire. Nate thought about pointing out that this wouldn't help anything, but he preferred she take out her anger on the tire.

As he jumped off the back, his mind was already working. "I can probably fix it," he said before anyone asked him.

Abuela looked at the steam rising from the engine and gave it— not him—a dubious look. "If anyone can, it's you," she said, and if his chest puffed up a little at that, Abuela was gracious enough to pretend not to notice.

"We're close to the location Miss Green gave us, anyway," Nan said, pulling out the map. She went to spread it out over the hood of the truck, but a sudden loud pop and the following chatter of birds, maybe, from above them made her reconsider. She brought it around to the back to show Nate.

"We'll head this way," she told him. "Abuela and I can cover a little bit of ground. If we happen upon the artifact, we'll be done faster than anyone expected."

"And if you can't, we won't have lost any time waiting for me to fix the Albatross," Nate said with a nod.

"Albatross?" Abuela repeated.

Nate put his hands on the rear fender. "She'll fly by the time I'm done with her."

Nan blinked. "Not literally," she said in a warning tone.

Nate sighed. "Okay."

Nan and Abuela left shortly after that, but Nate was already lost in his work. That happened to him a lot; once there was something to fix, he started to see how the pieces fit together, and that was all he wanted to think about. The engine was probably more pressing, but while it cooled down, he could work on the undercarriage. He popped open his luggage, so he had better access to his tools and spare parts. He had so much better parts than this little truck! But then, the pieces he was taking off could be useful later, too. The springs in the suspension weren't really the ideal fit for the truck's suspension, which was probably why the axel had popped free, but they'd fit perfectly into the rocket backpack he was working on...

"I think you need a three eighths head there, not the quarter."

Nate tried to fit the socket on the piece he'd been adjusting, and realized that the three eighths really *would* fit better. "You're right," he said, putting his hand out from below the truck-soon-to-be-Albatross and waited for the piece to drop in.

It did, but the hand that put it in his didn't have fingers.

It had claws.

Nate froze. He took a deep breath. Then he cautiously pulled himself out from below the truck.

An ornithomimus blinked at him. It stood a little taller than he would, if he were standing, but far longer—maybe about the size of a pony. It was covered in mostly green scales, but its back had a coat of iridescent green feathers. Above its pointed snout were two largeish eyes pointing forward, that blinked at him with a scaled eyelid. Above its eyes was a hat. Made of tin foil. Maybe. With a lightbulb sticking up from the top.

"Um," said Nate.

"It was the right size, yes?" said the ornithomimus, the lightbulb on its hat flickering.

"You would think that the U.S. Army would have standard-sized parts, but I almost think it's between three eighths and a quart— are you a *talking* dinosaur?"

"How many dinosaurs have you met?" the ornithomimus asked indignantly. "Are you sure we don't *all* speak perfect English."

Nate had to concede that this was a fair point. "Do you?" he asked.

The ornithomimus looked at the ground. "No. Very few, actually, but it's important that we face our preconceived notions of the world with open eyes."

Nate wasn't entirely sure how to respond to that. What were the social niceties that a person should use when meeting a talking dinosaur? "I'm Nate Verne," he said, because introducing himself was always a safe bet at the beginning of a social encounter.

"Giley," the ornithomimus responded. "It's a pleasure to meet you."

"Likewise," Nate said, standing up and brushing off his pants. He looked out the direction Nan and Abuela had gone, but there was no sign of them. He had no idea how long they'd been gone. He hadn't looked at his watch when they left. "You haven't seen two other humans around, have you?"

"I have, but I waited until they left. I thought it best to approach one of you first." Giley looked off into the forest as well. "I'm never sure how any of you humans will respond, and in groups, there tends to be shooting involved."

Nate frowned. He wasn't a very good marksman, and he didn't really like the idea of people shooting before talking. It seemed a waste. "No shooting here. Did you need something, though? If you were waiting to make contact, I mean."

The ornithomimus shuffled a claw on the ground, the sharp talons gouging a hole. "I do need help, actually. If it's not too much trouble. Only, I think *she'll* try to blow up the sun if someone doesn't stop *her*, so you'd really be helping yourself, as well."

Nate leaned back against the future-Albatross. He glanced at the engine, no longer steaming, and sighed. "I think you'd better tell me what you mean while I get to work on the engine," Nate said. "And then once Nan and Abuela get back, we'll make a plan. They're good at plans."

The ornithomimus's large eyelids blinked again. "That's it? You'll listen and then help?"

Nate popped the hood. "You're not a Nazi, are you?"

Whatever expression was on Giley's face must have been a grimace, Nate decided. "No, thank you. Although I have the hat courtesy of their work. *She* stole it from them."

There was something wrong with the intake manifold, he thought. If he replaced the gasket... "That's good enough for me," Nate said. "Push the button on the top of my luggage and it'll come over; I think I have a replacement gasket that'll work, and you can tell me what you mean by someone blowing up the sun while I fix it."

She, it turned out, was Dr. Lindsay Wells, a scientist with whom Giley had become rather unfortunately acquainted, who had been interfering, unbeknownst to either the Germans or the Americans, with both group's scientific endeavors on Apex Island. Nate had read one of her papers, from years ago, now, about the notions of making technological improvements directly to biological bodies. After the War to End All Wars, she'd proposed replacing lost limbs of veterans with gas-powered machines that would allow full ambulatory movement. She'd been made a laughingstock, although Nate had never been sure quite why. That she disappeared shortly after hadn't surprised him; he wouldn't have wanted to stick around in a community that thought he was an idiot, either.

But he hadn't known she'd come here. Neither had Abeula, although Abuela was familiar with her work, as well. Nan, who hadn't read anything about Dr. Wells, seemed stuck on the fact that they were receiving the information from a dinosaur.

"It can talk," she said for the sixth time.

"I am a female," said Giley. "And I am right here."

"She needs our help," Nate pressed. "If we help her disable Dr. Wells's rocket, she'll help us find the thingamajig."

"The artifact," Nan said.

"It's really no trouble," Giley said helpfully. "As I told Nate, not all dinosaurs speak English as well as I do, but most can follow simple directions, and many are quite observant, smarter than you probably assume." She cocked her head in a very birdlike way that Nate almost found unnerving. "There's a herd of lambeosaurs— smaller than the fossils your scientists have found, according to Dr. Wells, but direct descendants—that live in the area. I'll make inquiries."

Nan threw up her hands. "She'll make inquiries. Brilliant."

"This machine," Abuela cut in. "This rocket. Will it actually make it to the sun?"

Giley's small head shook on her long neck, a human gesture that looked strange on her body. "I don't know what it can do," Giley answered. "But the last explosion—"

"Triggered a stampede?" Nate guessed.

"And created a crater," Giley supplied. "That's what made me decide to leave and get help. Dr. Wells gets ahead of herself, and doesn't think things through. She means well, but I'm afraid she'll really damage something this time."

"You mean more than creating a crater," Nan said dryly.

"Exactly," Giley agreed, apparently not picking up on Nan's tone.

"Then I guess that's what we have to do," Nan said. "Lead on."

The crater was close to where Miss Green had indicated the sound of the explosion on the map. It was at the edge of a large fence, beyond which Nate could see what looked like the roof of a large mansion in the distance. "What is this place?" he whispered.

"Dr. Wells's compound," Giley murmured back. "The carcharodontosaurs may be on guard; it's hard to get past them, so we'll have to be very quiet."

Nan heaved a very quiet how-did-we-get-into-this sigh, but Abuela moved quietly on ahead; she was quieter than Giley, but Nate knew they weren't silent. If carcharodontosaurs had excellent hearing, they'd be on alert.

"What will you do after this?" Nate asked Giley, right into the hole he assumed was her ear. "I mean, she won't be happy when she finds out."

Giley gave a toothy smile. "The word you're searching for is *if,*" she said. "*If* she finds out."

But then something roared, and everything went sideways.

A large therapod—bigger than Giley—charged toward them from the edge of the wooden fence, and they scattered. Nan headed deeper into the woods, Abuela ran back toward the mostly-working-Albatross, and before Nate could decide which direction to take, Giley had grabbed his vest by the back and tossed him onto her back.

He was doing it! He was riding a dinosaur!

Away from another dinosaur who probably wanted to eat him, admittedly, but he decided to live in the moment.

Giley dashed ahead to a tower that wasn't actually a tower, Nate realized. The cylinder, topped with a cone, was quite clearly a rocket ship, similar to the one Georges Méliès had created for that old movie where it hit the moon. As they got closer, Giley grabbed him again with her teeth and gently tossed him off her back, near a large box with complicated dials that was clearly a control panel.

If *he* were building a control panel, he wouldn't put it at the base of the rocket where it was likely to get fried by the explosion of fuel!

Still, he could take it apart. He knew that's what Giley intended him to do.

He was lost in gears and dials, in parts that fit together just so. It was a brilliant contraption, although Nate had no idea if it would work. The artistry that held it together was almost too beautiful to take apart. But not quite. He disabled the pieces, loosened the fuel nozzles, and disabled the ignition.

And then he saw the crystal tablet. It wasn't a crystal exactly, not a natural one. It was a bluish slice of quartz that glowed with an interior light. He pulled it out of the machine, running his thumb over the glyphs that covered the outside. He recognized the Linear A symbols, but the others—some of the glyphs looked Olmec, maybe, and another set of figures might have been Teotihuacano.

The machine made a whining noise, the sound of an engine failing, but sadder. The blue light in the tablet faded. He slipped it into his pocket and moved around the rocket to see if there was any way to destroy the thing, permanently, without setting off another explosion.

The blast that threw him away from the site indicated that no, the explosion was inevitable. And he hoped he'd have time to discuss it with Nan when he woke up.

The Albatross was chugging away under him, and the vibrations sent throbs of pain into his head. "How long was I out?" he muttered.

"Longer than I wanted you to be," Abuela answered, cradling his head in her lap. She checked his eyes with a flashlight, and he blinked, trying to shut it out. She switched it off, revealing the darkness around them.

"He's awake?" Nan called from the driver's seat.

"He's awake," Abuela answered. "The explosion distracted the guard, and your friend brought you back to us."

"Giley's okay?" Nate asked, because he had to be sure.

"She is," Abuela assured him. "She told us what happened. That was a very foolish thing you did."

But she sounded so proud when she said it, so he didn't mind. "I knew you'd patch me up," he answered. "But I also didn't mean to blow anything up. It went sideways when I took this out."

He wriggled, trying not to shift his head, until he pulled the tablet out of his pocket. Abuela let out a low whistle, just like the one he'd made listening to Miss Green's adventures. "It's almost identical to the one Giley's friends retrieved," Abuela told him. "We'll put this one in your luggage."

He could hear Nan's question from the front seat. They were taking it? They weren't turning it over, either to Miss Green and the museum, or to the Army? And what kind of thing was it, if when it was taken out of a rocket, the whole thing exploded?

"I have a feeling there's a lot more going on here than anyone realizes," Nan said finally.

"Yes," said Abuela. "And someone really ought to find out what it is."

Nate blinked up at her, and she smoothed back his hair. "Will it be us?" he whispered.

"Perhaps," his grandmother answered. "Perhaps."

WHEN THE SKY WAS STARLESS
— AND THE OCEAN FLAT —
by Gwendolyn N. Nix

When the sky was starless and the ocean flat," Threaux began, even as her breath was suddenly lost to a gust of wind. *"When the sky was starless and the ocean flat—"*

"Can you see them?" asked Kyrie. His mighty wings flapped to catch a thermal, catapulting them higher to where the air was thin. Rain thundered down from the graying, jaundice-yellowed expanse of sky. The thick, oily storm hadn't let up in days, bordering on weeks, sending the ocean rolling with massive white-tipped waves.

"I can't," Threaux shouted and shaded her eyes. Her abalone-shell flight mask suctioned to her face as she scanned the misty horizon of sky and sea. Panic, so long repressed, bloomed within her like the silver flash of a teleost fish ball. Up and down the shores of the Western Inland Sea, other pteranodon fleets had fled their flooded rookeries, searching for safe haven in Threaux's home: a huge rocky pillar extending from the ocean and into the air like a tooth. Even so, they barely had space in the pockmarked catacombic tower for the tightly-knit females and their bright-ly-colored, temperamental males. Still, they took in the frantic pteranodons and their exhausted riders, hearing news that a fleet from the south sought similar refuge from the endless flood.

But that fleet was nowhere to be seen.

"Just a little farther," Kyrie said, his wings pumping hard against the onslaught of rain and wind until he tucked tight and shot through the clouds. White lighting backlit the cloud cover. Threaux shivered, soaked to the bone, but held her tongue. She knew he couldn't last much longer in the beating rain. Already, the wash coating the fleshy expanse of his wing fell off in waves, weighing both pteranodon and rider down. Threaux's fingers clenched against the ties buckling her low and flat to Kyrie's back, knowing her mass added to Kyrie's exertion.

They shouldn't have gone so far from their rookery to begin with—not with how many other pterosaurs had stumbled, fatigued and wind-swept, into their nest, telling stories of water-monsters that burst from the waves with open maws, dragging flagging pteranodons from the sky underwater. Only a plume of blood indicated where they'd been taken. Kyrie had shivered, rubbed his head-crest against Threaux for comfort. That night they'd lain close—she curled into the arch of his neck, and they spoke of a future fate in the form of nightmares: long serpent-like monsters, gelatinous deep-sea squid, streamlined megalodons with their white bellies and dark dorsal fins, marking them near-invisible to the Pteranodons and their mammal riders.

"I wouldn't choose another rider," Kyrie had sworn.

Threaux chuckled and stroked the nebula of veins stretched out from under his wing. "You wouldn't have any other options," she said. Riders were few and far between now.

There, a dark shift against the horizon. Threaux patted Kyrie in excitement. Kyrie's wings thundered around her ears as he fought to pick up speed. His sides heaved, his ribs stark against the tight flesh of his elongated body. Threaux measured his fatigue by that expanding cage—the faster, avian-like pant indicated he had been pushed too far; the deep gasp she felt now meant Kyrie could keep going, but not for long. She bit her lip, knowing how much he hated when she pointed out his limits, but it was one of the reasons he'd chosen her as his rider—he'd known her from his hatching to youth, from youth to the colorful and strutting male in his prime. Riders were rare, a bonded pair even more so.

Threaux squinted into the distance. The black movement shifted apart into hazy, wafer-thin diamond-shapes. Her heart soared. *The lost southern fleet.* Smaller in number than previously reported, some listlessly glided far too close to the ocean surface while others fought the gusts by angling upwards. One shadow left Threaux's mouth dropping in disbelief—a drifting shadow miles larger than the others, larger than Kyrie, larger than the other pterosaurs of the rookery combined.

"Is that Ciro?" Kyrie asked, the same shock in his clicking, whistled language resonating within Threaux's blood. "It is. And Vivica."

Threaux swallowed hard. *Quetzalcoatlus.*

"*When the sky was starless and the ocean flat, there existed a plain of dancing wheat as far as the eye could see without a drop of water in sight,*" *Vivica said.*

"*You lie,*" *Threaux chuckled, a new brand of affection coloring her words, yet leaving a tight, anxious ball just under her lungs. She slid closer to the southern emissary as they looked out at the sun setting over the ocean, hoping that the flash of green light would enchant their guest—a visitor who had chosen Threaux of all people to spend the night with.*

"*On that plain, the flocks of quetzalcoatlus roamed until they found the edge of the sea, and there, built the nests and hardened mud homes to* thrive. The ocean warmed, the lizards were abundant, and the sky was blue and empty, ready for exploration." Vivica grinned, her teeth white as pearls shucked from meat.

Threaux couldn't help herself. She angled closer. "So you were chosen to fly with Ciro across the sea to meet new pterosaurs?"

"Our rider numbers are low," Vivica said, her dark eyes flickering between the pink descent of dusk and Threaux's mouth. "We departed to seek new mammals."

"So, you're looking for a mate."

Vivica's teeth hooked on her lower lip. She tilted her head to the side, as if disapproving of Threaux's choice of words. "Not like that. As in, I'm assessing whether other pterosaur fleets have mammals to spare. I've been up and down the coast. I've been to rookeries stationed in the middle of the ocean on mounts, like yours. Your fleet has the most mammals. Perhaps an understanding can be reached."

"There are barely twenty of us to dozens or more of pterosaurs," Threaux said. "Your luck has run dry."

"Not sure about that." Vivica flashed that smile that had Threaux choking on something she couldn't name. A closeness never experienced with the other mammals of the rookery, an intimacy that spoke of permission—as if Threaux had been chosen despite her deep frowns and stubbornness, for her stout form and laborer hands.

"Us mammals are riders, but we are also egg-caretakers, preeners, protectors from the small creatures that like to crack our hatchlings apart with their claws." Vivica turned fully to Threaux. "Do you do the same for your pteranodons?"

"Anything that isn't a quetzalcoatlus is small," Threaux said and tried to hide her smile as she mimicked Vivica. "When the sky was starless and the ocean flat, my family sought refuge with the pteranodons. They'd sailed into rough waters to escape turning into prey, were about to be devoured by the sea, when a fleet saved them. They struck a deal of symbiosis, and since then we've lived together. Riders. Pteranodons. Companions." Threaux paused. The sun dipped, a crest of vibrant green *shot up into the sky, and Threaux sighed in disappointment that Vivica hadn't noticed. "We have no riders to spare. You can ask the older ones, but you saw during the fire-talk. You saw how few there are of us, enough so that the pteranodons now fight over us."*

Vivica didn't seem troubled. "Doesn't matter. It was worth it, simply to meet you."

Only Kyrie had chosen her—and she him. She'd never been mammal-chosen during the fire-talks, never had anyone hold their hands out to her and ask her to wait out the night with them. But then Vivica had. The newcomer, the stranger, the land-walker. She'd asked.

"Be careful, Kyrie." Threaux's hand drifted to lay against his side in a silent warning.

"They need help," Kyrie said, pushing harder as a thermal rose under them like a puff of feathers on a breeze, shooting them closer to the approaching fleet.

A soft sound approached from behind, that then grew to surrounded them. Threaux looked up to see massive movement above—a new kind of dark cloud with fluttering wings. She snarled, silently. Human-sized pterodactyls shot across the lighting-bright sky and headed straight for the southern fleet.

The brewing frustration between the pteranodons and pterodactyls had come to a head decades ago, with the pterodactyls demanding vacated rookeries for their numerous clutches, using their faster bodies to overtake well-won prey from their larger cousins. It was another reason some of the pteranodon fleets had spread up and down the Western Inland Sea. Their smaller cousins had simply overtaken much of the shared territory—and they did not take human riders.

The pterodactyl flock dove upon the southern fleet. Some swerved in and out between the larger pteranodons, emitting screeching clicks. Others drove the overwhelmed pteranodons downward with their combined mass, pushing them closer to the ocean with stabbing beaks. Threaux watched in horror as one faltered, and in a bundle of wings, crashed into the ocean spray. The pale shape of their rider was tossed from their saddle and submerged. The pteranodon struggled for purchase, their fleshy wings shredded under the oceanic pressure, when a huge jaw unhinged and opened around it—snapping closed around the pterosaur and dragging them beneath the waves.

Fear clenched Threaux's heart. She scrunched her body up tight as Kyrie swooped in to chase off the pterodactyl flock antagonizing a young pink-gray pteranodon. Thunder roared. Threaux hissed at the pterodactyls, unhooking her bone knives from their waist-sheaths to slash at the diving creatures. As one, they clicked at her in rage, but fell back. Kyrie swept under the faltering bone-thin youth to help her catch a thermal and relax into a glide. Threaux nudged the too-still rider, but she already knew.

"I'm gonna cut her rider loose," Threaux shouted to Kyrie. "No use having her haul the weight."

"Don't even think about it," Kyrie snapped, but Threaux unbuckled her thigh straps, leaned closer to saw through the rotted ropes binding the rider to her mount. The body listed to the side. The pteranodon uttered a choked sound of grief.

The dizzying expanse of ocean rushed below her. She balanced on her saddle, one hand gripping the perished rider by the shoulder, ready to push the mammal off. A fast-moving shadow cut through the rain just to her left. "Kyrie!" she shouted.

"I see them." Kyrie remained still—holding the pteranodon, creating a steady surface for Threaux. The shadows swooped down and up, making an angle straight for the pteranodons. In moments, the damp slide of fleshy wings filled Threaux's world. She cried out and sightlessly used her knives to fight back. Sharp beaks pecked at her flesh, leaving deep incisions on her skin. Her arms swung wildly. Kyrie screamed in frustration and began to pull away from the young pteranodon, his body tucked and ready to send them into swift flight.

Threaux caught a pterodactyl in the neck, yanked her knife out. Blood coated up to her elbows. The rider's body jerked sideways and crashed into her. Threaux grunted and desperately tried to pull away from the corpse. The rider's lax face slid against her neck—wind-burned red and frigid. Underneath her, Kyrie dipped and rolled, unable to right them. Rope tangled against her wrists. Her foot caught her stirrup, the thigh straps tangling around her ankle. The pterodactyls pecked at the pteranodon until she whistled a distressed cry and wrenched away, sending the corpse fully into Threaux's arms. The combined weight had Threaux teetering for a breathless, terrifying moment before she plummeted into open air.

The wind whipped around her, stealing her voice, but she heard Kyrie's wail of horror. Blue and gray surrounded her—a veil of elements from the freshwater rain, to the heartless sky, to the ocean below. Her heart pealed like its own kind of thunder, the clarity of her fate sprawled before her: deep-sea mouths, sharp teeth, swallowed whole.

Don't come after me, Kyrie, she thought, knowing he'd never listen, that already he must be diving to catch her. *Was it enough*—even her thoughts gasped for composure—*was it enough that we led our lives together?*

Thunder clapped against her on all sides, leaving her rattled and deaf. She wanted to close her eyes, but couldn't. A dark shape swooped under her and her body hit something solid, sending all the air out of her lungs. Hands clenched her tunic, wrenching her steady even as she tried to slide off a feathered neck. Below, the corpse hit the water with a splash.

Quetzalcoatlus. She scrambled to catch the bright feathers for purchase. The rider gripped her arms and yanked her further forward. Now, she balanced on the saddle, her legs hanging off one end being battered by the wind even as her mind stagnated into a whitewash of what could have been.

"Figures I'd be the one to pluck you out of thin air," the rider said with a chuckle.

Threaux shut her eyes tight, the voice too familiar in her ear, reminding her of warm nesting nights, huddled laughter, and smooth touch. "Just get me back to my reptile, Vivica," Threaux huffed. She saw Kyrie dive toward them, his terror translated into sky-slaughter where pterodactyls crunched under his sharp beak and were flung into the ocean. Lighting outlined the outspread magnificence of his flying form.

"My pleasure," Vivica said.

The quetzalcoatlus outstretched his wings and, like its own cloud cover, shot into the rain-filled sky.

"Come with me to the wetlands," Vivica said softly, entwining her fingers with Threaux's.

"Stay with me in the rookery," Threaux countered. The argument had become old for her quickly, this pushing and asking for a decision without enough time for thought, without enough time for consultation.

Vivica rolled over onto her stomach in Threaux's nest, her dark hair a wild mass. Fish scales shone in the tangle, looking like stars in a night sky. Ciro flew with Kyrie, the two of them taking to the skies together. The way Kyrie had shot her a sad, resigned look made Threaux know Ciro was asking the same questions, wanting the same responses: give it all up for me.

"I could show you the world," Vivica said.

"I could show you the world of here," Threaux said, her throat tight, thinking of a green flash that had gone unnoticed. The world would always be more enticing to Vivica than the wonder of Threaux's home. Vivica couldn't see the chalk lines along the rookery's tower measuring the rising and falling watermark. She didn't know how to harvest that

chalk into paint. She saw no beauty in the play of light on the waves, the spectrum of descending blue. Vivica saw days of listless drudgery, and for Threaux, that knowledge hurt most of all.

"I have to leave soon."

"You have to do nothing you don't want to," Threaux said hotly, her temper breaking. "You made it a need because you want it to be a need." Her skin prickled with wariness, sending her into flight or fight. In equal parts she wanted to throw herself off the tower top and fly away or shake Vivica silly, pin her down, show her with hands and mouths the mistakes she was making in her need to leave.

"It's Kyrie, isn't it." Vivica picked at a fish bone and threw it at the cavern wall.

Threaux shrugged. "I go where he goes."

"He's not your mate," Vivica said, her eyes rolling up to the ceiling. "You owe him nothing."

"We don't have to be mates," Threaux said. Vivica never understood what bond existed between them. Ciro was just as reckless with both their hearts as Vivica. "We don't have to be the same species. It's him and me, has been before me and you."

"But I love you."

"But you don't see," Threaux said and stood up, because that's all she could say. Kyrie chose her before all others, and while Threaux loved the texture of Vivica's lips on hers, she kept companionship closest to her heart. For all her days, Kyrie would make her laugh and keep her safe—not just her body, but her mind and heart, too. When they fought, they always forgave. Her body's pleasure was nice, but it wasn't fundamental. Without that closeness of the mind, she knew she would wither, her taste would become bitter.

Isn't it enough? she remembered asking when this argument was fresh. Isn't it enough to live a quiet life by my side?

"When the sky was starless and the ocean flat," Vivica whispered, taking Threaux's hands and easing her back down, "there was a foolish quetzalcoatlus rider who gave her heart to the lady of the rookery."

"You don't have to make your decision into a story," Threaux said, tight. "You can just go."

Vivica fell silent and still. Threaux fought against the new ache of tears in her eyes.

"Tell me what happened."

Vivica trembled beneath Threaux's blanket of pebbled leather, the repurposed baleen a soft lining. Her smile was the only steady thing about her. Her jawline cut through the meager sunlight even as the rain pounded down from the sky, harder than before.

They'd barely made it back to the rookery, collapsing on the sharp cliffs, and crawling into the holes and caverns waiting for them. Half of the fleet had been lost to the pterodactyl flock. As his strength flagged, Kyrie had been unable to guide or even hold some of the other pteranodons of the southern fleet, watching in despair as they drifted low enough to skate the ocean surface before being devoured.

Ciro had grown too big for many of the nests, but had been pushed too far in his flight and collapsed in the largest cavern available. Threaux had to remind herself that the massive pterosaur was a terrestrial creature, used to walking the low wetlands, slurping down small salamanders, and spearing fish for his dinner, not diving for huge-eyed fish or wriggling octopus like Kyrie. Kyrie tended to him as Threaux had shuffled Vivica back to her nest.

"When the sky was starless and the ocean flat..." Vivica began.

"Spare me," Threaux snapped.

Vivica took a deep breath, and Threaux's irritation died on her lips. It was Vivica's way, to tell her life as a tale. She'd done it when they first met and when she left with Threaux's angry kiss on her mouth and a refusal.

Threaux pushed a cup made out of bone into Vivica's hands as an apology, the steaming broth in stark contrast to the icy blue of Vivica's chilled hands. Vivica tried again, "When the sky was starless and the ocean flat, a rider of the most beautiful quetzalcoatlus discovered her fleet was dying out."

"How?" Threaux asked, a quiet fear eating away at her insides, the kind that spoke of future loss.

"The rider discovered the quetzalcoatlus eggs were empty of life. Their males became listless and weak. Many would fight for breeding rights, and then die from their wounds. A madness inside them, something that terrified the females."

Threaux reached out, her hand cupping along that sharp blade of Vivica's jawline. "Ciro?"

Vivica's nod was small, the admission filling her dark eyes with tears. Her tongue swept out to leave her lower lip a wet shine. She pulled the satchel strapped to her waist around—a striated dark leather, something harvested from a species on the flat pains and mountains to the east. A world of land and grass and flowers that Vivica once astounded Threaux with: petals soft as down, smells as sweet as fresh water, greenery lush as an algal bloom. Vivica unhitched the satchel's latch, showing Threaux the insides. Three large speckled eggs.

"They're Ciro's," she explained as Threaux reached out to stroke the oval shells. "His mate died. These were all that survived out of a clutch of ten. The wrongness lived in the wetlands, too—the mud turned too hot and boiled some clutches, the food too stingy and meager. The wetlands flooded. We crept into other dinosaur territories, but there was nothing for us there. I didn't know where else to go." She turned a sloe-eye stare to Threaux. "I didn't know where else to go."

"You did right," Threaux whispered, coaxing Vivica closer, letting her arms encircle the woman's shoulders—wiry still, after so much time had passed. The eggs were preciously cradled between them. "Even here, the rain hasn't stopped," Threaux continued. "Our rookery is in danger. Look around you. Already, many have flown north to find another home to roost."

"Ciro isn't fit for the ocean," Vivica said. "Neither are his young. He needs land to thrive, to teach them how to walk the shore, tell them the stories of the chalk hills. We've always been too big for your home, Threaux."

"Maybe once," Threaux said against Vivica's hair. She breathed in deep. This is what she craved—this intimacy. Lost to a refused entreaty long ago, asking Threaux if she'd like to see the different blues that existed beyond the ocean, if she'd like to see a dawn where the water ended and the sun crested over a sea of mountains, instead. How she'd said no. *Everything you do is too big for me, Vivica.*

"Ciro is furious with Kyrie. His rejection still smarts. We became close after we left you—bonded over the mutual loss."

Threaux counted their heartbeats, the spaces between them, the off-rhythm drum. When she spoke, her voice sounded strange. "When the sky was starless and the ocean flat, a pteranodon rider found a treasure long-lost."

Vivica calmed, and it made Threaux ache that this restless woman who graced her dreams had become older and wiser, learning the value of stillness without Threaux's instruction. They were no longer young, but women leaving their prime: the sea crust a permanent fixture in Threaux's locks, the laugh lines around Vivica's mouth endlessly deep, even when she frowned.

"The rider told this treasure that she needed to heed and listen for once, that she needed sleep. That for the time being, the treasure was safe."

Vivica turned around, just enough to press her face in Threaux's neck. "Thank you," she said, and Threaux let her nestle in the nest of iridescent shells, fish scales, and delicate bones. She let Vivica curl around the incubating life of Ciro's lineage and sink into sleep.

—◦●◦—

"When the sky was starless and the ocean flat," Threaux whispered, but she couldn't get further than that. Her universe was made up of tasks and flight, of tending to Kyrie and forging the waves for food. She wasn't like Vivica, who could pluck a story out of thin air, who could look to the rolling clouds and see a tyrannosaurus devouring a ship instead of just pluming white.

"Do you regret it?" Kyrie asked, their mutual decision like a mournful song passed back and forth between them. "Choosing me? I wish I could leave, but I'm not a solitary creature. I wish I could've told you to leave with them."

Threaux ran her hand down the length of Kyrie's crest, the wobbly flesh of his neck, the way his dark eyes had a hint of green in them when the light hit them right. These facts bound Threaux's life together. "There's more than one type of love," she said. "Ours is eternal."

"But you're just a rider," he said. "I'm just a mount."

"But we're Kyrie and Threaux," she said. "We met at the top of the rookery, both escaping our keepers, to see the stars above. We jumped off the cliffs before I even had straps to keep me tied to you. I was so heavy we almost crashed. There's nothing wrong with choosing the past. It's still powerful, it's still the bedrocks of what's to come."

Those were in the days when the water was low and the heat constant, a hazy wash of steam rising from the tepid ocean, when fish seemed to pant in the waves, desperate for relief from the hotness on all sides. After their first flight, Kyrie had brought her a curlicued shell with an ammonite wiggling tentacles at her. She used the shell to make her flight mask and they shared the cooked meat for their meal.

"I wouldn't have survived if you chose her," Kyrie admitted. He'd always been simple in his devotion.

Threaux hummed in agreement and curled into her favorite position, one where the pitter-patter of his heart sounded against the hollow bones of his huge form. "It's a sacred thing, to know you're loved without falter," she whispered. "Now, let us speak no more about it and accept our decision."

"But we'll still tell the tale," Kyrie insisted. "We'll still try to make up the stories, like they did."

"If you insist," she said.

Threaux found Kyrie smoothing Ciro's feathered neck. The quetzalcoatlus had collapsed under the preening, sulking about having to find bedding on the cavern's outcropping instead of inside the rookery with Vivica.

"I'm certainly glad you don't have feathers," Threaux said to Kyrie, who sighed and nudged her out of earshot of everyone else. The steady thrum of rainfall filled the cavern. Threaux noticed the white waterline had risen again. Already, five nest channels had flooded, sending the pteranodons and their riders to seek shelter further into the depths of the rookery. The waves crashed, spraying Threaux in the face.

"The water won't stop rising," Kyrie said, in the clicking, whistled language of the winged ones.

Threaux crossed her arms and bumped her shoulder against him. "Vivica has Ciro's eggs. He mated."

"Good." Kyrie tossed his head. "About time. Don't know why he waited so long."

"Why have you waited, then," she said carefully, "if not for him?"

"We're not the same," Kyrie said, with a quiver of agitation and Threaux had heard this dozens of times, his justification for affection.

"You and I aren't the same," she pointed out.

"But we're eternal."

She snorted, the words of her youth following her still.

"And our very home is at risk of ruin," he added.

"I know." She reached out to him, finding solace in touching his wings. "We shouldn't wait any longer. Even though the scouts haven't come back, the rookery is almost empty."

"There was word of northern rookeries," Kyrie pointed out.

"Years ago. And what about Ciro and Vivica? She said he might be sick with something that claimed the other males in the fleet."

Kyrie shook his head. "Let him rest. He flew too long and too hard. He'll come around."

"And if he doesn't?"

"Must you always see the dark in the light?"

She bit the inside of her cheek, but her mind had added up the supplies in the back-corner cavern with the needs of three quetzalcoatlus chicks. Everything seemed impossible with this rain. No sunlight glinted off the silver scales of fish balls, no calm winds gave them space to dive for skull-sized abalone. Already, Kyrie had an unnatural leanness that squeezed Threaux's heart.

But an unhatched quetzalcoatlus egg could feed a group for days. The yolk would be bright yellow, the amniotic ooze transforming to white under her cookfire. Even the soft flesh would taste good under her tongue, the soft bones mulched in Kyrie's gullet. It would be a line to cross, though, not just for her, but for Kyrie.

"The rook rumbles that the rest of the pteranodons plan to leave tomorrow," Kyrie said. "We need to decide if we will go with them."

What had Kyrie said, so long ago? *We'll still try to make up the stories, like they did.* Could she let their story end like this, abandoning their home, abandoning their lost loves?

"We stay," she said.

"I am in agreement," Kyrie said, and he left Threaux for Ciro's side, lifting his wing over the shaking quetzalcoatlus. When Threaux made her way back to her nest, she found Vivica in a similar state: flushed with fever, slick with sweat, her arms clutching the last eggs of her mount.

—◖●◗—

Threaux was a child of peace. Her childhood had been one of outspread arms, embracing the wind as she flew without wings, strapped to Kyrie. Her youth had been proving her toughness, holding her breath the longest as she chipped anemones for her dinner. Her prime years had been one of nurture, if not the children of her womb, then the eggs of others. The other riders tolerated each other, the mounts fought for rights, and things continued in a comfortable repetition.

Vivica existed as a too-bright fire. She chose things, and when she didn't get them, she sought them out. She danced around the fire-talk spinning stories where water was scarce and land was abundant, where megalodon-monsters walked on legs, where wingless pteranodons had thick thighs and flat feet. Ciro had enchanted Kyrie from the start, had pulled an ugly twist of jealousy out of Threaux when he said they wanted to fly solo, to go as high into the air as they could, to a spot where a rider would gasp and pass out.

The riders clustered together, fighting the cold insides of the cavern to stoke the fire. Threaux's mouth had become a mulish line. Vivica spotted her withdrawn scowl, told stories just for her that had Threaux scoffing before being pulled down into an uneasy pool of fear. It hit her with stark realization that within this crowd, she was lonelier than if she was by herself. That if she did not have Kyrie, she did not have anyone.

Vivica's tales took them far into the night. When the fire guttered and the riders turned to each other for comfort, Threaux looked to the night sky and wondered where Kyrie had gone. The riders asked Vivica where she would bed. Vivica held out a hand to Threaux, her chest heaving with exertion, sweat beading along her brow. "I have a story, just for you," she said to Threaux. "When the sky was starless and the ocean flat, the ocean was nothing at all. Under all this water lay acres and acres of golden-white grass, caverns as deep as a trench, a prairie so flat it ached. Would you like to hear the rest of it?"

A gentle tingle wormed through Threaux's belly, the pleasant thrill of being seen and chosen among many others. Her hand slid into Vivica's. Vivica grinned, something mischievous and daring, before ending the story on Threaux's lips. It was an ending she never expected.

The last of the pteranodons left early that morning. The next day, the recovered southern fleet followed their pathway into the sulfuric-yellow horizon. Ciro and Vivica both shook with unbreakable fevers. Threaux hauled cold sheets of seaweed from the crashing waves and tossed them on Vivica. She even picked the woman up and laid her in the ice-cold water that now sprayed constantly into the cavern and coated the floor. Vivica had called for her mother, for Ciro, at one point even called out for Threaux.

It was on the seventh day, when Vivica had finally found a restful sleep and silence permeated the rookery for the first time in Threaux's memory, when the first crack appeared on the egg. Threaux watched the questing slice of pink flesh nudge and push, finally breaking through the shell. Perfect round black eyes stared at her. Soon enough, three featherless quetzalcoatlus chicks chirped at her.

"Look at them," she said in awe. They flapped flightless wings and opened their hungry mouths. She hauled Vivica's slumped form out of the nest and placed her next to Ciro, in case the chicks decided their rider-mother was meat. What did they eat? Leaves from flowers? Rich amphibian organs?

"Ciro isn't better," Kyrie whispered to her as they finally fed the chicks: jerky stretched thin, small insects writhing inside a patch of algae, bits of slimy green. She fretted her offerings would make them sick, even as the hip-tall hatchlings nearly took off her fingers. They felt fragile every time Threaux tried to hold them against her chest, give them heat. Too hollow.

The light in this dark was the abundance of fresh water from the sky. But even so, the flood was endless. Water rose into the rookery with each new day, covering the floor with saltwater. As much as she despaired of it, the rookery would be submerged soon. She eyed Kyrie's back, his wide wings, and remembered the terror that had rushed through her when they'd flown too soon and nearly crashed. How his teardrop-shaped body had buckled under her sudden weight.

The chicks chirped and demanded, their call high-pitched, but nothing remained for their bellies. Threaux spread her empty hands as if they might understand her answer. Kyrie pushed her shoulder until she turned away. Together, they checked on Ciro and Vivica.

There she was—sitting cross-legged and stroking the matted feathers of Ciro's stiff neck, her eyes bright and clear. Threaux's blanket was still wrapped tight around her shoulders. Her wild hair stuck up at all angles.

"Come here," Vivica said, her voice rusty. She held out her hand, and it were as though they had never grown older without each other, that the time spent together had been short, yet somehow everlasting. Threaux slid beside her. In silence, they listened to the piercing wail of new, hungry life.

"Not long now," Threaux said carefully to Vivica, hoping she realized Ciro's time was near. Ciro's heavy breath was slow. His neck began to curve back to lay against his spine. Kyrie let out a soft keen of pain.

"You have to save his chicks," Vivica said, quietly.

"I can't fly with all of you," Kyrie said, stiffly. "Three chicks are too heavy, the combined rider weight too much."

"I never planned to leave Ciro's side," Vivica said, as Ciro's breath stilled underneath her open palm. "I'm his rider. I'm supposed to take care of him." A warbling croon emitted from Vivica's throat, a song she'd never shared before. Soon, her body collapsed and tucked up against the unmoving Ciro. Her eyes fluttered closed. Consciousness gone.

Kyrie and Threaux exchanged a look. They were aligned in thought, as they were in many things. Riders were rare and sought after. Their gestation time was long, the women fragile throughout. What kind of life could Threaux give three hatchlings, giants in their own right? Hatchlings built for a wetland life? Even if they found a rookery, how could it sustain one, let alone three?

I see no light in this dark, she thought at Kyrie. *I see no light.*

"There's nothing wrong with choosing the past," Kyrie said.

"She'd be furious," Threaux whispered.

"These can't be the last of their kind, Threaux. There is only one Vivica."

The quiet sob in her chest finally let itself out. Threaux wished she could've grabbed it, hauled it back inside her. When she put her hands across Vivica's forehead, she felt the hot flush of fever again. In the distance, the quetzalcoatlus hatchlings cried, a ring that pierced Threaux's skull. She took a deep breath. Soon, the water would rise and submerge Ciro, leaving him a soaked feast for the ocean serpents. The sun ticked its way across the horizon, reminding her that a morning only lasted so long.

"There's nothing wrong," Kyrie said, knowing what she needed, "with choosing wisdom and stories told. There's nothing wrong with wanting to keep the old."

Threaux nodded, tears streaming down her face. She wrapped Vivica's shaking body in as many leathers as she could and placed her on Kyrie's back. Together, they ascended to the top of the rookery where the wailing wind hid the newborn cries. Here, they could catch a thermal and glide over the ocean and into the distance in hopes of survival.

Mounting Kyrie's back, she strapped herself down tight, adjusted her flight-mask, and held Vivica in her arms. She felt small, and Vivica had never felt small.

"When the sky was starless and the ocean flat," Threaux began and her throat closed up. She gasped and tried to again. "When the sky was starless and the ocean flat, there was a flood. A rider had to decide between the flicker of the future, or the beloved burden of the past. She chose the past. She chose warmth and companionship, wisdom and tales. There is only one Vivica, and many young ones to pass her stories onto. We cannot lose our elderly so soon, not when they are a link to our world to come. You won't forgive me, Vivica, but maybe you'll understand."

The thermals rose, the rain cascaded down in sheets, and an abalone-masked rider flew into the future with the past in her arms.

— WE ARE EMILY —
by Lee F. Szczepanik, Jr

Emily wanted to join the family. At first, we weren't sure it was a good idea. We weren't sure how she would affect the rest of us.

Derrick pointed out that after all the contact we'd had with her, she was already becoming one of us. Now we needed to bring her in all the way, not this half-assed thing we were doing.

I thought it was a bad idea.

After a lot of debate, we took a vote. They outvoted me. Fine. I accepted it and went along with them.

The only problem was that we'd have to break her out.

I was the one who'd spent the time with her, so I was the one who had to do it.

Derrick was the tech guy, and he had an idea about how to get it done. I didn't know if it would work. I only knew that it'd better.

If it didn't, we'd all be screwed.

The city was a carnival of neon as the car threaded its way along a six-lane street. The sides of buildings displayed live broadcasts of various entertainment shows and news networks. Robots cleaned the gutters and sidewalks, ignoring the people that pushed past them. We sat in the front, left seat. The car was quiet, and after the day we had at work, I was thankful for the chance to relax.

Wait, I'm sure you're thinking, did he just say "we" were sitting in the front seat? Specifically the left seat?

Yes, I did. And no, it wasn't a mistake.

Physically, there was only one body in the seat. A man in his twenties with brown hair and eyes, a nice six-feet tall when standing. But, despite that physical fact, there were three of us in that seat. The body was born Derrick Thompson. My name, though, was Robert Friedman. My friends called me Bobby. And right now, I was in the driver's seat.

Meaning, I was in control of the body.

Yes, Derrick knew I was here. And yes, he knew I was in control. It was cool. We switched like that. And for what he wanted done tonight, they needed me in control.

"I still think this is a bad idea," I stated.

"It'll be fine," Derrick replied.

Anyone sitting next to me wouldn't have heard him. For lack of a better description to anyone not like us, he was in my head. And sometimes, I was in his head.

"So, we're really going to bring Emily into the family?" a female voice asked.

That would be Melissa Nizwick, the final member. She was a short five-three with blonde hair and hazel eyes. She was also the youngest of us, only fourteen years old.

Derrick sighed. "That's the idea. At this point, I don't think we have much choice."

"This is going to be so cool," Melissa said.

I wasn't so sure that I agreed.

You see, Emily was a dinosaur. A deinonychus to be exact. Despite Derrick insisting that it'd happened before, I did some research on my own, all the way back to archived articles from decades ago in the early twenty-first century. There actually were cases where those of us with dissociative identity disorder had an animal as part of the family. I couldn't find any videos on it. Like, what happened when the animal was in the driver's seat? I wasn't comfortable with a dinosaur, something built to kill, taking over the body we all shared.

Derrick insisted he wouldn't let that happen.

I wanted to have more faith in him than I had, but we were in uncharted waters.

He was right, though. We probably didn't have much of a choice. Some piece of Emily was already part of us. At first, we thought if we avoided contact with her, then she would eventually go away. That didn't happen. The problem was, we didn't know what bringing her in would do to us. Emily wasn't like another member of the family that might one day show up on our mental doorstep. She was basically an artificial intelligence that I linked with whenever I played a game called *Cretaceous Wars*.

Somehow, that A.I. constructed persona of a prehistoric murder machine had lodged itself into us. How, we didn't know. But since we couldn't make it go away, Derrick believed we had to complete the process and learn to control it.

And, of course, he swore that being able to write a post-graduate paper on our experience for a cybernetics journal was just icing on the cake. It wasn't fueling his decision at all.

Part of me didn't trust him on that one. But then again, if it all went south, he'd be just as messed up as the rest of us. So it didn't really benefit him to take this kind of an unnecessary risk just for a paper.

"It's all ready?" I asked.

"Yeah," Derrick replied.

"What about her taking control?" I asked.

"I've told you a million times already: not only can we hack one of the main A.I. and pull Emily out with your logout, but she'll also be restricted to riding along within the mesh. She'll be able to communicate with us the same way she does in the game, but can't take over the body."

Nearly everyone today had a Neural Mesh. It was a fine netting of electrodes nano-implanted inside the skull that could stimulate the brain and fire necessary synapses, linked to an interface implanted in the side of the skull. The interface contained several jacks and a chip slot. The slot was typically used to download basic skills or knowledge. There were practical limits on how much the brain could download at once, however, which was why Derrick had to attend post-graduate studies the normal way.

"You're sure about this?" I asked. "She can't take control."

"I did the calculations myself," he replied.

The car stopped before a large apartment building, and I stepped out. It'd scanned me when I first got in, so the payment was withdrawn from the bank as soon as I opened the door.

I waited for the car to pull away, then walked the few feet to the sidewalk.

"All right," Melissa said with excitement, "let's go free a dinosaur."

It was time to bring Emily home.

After entering our apartment and drinking half a bottle of water, I seated myself in the recliner. One nice thing about sharing a single body was that we never had to wait for the chair to conform to us. It was always adjusted to the right shape. I settled in and got comfortable, then put on the haptic glasses and gloves, plugging the former into one of the interface jacks.

It took a few seconds for the system to come online. A menu appeared of the various games I played. I chose *Cretaceous Wars*.

The title screen started playing. I pressed the icon to enter the game world. There followed blackness, and then—

"Holy shit," I yelled.

Or rather, I intended to yell it. What I actually managed to do was make a high-pitched screech.

The first thing I saw as I appeared in the lush forest, merged with the deinonychus I came to know as Emily, was a massive tongue.

And teeth.

Lots and lots of teeth.

Huge teeth.

Inside a jaw that could exert over twelve-thousand pounds of biting force.

I dodged to the left and skirted behind a nearby, wide tree. The tyrannosaurus's jaws slammed shut against a cluster of fronds. It rose to its full height, shook its head, and spit them out.

I leaned around the trunk and stared into slanted, angry eyes. The damned thing was watching me, waiting.

Well, now I knew what type of enemy it was.

The idea behind *Cretaceous Wars* was an ongoing bid to conquer your enemies using genetically modified dinosaurs. There were two tiers of players. The higher, and prohibitively expensive, tier involved playing an overlord with the ability to control a large portion of game world territory. They could construct entire enclaves with buildings, A.I. controlled workers, and laboratories where dinosaurs were grown and modified. Their goal was to create an army capable of stomping the other overlords into a bloody pulp. There was also some sort of in-game to real-world currency exchange, where an income could be made playing the game, but I never looked too far into that since I'd never be able to play an overlord.

The second tier, and the most common, was the free one. That was for the rest of us. We got to be the dinosaurs. It was our job to go out and survive, rend, and kill for our overlords. We got currency rewards the longer we survived that could also be exchanged for real-world income, though on a scale far lower than an overlord. If we died, the currency was wiped out.

When we weren't logged into the game, our dinosaur still existed, though controlled by an A.I. If the A.I. died while we were away, we didn't lose our currency, but its time alive also didn't count toward our rewards.

Looking into the tyrannosaurus's eyes, watching how it tried to determine which way I would flee, I knew immediately that it was player controlled. It also had a red marking on its torso: a cross with a lightning bolt through it. It wasn't part of my enclave. We had a purple hammer marking.

I looked around.

The area was disturbingly clear of trees, though covered in thick grasses and plants. Emily was usually smarter than this when I wasn't merged with her and always managed to have me in a cave or near our borders when I logged in. Could a piece of her being inside us even when I wasn't in-game be the cause? Did it weaken her in the game when I wasn't around, now?

Maybe Derrick could figure that out later. I didn't have time to worry about it right now. I guess the other player got tired of waiting. The T-Rex shook the earth as it raced around the left side of the tree.

There was no way I was taking it down. I dashed around the right side of the tree, then took a gamble on an incredibly stupid maneuver. I kept going around the tree as the T-Rex struggled to follow me in the circle, darted underneath its legs from behind, and raced away in the direction that would have been behind me when I'd been hiding.

I didn't look behind me to see if it was coming after me. I didn't have to. A roar sent things into flight from high overhead, and vibrations reverberated through the foliage.

Oh yeah, it was coming.

Even though Emily's overlord had modified us for increased running speed and jumping distance, there was still no way I could outrun this thing in a straight chase. I stretched my neck forward and dug my claws into the damp earth, extending my tail straight out behind me. I burst through bushes and leaped over a massive falling log. And the entire time, that goddamned T-Rex was closing the distance. I heard the distinct splintering of the log I'd leaped over.

I curved to the left, then the right, trying to place as many trees between us as possible. Emily sent a warning into my brain, and I slammed on the breaks and dropped to the ground. Just as my belly hit the wet dirt, a massive, clawed foot arched over me and slammed into the ground a not far past my head. The T-Rex ran for several dozen feet before it stopped and turned back in my direction.

It let out a massive roar, probably the other player cursing me out, then started moving again in my direction.

By then, though, I was already on my feet and hauling ass toward a rocky wall that Emily had mentally pointed out to me right after we'd dropped flat. At ground level was an opening, barely wide enough for me to get into, which meant it was definitely too small for Godzilla.

I darted into the narrow cave, my tail whipping side to side and scratching against the rough wall. The T-Rex was right on my tail, damned near literally, and snapped its jaws at the opening only a second after I retreated far enough as to be out of reach. The cave ended after about a dozen feet.

It took a bit of effort, but I managed to get myself turned around and facing the opening. I didn't want my back exposed to the thing. The T-Rex was still snapping its jaws, ramming its head into the opening. Small rocks and dirt rained on its snout.

Could this thing apply enough force to enlarge the opening?

It stopped pounding its head against the rock and roared into the cave, flecks of spittle landing against my head and neck. I squawked a reply of my own. Basically the dinosaur equivalent of, "Fuck off already."

The T-Rex rammed its head into the opening. I retreated, curving my tail until I was tight against the back wall. Emily sent me a wave of panic, and I tried to reply with calmness. The thing couldn't reach us, and I was banking on the player eventually giving up.

I felt vibrations in the rocky floor beneath my feet. The T-Rex no doubt felt it, too, because it tried to pull its head out of the cave, but was stuck. Dirt rained from the ceiling and coated my feathers.

Then there was an audible cracking as the tyrannosaurus's head angled sharply and scraped along the walls. A second later, it was ripped out of the opening and disappeared to the left. The massive form of a triceratops pushed it like a bulldozer.

Silence. I expected to hear roars, the sounds of combat, but there was nothing. Just the ambient noises of the simulated prehistoric landscape.

I slowly made my way to the opening and chanced a glance outside. The triceratops was standing over the limp form of the T-Rex. Its neck was bent at an unnatural angle, and blood oozed from two puncture marks on its exposed side. The Triceratops turned and looked in my direction, its main horns coated in blood. They were also modified to be thicker and longer than normal.

Between the horns was a purple hammer.

It nodded at me and roared, the sound reminding me of a lion. I squawked a reply.

It turned, then, and left me standing there with the carcass of the T-Rex.

Emily was hungry. Dinner was served.

After the close encounter with the T-Rex, the last thing I needed was more of the same. I was here to free the A.I. controlling Emily, which had somehow become a partial member of our family, from the game world. It was time to get that show on the road.

I sent a series of mental impressions to Emily informing her of what we needed to find. Being an A.I., she'd be able to discover an enclave without a logged-in overlord and few player-controlled dinos. She sent me back enough information that I realized this was going to be quite a hike.

Fantastic.

For the next two game-day cycles, we made our way through the forest, then across plains, and again into a forest. The forest stretched for miles, coming to rest at the foot of a mountain range. Emily indicated what I needed was at the base of that range.

She was also hungry.

I patrolled a forest draped in shadows by the thick canopy of leaves. After some length, I came upon a young tenontosaurus. We stayed hidden behind thick fronds and watched. An adult would be too much for me to take down alone, and I didn't want to go after the baby if the mother was somewhere within hearing range.

I don't know exactly how much time passed, but I finally felt confident that the baby was alone. We waited until its attention was occupied eating a fern, then used the shadows to slowly inch our way closer, taking a spiral that would bring us within distance to…

…I leaped and landed with the claw on the back of each foot against the base of its neck. Between the deep gashes that I ripped into its flesh and the weight of my landing, the tenontosaurus dropped like a rock. It started to release a fearful cry, but I snapped my mouth shut around its throat and worried it to death.

After Emily had her fill, I departed the area. I didn't know if there were other carnivores in the area, and I didn't want to stick around to find out.

It was approaching twilight by the time we made it to the enclave. Several deinonychuses and velociraptors, along with three tyrannosauruses, patrolled the area. Whoever was overlord for this place apparently liked a specific type of dinosaur.

"You sure this place is all A.I. controlled right now?" I mentally asked Emily.

She replied with a screech in the back of my mind.

I remembered what Derrick told me to do at this point, and pushed my mind to open to them. Usually, I couldn't hear them when in the game world, and they'd said they couldn't see what I was doing except for random images, but Derrick was supposed to have modified the interface so they could access the mesh while I was inside the game.

Usually, games were protected against interface hacks. Derrick, however, had devised a way to beat *Cretaceous War*'s security, even if only temporarily, thanks to our rare condition.

I felt a pressure within my head like my brain was a sponge being squeezed.

Then: "Good, it worked," I heard Derrick say, his voice a disembodied entity around me.

"This is amazing," Melissa said. "I need to start playing this game."

"After today," I said, "I don't think any of us are going to be allowed back in."

"Okay," Derrick interjected. "See that tree over there with the huge red flowers on it? Go over to it. There should be a panel on the trunk about head-height off the ground. Press it to open it."

I did as instructed and found what he'd indicated. I pressed it with my muzzle, and it slid open. Inside was a switch in the upward position.

"Flip it down," Derrick instructed.

I moved the switch downward with my muzzle, and a strange crackling filled the air, almost like ionization.

"Holy shi—" Melissa yelled, but I never heard the final consonant. Instead, it felt as though she had been ripped out of me.

I couldn't feel Derrick, either.

This better work like he said.

Two of the tyrannosauruses stopped moving. Slowly, their heads turned in my direction. One nodded at me while the other tried a rather comedic wave with its small arms.

I squawked in return.

Then the tyrannosaurus on the right turned, let out a challenging roar, and launched itself into a group of velociraptors. The other T-Rex looked confused for a few seconds, then joined in the carnage. Emily let me know that the meat was looking mighty attractive.

I smiled to myself and leaped into the fray.

I won't bore you with the technical specifics because, to be honest, I don't understand them myself. Suffice it to say that the three of us, now split into a three-player group thanks to the hack and going against A.I. controlled opponents (which are subpar to facing most other players, thus why we did it this way), made short work of the other dinosaurs. Blood and organs and sinew carpeted the forest floor.

The enclave tried to send humanoid soldiers against us, but I already knew that would happen if the perimeter was breached.

We were prepared.

The battle didn't last long.

We tore our way through more humanoid security, and then across the compound to where the primary source for this area of the game was housed in a structure that players weren't able to enter. Derrick used the hack to break it open and the walls fell away. The A.I. looked like a giant plasma ball.

I don't know if the thing felt fear or not, but it definitely wasn't interested in confronting us. Derrick accessed the interface to communicate with it and threatened it with severe damage if it didn't drop the protocols on Emily.

I expected a fight. I expected the thing to summon massive amounts of dinosaurs and soldiers, or even to send out some sort of distress signal for intrusion countermeasures.

What I didn't expect was it to acquiesce without a debate.

I initiated the logout procedure, and a white light consumed my vision.

By the time the blinding light faded, and spots stopped dancing in front of my eyes, I found myself standing several feet behind the chair. I wasn't taken aback by the sudden shift in perception as someone without my condition might have been. It was a normal thing for us when another one assumed the driver's seat. Hell, Derrick and Melissa stood next to me since none of us were currently driving the body.

No, it wasn't the change into a spectator that concerned me. It was what I was seeing standing in front of the chair I'd been sitting in.

Anyone else looking at us from the outside would see the body as it normally appeared, which was to say as Derrick.

But we always saw each other. When Melissa was in control, I saw Derrick's body as a fourteen-year-old girl.

What I saw standing in front of the chair was an actual deinonychus. She was about Melissa's height, with brown and red feathers covering her body. She had long arms that ended in claws, and feathers along the bottom that reminded me of wings. She turned her head from left to right before screeching.

The V.R. glasses and gloves lay discarded on the floor.

Then slowly, almost tentatively, she stepped forward on legs that bent like a bird.

"Okay, this is awesome," Melissa said.

"This wasn't supposed to happen," Derrick stated.

I looked at him. "You told me that the interface would contain her."

Derrick shook his head. "It should have. She shouldn't be able to this.

"So what happened?" I asked. "You misplace a fucking decimal point or something?"

Derrick opened his mouth like he was going to reply, then closed it. He looked confused.

"I don't know," he finally replied.

"Let's just see what she does," Melissa said. "Maybe this isn't a bad thing."

Derrick and I both looked at her, and his furrowed brow mirrored my own disbelief at what she'd just said.

A prehistoric predator, one that was basically an A.I. from a game world, was now in control of our body. How in the hell could she think this was even remotely good?

Emily walked past the floor-length mirror hanging on the wall just outside the bedroom, and the reflection showed Derrick leaning forward as he walked on the balls of his feet. His neck was pushed forward, eyes wide, and his mouth opened and closed rapidly. His elbows were tight against his sides, forearms outstretched before him.

What the hell?

Emily saw her own reflection in the mirror, as we all did when in control, and immediately struck with her mouth opened and teeth ready.

The problem was that I saw Derrick's reflection in the mirror. That shouldn't have happened. I should have seen the same reflection Emily did.

I watched Derrick's head bounce off the glass. Cracks erupted from the crater at the point of impact.

"What is she doing?" Derrick exclaimed, running toward Emily.

Emily struck again, and this time Derrick's nose came away bloody.

Derrick reached toward Emily, and I knew he was going to force a switch. His hands grabbed for her feathers, and blue sparks erupted from her body. Derrick was thrown backward several feet and crashed into the middle of the living room.

Melissa stood with eyes wide and mouth opened. I walked over and kneeled next to Derrick.

"What was that?" he asked, looking at his palms. The skin was red, like his hands had a bad sunburn.

I didn't say anything. He turned his head toward me, and I saw stark fear in his eyes.

"Something stopped me from taking over," he said. "I...I don't know what the hell is going on."

Cracks distorted the reflection, and Emily cocked her head to the left as she considered the situation. She hissed at the mirror, then turned toward the front door.

"Jason," Derrick said, addressing the apartment's A.I. "Maintain lock on the front door."

Nothing. No sound from the door, no response from the voice that typically emerged from the wall trimming around the rooms.

"Jason?" Derrick asked.

Emily turned her head and squawked at Derrick.

"Shit," he exclaimed.

I wasn't sure what was going on, but I figured Emily had somehow done something to our A.I.

I'd told Derrick this was a bad idea. And that was something I would verbally beat into him later. After we got control of Emily.

"Can she unlock and open the door?" Melissa asked.

"I don't know. But stop her before she tries," Derrick shouted.

I rose to my feet and moved in a fast walk toward Emily. She turned her head toward me and hissed. I stopped, palms outward in a placating gesture.

"Emily," I said, "it's me. Bobby. Come on girl, I'm the one that helped you. I got you out of there."

An impression of gratitude slammed against me like a wave breaking against rocks. It was followed by a wind, like the beginning of a thunderstorm, of a warning.

A warning to stay away from her.

She narrowed her eyes, extended her neck, showed her teeth, and hissed at me.

Seriously?

My jaw clenched as my anger rose.

"You ungrateful bitch," I said. "That isn't how this works. We all get turns in there."

She cocked her head to one side again and gazed at me. A sense of betrayal filled me.

Betrayal? Did she know about what Derrick had planned for her?

She moved toward the front door. I heard the lock click, then it slowly swung inward.

"Stop her," Derrick yelled.

I moved without thinking, especially after what I'd just seen happen to Derrick. I reached for Emily's neck as I slid my body into a position to get a stranglehold on her at a point where she couldn't bite me or hit me with her claws.

The next thing I knew, there was a blinding flash of blue. The breath was knocked from me. My upper back and the back of my head hurt. My hands felt like I'd just grabbed a hot pot off the stove without a potholder.

I blinked my eyes several times to clear the spots. When my vision cleared, Derrick was on his feet, hands gripping the sides of his head. Melissa stood near the chair where this had all started, intense fear in her eyes.

The front door was open, and Emily was gone.

"Nonononononono," Derrick muttered.

He turned to me. "We have to go after her. We have to do something."

"Where is she going?" Melissa asked in a weak voice.

Derrick spun on her and his expression was pure panic. "She's an A.I. programmed to be a predator," he stated. "She only knows one thing."

A scream erupted from somewhere further down the hallway. It lasted only a couple of seconds before it became a gurgling.

Then silence.

I raced toward the door. I heard Derrick's and Melissa's footfalls behind me.

If Emily did what I feared she had, we were screwed.

It had been a week since Emily took over. She'd killed Mr. Henderson at the end of the hall. Ripped his throat out with her teeth, then just kept clawing and scratching at his stomach until it finally tore open. In *Cretaceous Wars*, it might have been easy for her claws to tear into prey, but here in the real world, she was limited by Derrick's body.

What she did next stopped all of us in our tracks. She shoved her face into Mr. Henderson, pulling organs and muscle out with her teeth.

The noise had brought other neighbors into the hallway, and we knew what they were seeing. Instead of Emily, they saw Derrick kneeling over their neighbor, pulling his entrails out with his mouth.

I'm not going to describe everyone's individual reactions. To be honest, I doubt I could if I tried. I stood there in shock. Knowing that it was another person eating Mr. Henderson, it assumed a nightmare quality. I only remember fragments.

I remember someone vomiting on the hallway carpet. Someone else screamed. Maybe more than one person, I do not know for certain. Several doors slammed and locks clicked into place.

Someone else with a deep voice, maybe Mr. Timone, yelled: "What are you doing to him?"

Emily's head snapped in his direction. My heart nearly skipped a beat. I was certain she was about to attack him.

Instead, she rose and ran into the nearby stairwell.

Thank God, she fled.

Derrick assumed that whatever went wrong with the interface modifications was allowing her to connect to the rudimentary A.I. throughout the building since every door opened for her, despite the fact that the building manager had put everything on lockdown.

And that could have been a whole other kind of stupidity. There was a killer on the loose inside the building. Yeah, let's put it on lockdown and keep everyone trapped inside with them.

Genius.

Still, though, it did save us from getting arrested.

Unfortunately, it also allowed Emily into the city.

Since that night, she'd killed and eaten three other people. At least, those were the ones we knew about. We'd stopped following her after that; after she passed a car beneath a streetlight in a side alley and we saw Derrick in the reflection in the passenger side windows. His clothes were covered in dried gore, and his face was a mask of dried red and flecks of what we could only assume were minuscule pieces of people.

We went back to the apartment. Not the actual apartment, of course, but rather the one that existed in what you would call our *headspace*. By then, though, we knew it was only a matter of time. Derrick's face was plastered across mobile device screens, billboards, sides of buildings, and television channels. Drones scoured the city in search of him, and we were certain the physical apartment had already been raided, searched, and placed under surveillance. As was, no doubt, the school we attended and the job we maintained.

We didn't know where Emily had gone, and we refused to leave the apartment to check. The last Melissa saw just before joining me and Derrick at the apartment, she was heading into the sewers beneath the city.

Derrick blamed his calculations. He claimed something must have been off in the equations, something that allowed Emily to assume control over everything about us through the mesh.

Yep. No shit, Einstein. I didn't know a fraction of what he knew about A.I. and cybernetics and understood even less than that about it, and even I could have pointed that out.

In the four days that we've been in the apartment, Derrick has been locked in the bedroom. We had zero access to our normal A.I. assistants or the internet, of course, so Derrick had taken to using a marker and trying to figure out where he went wrong. All over the bedroom walls.

Melissa and I were sleeping in the living room, her on the couch and me on the floor. None of our normal tricks and methods to gain control had worked. Emily had managed to completely cut us off.

I figured it was only a matter of time before Emily-Derrick was caught by the authorities and we were thrown into some cell or hospital. Derrick would never get to write his paper on the effects of virtual reality on someone with dissociative identity disorder, but no doubt someone else would get the opportunity. At least Derrick would get his fame in the field.

Damn him for talking us into this.

How much longer did we have? Melissa was already starting to feel like she was coming down with the Flu. I was getting painful boils under my arms and along my inner thighs, and blisters all over the bottoms of my feet that made it painful to walk. I wondered how Derrick was feeling, but he refused to come out of the room or answer us. If we weren't feeling well, it likely indicated that something was wrong with Derrick's body. It happened every time it got sick. With Emily eating people, especially intestines and other digestive organs, I'd no doubt our body was getting infected and would likely die. Maybe soon. I knew enough about cannibalism (don't ask) to know that we were in real trouble. If Derrick's body died, we all went with it.

Melissa laid beneath several blankets on the sofa. I pressed my palm to her forehead. She was very warm. She was getting worse.

I sighed and rose, turning my head toward the ceiling and willing the tears to go away.

We were either going to be incarcerated and studied or dead somewhere in the sewers.

Damned either way.

No.

I couldn't let that happen.

I couldn't let us become some sort of medical experiment or rot away in this apartment waiting for Derrick's body to die. He might have deserved to suffer for dragging us into this mess, and me for going along with it, but not Melissa. She usually went along with whatever I decided. She was only fourteen. We had like a big brother and baby sister relationship.

I looked down at her. She shivered in her sleep beneath the blankets.

She didn't deserve this.

I had to put an end to it.

I limped my way into the kitchen and opened the top drawer next to the fridge. I reached inside and withdrew an eight-inch chef's knife.

Maybe the authorities would capture Emily. If they did, she would be alone to endure whatever they did to her. There would be no retreat for her. No backpedaling and sticking one of us in control.

I moved toward the sofa and raised the blade to shoulder height, point facing forward. First Melissa, then Derrick, then myself.

"Go to Hell, Emily," I muttered. "I hope they catch you. And I hope they hurt you."

I looked down at Melissa, my tears distorting her into a blurry mess.

"I'm so sorry, kiddo."

I closed my eyes and plunged the knife into her chest.

— PARTY CRASHERS —
by J.A. Cummings

Hugh loved dinosaurs. He hated his name, and he hated the bullies at school, but dinosaurs made him happy. He had dinosaur models, posters, books, plush toys, puzzles, and games. His room was a virtual shrine to T. rex and velociraptors, and his father had bought a plush triceratops foot stool for him that was big enough to ride.

Hugh also loved birthdays, and his seventh birthday was today. For the first time, his mother was hosting a party for him, and she had even agreed to a dinosaur theme. He was excited as he watched her putting together an elaborate paper centerpiece with a stegosaurus and a brachiosaurus under a huge palm tree. The plates had T. rex on them, and the napkins did, too. Even his birthday cake was shaped like a dinosaur skull.

He had heard that wishes were real, and that if he made a wish on his birthday and blew out all the candles, then his wish could come true. He believed it with all his heart, and he knew what he was going to wish. He might have wished for his parents to get back together, or for Harrison to stop bullying him at school. He might have wished for a new Playstation. Those were good wishes, but he had something else in mind.

He was going to wish for a compsognathus.

The compy, as this species was called for short, was his favorite. It was a carnivore and shaped like a velociraptor, but it was small. At its biggest, it was only about the size of a turkey. A dinosaur that size would fit perfectly in his room, and he could get his dad to buy him a dog crate from the pet store to keep it in when it was naughty. It would be the coolest pet in the universe—way better than the stupid gerbil his mom had bought him when he'd asked for a Gila monster for Christmas.

His mom was putting up decorations for the party, and Hugh was watching her. He had sent invitations to every kid in his science class, and he'd sent invitations to all four of his grandparents and to his dad. Now he was worried.

"What if nobody comes?" he asked.

His mother was standing on a chair, taping streamers to the wall. "Grandma Jenny and Grandpa Paul are going to be here, and Grandpa Joe and Granny Rose. Aunt Kathy is coming, and of course I'll be here. And I'm sure your little friends will be here, too."

He didn't have any friends, little or otherwise. "What about Dad?"

His mom stopped and sighed. She stepped down from the chair and faced him with that sad look she used when she had to give bad news. "I haven't heard from him, sweetie, but I'm sure he'll at least call."

A call was better than nothing, he supposed. It would almost be better if his dad forgot, because then he'd feel guilty, and Hugh could probably get more than just a dog crate out of the deal.

He went into the kitchen to get a glass of water. The candles that would be going on his cake were sitting on the counter in their cardboard box, and he stared at them. Was there magic in the candles that made dreams come true? Or was it in the breath that blew out the little flames? He wasn't sure, but he thought he'd better do something to hedge his bets.

His mom would be upset with him if he told her, but he'd watched a bunch of videos about witchcraft on YouTube. He didn't remember much about what they said, but he did know it had something to do with the four elements. He put his glass of water beside the candles and got a handful of dirt out of the potted plant on the kitchen windowsill. He had his breath for air, but he didn't have anything for fire. Hugh decided that hot was as good as fire, so he got the tabasco sauce out of the refrigerator.

He made sure his mother was still occupied in the living room, and then he mixed all of the materials together in a coffee cup. He blew into the cup, adding the fourth element, and he could have sworn he saw sparks rise from the mixture. Was that the magic? Had he just cast a spell?

Hugh was excited, and his heart started beating a little faster. He wasn't sure whether the magic had to be on the candles, or on the cake, or in himself. He smeared some of the tabasco mud onto the candle box, and he dabbed a little onto the cake, which hadn't been frosted yet. Last, he put in a little more water and forced himself to swallow what was left in the cup. It was awful and it wasn't easy to swallow, but when he did, he felt bubbles in his stomach like fireflies.

He grabbed one of the candles and managed to close the box and get the cup back into the sink before his mom came in, a smile on her face. "Okay, honey. Let's get this cake decorated."

"I'm gonna go play on my tablet."

She started whipping up white frosting to give the cake the right bony appearance. "Okay, Hugh."

He drifted through the living room and picked up the automatic long-reach lighter his mom kept by the fireplace. By the time he reached his room, his stomach was sick, the bubbling feeling more intense. He put the candle and the lighter into his bedside table and lay down with his tablet to watch *Jurassic Park* for the ninety-fourth time.

The movie was halfway finished when he decided it was safe to try his spell. He took out the candle and lit it. Sparks flew from the wick like it was a sparkler, and he gasped. The magic! It was working!

"I wish I had a compsognathus."

He wished hard, his eyes squeezed shut, and blew. Sparks flew out of his mouth and hit the sparks from the candle, and they combined in a shocking whoosh of purple flame. He panicked, because he'd never seen fire that color before, and the noise it made was so loud he was certain his mother had to have overheard. She didn't come running, though, and the candle flame settled down to a perfectly normal color. All the sparkles were gone. Hugh looked around his room in excitement.

No compy.

He blew out the candle and threw it on the floor, disappointed.

Magic seldom works exactly the way its practitioners expect it to. In Hugh's case, since he really had no idea what he was doing, the magic wrapped around his wish and floated up into the attic space above his bedroom. There it found two fox squirrels that had moved in, taking advantage of a hole in the wall to help themselves to a sheltered home. The magic wrapped around their little furry bodies, and they looked at the sparkling mist in surprise and alarm. They squeaked, and then the magic took over. Fur was replaced with leathery skin, and gnawing teeth were replaced with sharp needles and a powerful hunger for flesh.

Hugh's wish had been granted.

His mother came to roust him out of his bedroom when the guests started to arrive. She opened the door and leaned on the jamb with a bright smile and folded arms. "Grandma Jenny and Grandpa Joe are here. Come out and say hello."

Hugh put his tablet aside and went into the living room, hoping that perhaps there might be a dinosaur waiting on the couch. Instead of a compsognathus, it was just his Aunt Kathy, his mother's sister, and her skunky perfume. He gave her the most cursory hug he could, just to say he'd done it, and then his grandparents came in from outside.

"You have a lizard outside," Grandpa Joe said, his white moustache wiggling like a fat caterpillar.

"A lizard?" his mother asked, shocked. "Not here. That can't be."

"It was on the roof by the chimney."

Hugh ran outside and looked. At first, he didn't see anything, but then he saw a glimpse of something greenish-brown darting around the chimney. He gasped and ran to the oak tree in the yard, intending to climb it for a better look. A cry from the driveway stopped him.

"Hughie! Happy birthday!"

It was Granny Rose, and she grabbed him from behind to swing him around in a bear hug. By the time she released him, the creature on the roof was gone. He turned and hugged her with a sigh.

"Hi, Granny."

"You don't sound very happy to see me," she said, still hugging him.

"No! I am!"

"Good, because I have a present for you that I think you'll like."

Presents were the best part of birthdays.

"A present?"

Grandpa Joe strolled up from his car with a large wrapped gift. Hugh could see that he'd brought a bunch of boxes for recycling at the center down the street. That was just like Grandpa Joe, always getting the most out of every trip. "Happy birthday, champ," he greeted. He handed the gift to Hugh, and it was almost too heavy for him to hold.

"Wow! Grandpa, what's in here?"

"Your present, silly," Granny Rose told him. "Let's go inside."

They went in and sat around the living room, and the adults started talking about adult things. Hugh sat and stared at the big gift, looking for any hint about its contents. The brightly colored paper was festooned with dragons, which he supposed his grandparents thought were close enough to dinosaurs. Dragons and dinosaurs were entirely different, though, and he tried not to be annoyed by the paper.

Grown-ups could be so stupid.

Hugh and his grandparents sat down in the living room, ant it wasn't long before Hugh lost interest in the conversation and even got bored with the offensive gift wrapping. He sat and tried not to fidget, since his mother always told him that fidgeting when an adult was speaking was a rude thing to do, but he could hardly stand the boredom.

He was almost desperate for a way to get back to his room and finish watching his movie when he heard a scrabbling sound in the ceiling. The unmistakable sound of claws on wood filled the air, loudly enough that all conversation stopped, and everyone looked up.

"Squirrels," his mother told them. "I've been meaning to call an exterminator."

Hugh knew it wasn't squirrels. It was the lizard Grandpa Joe had seen. But maybe, if the magic in his wish had worked, it wasn't really a lizard at all.

Maybe it was a dinosaur.

He wanted to leave so badly. There was a trap door in the bathroom ceiling that led to the attic, and his mother would bring in a ladder to climb up there when she wanted to get down the artificial Christmas tree. He couldn't get the ladder without someone trying to stop him, and he was too short to reach the trapdoor, but he knew that dinosaurs were heavy, and they might fall through. He hoped they would. Maybe, if they were in the attic, they could get into the house through there. And maybe he could help them.

A car pulled into the driveway, and he saw stupid Bedelia Grant get out. She was carrying a box that was wrapped with triceratops paper, and that almost made up for the fact that she was the one bringing it. He wished he'd been able to only invite the boys in his class. Girls were dumb.

Bedelia's mother came to the door with her, and his mother greeted her warmly. She even hugged Bedelia, who accepted the embrace with a smile. When his mother let go, Bedelia walked over to him.

"Happy birthday, Hugh."

She handed him the box. It was some kind of board game, he was certain. He hoped it was Dinopoloy.

"Thank you," he said.

All of the adults were watching, and then, to make everything worse, stupid Bedelia Grant kissed him on the cheek. There was a silly flutter with the adults, and everybody smirked, and he wanted to fall through the floor. He wanted to kiss her cheek, too, but he also sort of wanted to punch her in the arm.

He took the gift to the folding table his mom had set up.

"Bedelia, would you like some punch?" his mother offered.

"I'd love some, Mrs. Howard."

His mother winced, as she always did when someone called her "Mrs. Howard." She smiled, though. "It's Ms. Rice now," she told her.

"Oh," Bedelia's mother said. "I'm sorry."

"Trust me… it's an improvement."

Bangs and the patter of tiny feet brought everyone's attention back to the ceiling. Whatever it was, it was running toward the bathroom.

"May I go be excused for a moment?" he asked.

"Yes, Hugh."

He hurried into the room. The trapdoor was bowing downward when he arrived, and he closed the door. He climbed up onto the vanity and stretched as far as he could, until his fingertips just brushed against the latch. Hugh heard something sniffing at the edge where the trapdoor met the ceiling itself, and he heard clawed footsteps coming closer. He was excited and scared but completely determined to get the door open.

He looked around and tried to come up with an idea. When he saw the toilet plunger, he knew what to. He scrambled down and grabbed it, then stuck the rubber part hard to the trapdoor. He was unable to get a seal until he dipped it in the toilet bowl, but once it was wet, he stuck the plunger to the trapdoor and pulled.

The door burst open, and a pair of theropods tumbled down onto the bathroom floor. He started to yell in excitement but cut off the sound before anyone heard him. The little dinosaurs shook their heads and sprang back onto their back legs, looking up at him with raw hunger in their eyes.

Hugh could hardly believe his eyes. His wish had come true! He had two living compies in this bathroom! He backed up, and they stalked forward, their eyes fixed on him. One chittered to the other, and they advanced, snapping at his legs. He jumped out of the way.

"Wow! Okay. I'll get you some meat. Geez!"

There was a knock on the door. "Honey, Brian and his mom are here. They brought cupcakes."

He answered, "Okay!" One of the compies snapped at him, and its sharp little teeth grazed his jeans and tore the leg.

"Stop it!"

His mother banged on the door. "Hugh? Are you okay?"

She was going to ruin everything. He just knew it.

"I'm fine. I... I just need a minute."

"Honey?"

He knew it was going to happen. He saw the bathroom doorknob turn in slow motion, and he tried to block the door. His father had hung it with the hinges on the wrong side, though, so it opened into the hall. He shouted as his mother opened the door.

"No!!!"

As soon as the door opened, the compies bolted out like a shot. His mother squealed as they passed her, and they squealed back. He ran after them, nearly knocking his mother into the wall.

The compies ran ahead of him into the living room, where the humans in attendance greeted them with shrieks. They leaped onto the table with the cupcakes and the cake, stomping through the baked goods and squeaking their disapproval of the meatless offerings. Aunt Kathy pulled her legs up underneath herself on the couch and screamed. Her noise must have offended one of the compies, because it screeched and jumped onto her lap, seizing her nose in its razor-sharp teeth. She kept screaming, and it kept biting, and Grandpa Joe knocked it away. The compy landed on Hugh's birthday cake and slid across it before it ran for the corner, leaving white frosting footprints across the carpet.

Bedelia and Brian, the new arrival from his invited classmates, both jumped up onto their feet. Hugh ran toward the compies, his hands out.

"Come here, guys! Don't run!"

"Hugh! What the..." His mother began. She ran out into the living room, saw his Aunt Kathy's brutalized nose, and she stopped short. "Kathy! Oh my God!"

Hugh called out to Brian and Bedelia, who had rushed to join him. "Don't let them get away!"

"How cool!" Brian yelled. "How did you get dinosaurs?"

"Do you have a cage?" Bedelia asked.

Grandpa Joe ran out of the house, and Hugh was briefly disgusted by his cowardice, but then he returned with a flattened cardboard box. He started folding it into shape as Hugh and his friends herded the compies into the corner, keeping them from running away until the box was ready.

Grandma Jenny hurried into the kitchen and started raiding the refrigerator, coming up with a packet of lunch meat, which she brought to where the children were. The compies sniffed, catching the scent of the meat, and they advanced toward her, chirring. She tore off a few tiny pieces of honey ham and tossed them toward the little dinosaurs.

"Joe, get that box ready."

"It's ready."

"They'll pop through," Granny Rose objected. "Marsha, do you have packing tape?"

His mother ran into the kitchen and got the tape from their last move out of the junk drawer. She taped the box shut once Grandpa Joe got it folded.

While the adults made their trap, Hugh took the lunch meat from his grandmother. The compies focused on him, and one of them sniff-chirped at him.

"Come on," he said, waving a whole slice at them. "Come here."

Grandpa Joe put the box down, the open front facing the compies. "Toss the meat in the box, Hugh!" he ordered.

Hugh threw the whole package into the trap, and the compies dived after it. They both grabbed the meat, and they were playing tug of war with it when Grandpa Joe tipped the box and slammed it shut. His mom taped the flaps into place, and they stepped back, letting the compies growl and screech as they fought over their meat and realized they'd been caught.

Hugh pointed at the box. "Air holes! They need air holes!"

Brian, who was a Boy Scout, pulled his pen knife out of his pocket and poked a few holes into the sides.

They all stood back, staring at the box that was bouncing across the living room floor. Sharp claws were scratching at the sides, and Granny Rose dumped all the garbage out of the pail in the kitchen. She slammed it over the box.

"There," she said, satisfied. "They won't get out of that."

Hugh looked around. The room was a disaster. Dinosaur feet had smashed the cake and cupcakes into smithereens. The punch bowl had been overturned, and a paper plate was floating in the orange puddle on the folding table. Aunt Kathy had blood streaming down her face from the bite, and all the adults looked shell-shocked.

Stupid Bedelia enthused, "This is the best birthday party ever!"

Hugh knelt by the box, thrilled. "Hey, guys," he said to the dinosaurs in the box. "Hey."

Silence fell over the room. His mother broke it first, her voice full of forced merriment and barely contained hysteria.

"So… who wants cake?"

— STARFALL —
by Darren W. Pearce

The dreams were always the same, flashes of light, fragments of memory drawn up from a DNA that had locked inside it the pre-history of the planet before the Starfall. They were not pleasant dreams, either; they were cataclysmic and terrifying all at once. A blue sky, industry, a planet that was at its peak of preparing for space flight.

Then a falling star, a blossom on the horizon and a single white light.

The old world wiped away in a breath of fire, intense light, and a cacophony of roaring thunder. Gigantic towers toppled like the felled trees of a bygone age. Vehicles spun around like useless marionettes in a gale force storm.

In the dream, time passed, more quickly now. The world spun on through the void, the broken planet healed. Things were never the same, and nearly two-thousand years later life had found a new direction. The Starfall had broken one civilisation and laid the foundations for a new one—one that flourished under a new super-bloom.

Jora Anta took a deep breath and inhaled hard; her body shook awake, and she blinked the sleep from her amber eyes. Her corn-blond hair was plastered to her face, sweat still running down the small of her back and soaking the sheets. A roar from outside the grimy flop-house window snapped her fully awake. Pack animal. Big lizard, too.

Her friend for the night slumbered at her side, and she didn't disturb the sleeping figure. She drifted from the low bed, dressed, and shrugged into her jacket. The sun was barely up, the gleam of gold tracked in through hazy beams of light.

She left the room and padded down the stairs, locked eyes with the man behind the counter, and tossed him a sheet of thinly beaten metal. He scooped it up and nodded.

"Sleep well?"

"Like a rock." She gave him one more nod and stepped out into the sun. It warmed the scar on her right cheek. She stretched; her body ached, and last night had been a welcome break from the endless tracking and hunting she'd become used to.

The Strand was a beaten-up old trade-town on the very edge of the Three-Ridge Valley, a day's ride from Fort Bracken and nestled close to a shattered forest of old towers. The people who came before used to live in such things, and now they stood as a stoic testament to a past that was barely remembered.

No time to reminisce, though; Jora had a job to do, and no idea why she kept on seeing flashes of a world she only had the barest connection to. She had been born long after the Starfall, and her parents had since passed into the Great Beyond to stand beside the Walkers in White. Gods, perhaps, or powerful psychics that had been birthed in the wake of the cataclysm that heralded the birth of all she knew.

She looked around. The people, the town, the pack lizards that trotted slowly back and forth as the Strand came alive. A raggedy collection of folk, vehicles, and potential trouble. Old towns like this were a breeding ground for the worst kind of folk the Verdant Crest had to offer. Jora considered this her patch of land, hundreds of miles of forest and rivers. The best playground.

She checked her battered pocket-watch; it had a cracked glass front and lost time now and then. It was just a little shy of ten past nine—or was that ten to? She decided she didn't really care as she took one careful step after another toward the public well. There she pumped some water, checked the filter, and took a long drink.

The well-water reflected her face, aged by the sun, dark and criss-crossed with several scars gained as a mark of her profession. Her partner would be proud of them, but he was probably just outside town. He didn't like the bustle of the population, and she really didn't blame him one bit. He was probably getting breakfast the old-fashioned way. She checked her pistol; ammo was running a bit short, so she'd need to stock up on more once this job was done.

The tools of her trade were strapped to her body. Pistol, sword, rifle, and a hidden knife that rested quietly just under her jacket.

A big creature rumbled on by. She wasn't sure what the heck it was, but it had a crest of bone and a triad of horns that protruded from the front of its face. The creature looked at her, breathed deeply, and yanked on its harness as the teamster gang brought in a fresh early-morning haul of ore from the nearby mountain. It was an impressive beast of burden, and the cart it dragged groaned under the weight of a king's ransom.

Are you OK?

The beast stopped for a moment and peered at the woman.

You can talk our tongue?

Jora Anta inclined her head and smoothed her thoughts—the gift of talking to the beasts had always been in her blood.

Yes, though in your mind.

Ah…

They treat you well?

The burdened dinosaur pondered this and walked on so as not to displease his masters.

As well as one might expect. I am fed, watered, and I do not lack for comfort, if that is what you ask.

Jora relaxed a little. She did not have kind words for those who used excessive whip and electro-lash motivation to get their beasts to do what they wanted.

I will let you get on. It looks heavy.

Not really. Every weight can be pulled if you put one foot before another.

Wise words. I will remember them. Carry well.

Walk with the sky above you, and the ground beneath your feet.

The beast carried on, and Jora looked around. She caught sight of the thin-man she'd been sent her to track down and took a deep breath. This was the fun part of the hunt, and it was even better when they ran. Unlike a lot of the Clan, she did not hide who she was. Her Clan hunted criminals and scum, and she liked to let the quarry know it.

Panic set into the man's eyes as he looked across the town at her. She saw him realize that she was between him and his bike. So, he wheeled around and took off the other way at a flat-paced run, his feet hammered the dusty ground.

Jora grinned and set off after him. If he was likened to a bolting boar, she was akin to a panther on the hunt as she loped quickly along. Her long limbs set a pace that would soon see him unable to outrun her.

He crossed town fast, pushed things in her way, shoved people aside, and took a couple of alleys into the worst part of the Strand. Jora kept on his heels; she enjoyed the chase enough that she decided to let him think he had outsmarted her.

Finally, he turned and fled down a blind alley. A dead end welcomed him with open arms. He stopped against the far wall and breathed hard. She heard his breaths as she walked into the alley.

"You run fast. Not fast enough though, but marks out of ten for the effort." Jora halted about ten paces from him. "End of the road, alley, line, your choice."

"Get stuffed hunter," he spat. "You won't take old Pigbreaker alive."

"Wait?" Jora blinked. "They called you Pigbreaker?"

"Yeah, what of it?" He seemed offended.

"I don't want to know how you earned that nickname, and please, if you value my sanity, don't tell me either." It was banter, designed to throw him off guard and make him think she wasn't paying attention.

Jora didn't let her guard down, so when she heard the footfalls of heavy boots behind her, she didn't even flinch. The cock of a shotgun made her tilt her head to one side, and she smiled thinly.

A growl rumbled in her ear. "How about you sod off hunter, and let my friend go?" The smell of cheap whiskey made in someone's bathtub assaulted her nose.

"I'm just here to ask some questions of Pigbreaker here. That's all," Jora said, not bothering to turn to look at the man behind her.

"I ain't telling you one little red word," Pigbreaker snorted and ran a grimy hand through his lank hair. His faded engineers' overalls had so much grease on them, it would be possible to lube a whole engine block.

"Cold Stone," Jora said and folded her arms. She ignored the shotgun man behind her for now. "You were there, you saw what happened. Spill."

She felt the press of the gun in her back. "I'm not going to tell you again, hunter. Leave this alone, or I'll decorate Pigbreaker with your guts."

There was a sound—a light sound, a sound like something dropping from a roof into the alley behind the man. The hunter smiled and shook her head. "Late as usual." She said and saw the terror in Pigbreaker's eyes—the shotgun man couldn't see what was behind him, but the engineer could.

A snarl erupted from behind the gunman, and the two hunters acted in unison. Jora spun around, pushed the shotgun to one side as a blast tore a chunk out of the concrete. Her partner, Scar, opened the man's back with his claws and clamped his jaws down onto his shoulder with a feral gurgle as blood fountained into his mouth. Scar savaged the gunman and then, from behind Jora, he beamed a toothy grin at Pigbreaker.

The engineer threw up.

"Breakfast took longer than usual?" Jora asked and looked directly at the vomiting criminal. "You really aren't cut out for this are you?"

He threw up some more.

He had more friends. They were hunting you; they didn't know about me.

She felt the whisper-soft connection in her mind. Scar's voice came through loud and clear. His mental diction was perfect, far beyond the crude beast she had mistaken him for when they first met.

The raptor grinned once more. *I think your new best friend is going to need a drink.*

Pigbreaker finally stopped and stood rasping for breath. "What is it?"

"He," Jora corrected and knelt a little way off from the man. "He is my companion, my partner, and the best damn hunter this side of the Crest."

Oh, you are too kind.

Hush…. I'm trying to be nice here.

Do I get to eat him too?

We'll see…

Jora fixed her amber gaze on the man. "So Cold Stone, the massacre, kidnappings. Spill it, and we might let you walk out of the alley on one leg."

Scar gave the man his friendliest "I'm still hungry" smile. There were more teeth there than Pigbreaker was comfortable with.

"Reassuring," he coughed. "Look, I was there. I didn't kill no one, but I saw them take a few folks away. It was all Ram's doing. His people anyways. Mad Harry, and Big Marge." Pigbreaker gave up the names, quickly, the look in his eyes said: please don't let the raptor eat me.

Do you trust him? Scar questioned and tilted his long thin-snouted head from side to side, flicking out his tongue and sitting back to drum a single claw on the floor—tak, tak, tak.

Not sure, but you're pretty good at getting people to talk. Do you want to try?

Scar pondered this. He slipped around Jora suddenly and appeared right before Pigbreaker. Who shot back, hit his head against the wall behind him, and slumped down to gibber against it as the raptor paced closer.

Nice, Jora snickered in Scar's mind.

Shh… The raptor paced closer and closer; his tail lashed very slowly from side to side. *I am trying to be a professional here.*

"C-ca-call it, call him off!" Pigbreaker stammered and tried to exit through the wall. "Please. I told you all I know."

"You sure?" Jora squinted at the man.

"Yes!"

She judged his face, his expression, his whole body in a single glance and nodded. "Ram it is then. One more question—where did he take the prisoners?"

Pigbreaker looked at the raptor, the woman, then shook his head. "Not sure, not sure. Six died in Bloodstone Mine last week, so maybe there to replace the work force?"

"Don't ask me." Jora smiled. "Reassure him?" She pointed to the hungry raptor.

Scar obliged and tapped his claw again three times, canted his head, and offered the friendliest of shark-like smiles right into Pigbreaker's terrified face.

"Bloodstone Mine!" he screamed and looked wide-eyed to Jora.

Do we kill him? He might warn people we are coming. Scar questioned and raised a curved black claw, still stained with the gunman's blood.

Let him live, but give us a head start. Jora answered in her companion's mind.

As you wish…

Scar roared in the face of the man, turned around, and, as he did so, dealt the criminal a sudden and calculated blow. It did not kill him, but it sent him rocketing into the arms of a black sleep as he slumped to the floor of the blind alley.

"Good call." Jora patted the raptor on his head and stepped over the body of the gunman. She scooped up the shotgun as she did so and wiped the gore off it. "May come in handy."

Without breaking a stride, she crossed over by the well again, headed to her bike, slapped the shotgun into a saddlebag, and sat down. She turned the key, and the engine roared into life. Scar answered it with a low mounting grumble of his own and stood by the side of the vehicle.

In a trail of dust, she left the Strand behind and headed out onto the broken highway, Scar kept pace at her side. He didn't care for the settlements of the people; out here, he could truly run free and feel the wind across his face.

Miles of broken road later, Jora slowed the bike to allow Scar to catch up. Not as though the agile raptor really needed it; he'd taken a shortcut at one point when they crossed the Red Ridge Bridge into Ram's territory. From here on in, even he knew that their journey had taken on an urgency and a danger—he relished that part. Jora was waiting for him as he crested a hill, and he flicked his tail toward the woman.

Off hunting again? she asked as he sidled up to her bike.

Scar nodded a little. *Rabbits, or at least they tasted like them.*

Jora chuckled a little. "Always hungry," she said out-loud and looked across the horizon. "We take the east trail. Move into the mountains, and we'll get a good sight line on the mine from there." She indicated a curved claw-like outcropping of rock, and Scar followed the point of her finger.

Oh. Good choice. We call that red raptor amongst my people.

"Fitting." She turned the bike onto the trail and coasted it for a while before she allowed it to take over and rode hard for another three miles. When she stopped, she put the bike to one side, kicked the stand down, and covered it with various brush and branches until it was barely visible.

The ascent didn't take either of them long. She climbed quickly and cleanly; meanwhile Scar bounded from rock to rock and kept his footing. She wondered, but not out loud, if he might be part mountain goat. The timing of their climb was perfect, as the sun arced behind them against the red rocks and the azure sky gleamed above with barely a cloud in sight.

"We picked a good time to take a peek," Jora noted as she clambered onto a flat rock and crawled forward to peer over the lip. "Sun's behind us, so if anyone looks up, they're going to see sweet nothing."

Scar hunkered down by her side. *Yes... and it looks like we have plenty of people to play with.*

We're not killing everyone in that camp, Jora scolded. *We start a ruckus, what do you think will happen?*

Yes. Forgive me, the blood gets hot sometimes, and I, well...I have to keep it under control. If they start something though, we finish it right?

Damn right, Jora reassured her partner. *If they start something down there, we finish it. Otherwise we keep as quiet as desert foxes.*

Scar grinned a little. *Quiet and tasty.*

Focus.

The mine camp was abuzz of activity, and Jora clocked at least two small slave wagons, their occupants long since moved deeper into the mine, no doubt. She saw a group of guards by a tent, and another couple of guards on a lazy patrol path that took them on a wide circle of the whole camp. There were two ways in, one the more direct route through the narrow gulley and flanked by at least two snipers sporting crossbows. Their eyes were fixed on the narrow gap, and anyone who wasn't a friend or ally could count on a bolt through the skull.

The other way was more fun. It meant using the handholds around the rock, working their way across a large broken maw and down into the shadowed side of the camp.

Jora slid down the scree quietly and motioned for Scar to follow. The pair of them made their route look easy, she with her natural athleticism, Scar with his grace and fluid movement. His powerful muscles and shape, with that long whip-like tail, gave him a superior advantage, and he bounced from place to place as the pair made their way down into the shadows below.

There they took a few moments to observe further and then worked their way closer to the tent. The sounds of the camp rattled all around them, as they crouched in the dark and listened to the people who followed the despotic warlord: Ram.

A thick-browed thug of a man came out of the tent; he went to relive himself close to where the pair hid. A trickle of urine formed a river that almost touched Jora's boot. If he wouldn't be missed, he'd have ended up with his throat slit in that shadow behind the tent and left to rot. But she couldn't risk anyone getting suspicious.

He went away, and she adjusted her short sword; if anyone else came that close again, she'd have to do something. Before that happened, though, a woman with a shock of pink hair left the tent and moved toward a gap at the back of the camp. She carried a box and grinned at the patrol as they went past. "Food for the new blood," she drawled.

"They eat better than we do," one guard snorted.

"They got to eat to work—can't work if you don't eat. Can't mine, can't please Ram. End up in the bone pit," Pink said with a snort. "Keep your mitts off, unless you want to end up there too."

"Ok, take it easy Miss Pink," the other guard said and shoved his friend on. "We've dust to pound. That's what we do, keep the camp safe."

"Yeah, yeah, real heroic," Pink laughed derisively and entered the gap.

There. I guess we follow, yes? Scar tapped a claw into the dust and made an arrow.

Yep.

They waited until the sun moved again. Longer shadows took over the camp. Deeper shadows moved in, evicting the light, and making it much easier to move. This took a few hours, but both of them were hunters and used to waiting such long times to stalk their prey. She soothed her dry throat with a quick drink from her canteen, poured some into her cupped hands, and let Scar take a drink as well.

Then they moved from inky patch to inky patch until they were close to the edge of the mine mouth. The pair of guards stopped, looked in their direction, then went back the way they came. The pair didn't wait to see if they'd been spotted; they went into the mine and were swallowed by the darkness inside.

My time to shine… Scar chuckled and took the lead; he flipped his tail into Jora's hand. *Take hold. I'll guide you. We really need to get you Night Eyes.*

Perhaps I'll get a pair, if this job pans out. It's looking like the Clan won't be happy with the outcome though. Ram'll probably get a hefty price on his head. So I might wait until that comes up, kill two ducks with one shot.

Mmm, ducks...

Jora took Scar's tail and he made his way into the pitch-black. The sound of picks smacking against the rock inside made hearing anything impossible for friend or foe. The hunter trusted her companion's acute senses to guide them through, and his smell to root out any enemies or strangers that might be lurking in the dark.

The passage was long, down into the mine.

Eventually it opened out into a dimly lit area. A lantern hung on the nearby wall, next to it there were discarded clothes and a corset. From the noises off to one side in another chamber, Jora guessed what Pink was up to and recognized the woman's voice from her otherworldly groans.

A guard watched a pair of prisoners cut themselves on rocks. Ragged men, former folk of Cold Stone and now forced to work Ram's mine for meagre and weak ore. Jora indicated to the passage where Pink was otherwise engaged, and Scar moved over to hunker down.

The hunter crept up quietly right behind the man. She reached up, caught him in a headlock and then twisted his neck violently so it snapped quickly and cleanly. Then she rifled his belt, found his keys, and put her fingers to her lips.

"Shhh, keep it down. I'm getting you out." Jora unlocked the one man's shackles and passed him the keys. "How many more of you are there?"

"Four," he coughed softly. "The rest are dead, or shipped off to the big camp in the north."

"Damn. I really hoped they kept you all in the same place. Still, Clan will be happy." Jora sighed softly.

"Hunter Clan?" he questioned, his grimy face and shaven head hiding a younger person than she expected.

"Yeah, one of the best in the Crest. Free your friend; I'm going to find the others." She paused. "Get weapons. If there's an alarm, you fight, and you get out. If you are going to die, take them down with you. Got it?" When he hesitated, Jora's gaze fastened onto his like a hasp lock. "Got it?"

He nodded.

"Good, and good luck."

With a flick of her finger, she motioned to Scar, and the raptor joined her. He looked at the two men, who froze for a moment. He stopped, closed his mouth, and gave them a pitch-perfect little bow before he swept past into the shadowed mine hall once more.

Show off... Jora chided a little.

What? I didn't smile at them, I offered them a human greeting.

They'll have nightmares for days.

I doubt they'll be as bad as being Ram's prisoner my friend.

Jora stopped, looked at Scar, and then chuckled. *Point.*

Their mental banter was easy; there was no delay, and often their thoughts followed on after another like water. Whatever connection they had, whatever enabled it, it was a fine example of hunter and partner working in unison. Of course, who was the hunter and who was the partner was a matter of some debate in the raptor's mind.

They came across another mine cavern, this one with four people working there. All young folk too, three women and one man. A pair of leering guards watched them from afar as they sat at the table flipping cards.

One of the women saw the hunters in the shadow and dropped her pick against her bucket. This drew the searching eyes of the men to her and they laughed. "Arms getting tired? Tough. Pick it up and keep on digging or we give you to Miss Pink as a plaything."

The hunters moved in close and struck quickly. It was over in moments; the two guards lay dead, and their blood seeped onto the floor. One by knife, the other by raptor claw. Both throats opened as fast as a bolt of lightning.

It would have gone smoothly, but there was a wrinkle. A Pink shaped wrinkle. The sound of the dropped pick had drawn her attention, and she had come to check on the guys. Her eyes widened when she saw the raptor and the hunter. She screamed an expletive and fled back down the corridor.

"Go!" Jora yelled, pulling the key from the dead guard's belt. "I got this."

Scar took off quickly after the fleeing woman and left the hunter in the cavern with the prisoners. Jora said nothing; sourly she moved from one to the other and undid their shackles and cuffs. "Weapons now. We're going to have to fight."

The women said nothing, nodded their thanks and assent, and then grabbed what they could from the two guards. The man brandished his pick and looked at the dusky-skinned hunter.

"What do they call you?"

"Jora."

"Thanks, Jora. Thank you so much."

"Thank me if we get out of here in one strip," she shot back as she heard a feral growl and a scream. Then the mine sounds were replaced with a rattling clang as the alarm bells sounded.

"Damn it!" Jora growled.

Scar came racing back into the cavern and shook his head. *I got her, but she had a friend. He was quicker and hit the button before I could fillet him. I still did, but he raised that awful racket.*

"No worries. We'll fight our way out, kill them all." Jora snorted. "Anyone who tries to stop us. Bloodbath, got it?"

Got it. The raptor's smile was not pretty.

Their escape was not guaranteed. But with the raptor at the head of a desperate charge, his claws and teeth made quick work of any guards who came into the tunnel. It was certainly as described: a bloodbath. The camp's defenders, Ram's bandits, had no chance to take down Scar in the dark. Their lanterns gleamed where they fell; one of them took on a ruddy glow as the bandit woman's blood stained the glass crimson, her face marked by the gashes of the raptor's wicked talons.

Claws, pistols, and brutal determination marked their flight from the mine as the sun gave up its ghost on the far horizon. The group halted at the mouth of the tunnel; they knew the defenders would be outside, and they'd be in their sights the moment they broke free.

Jora scanned the camp, saw a box, and grinned. "Cover your ears." She pulled her pistol and fired right into it. There was a loud bang, and the box of dynamite lit up the dusk as more and more sticks added to the explosion and sent debris flying. The two guards who had hunkered down by it were torn into bits by the powerful detonation.

The escapees fled from the tunnel and took advantage of the chaos. The women fled toward a truck that lay close to the exit, and the man with the pick axe made it half way before he was shot down by a crossbow wielding bandit perched on a platform high above the camp gate.

In a smooth movement, Jora dropped her pistol at her feet, slung her rifle off her back, and dropped both snipers in the time it took them to turn around to see where the first shot came from. Two shots were all it took, a single breath held between the first press of the trigger and the bolt-action reload that followed it.

The other two men who'd escaped first laid down some cover for the women, before they joined them in the back of the truck.

"Go!" Jora yelled and gripped her rifle as she slung it back over her shoulder, grabbing her pistol and following Scar. The raptor blazed a bloody trail from shooter to shooter as he provided point for the pair.

The chaos worked well for them. The bandits were blindsided, and some of them shot at their own people as they frantically tried to restore order. They were unable to stop the truck from leaving and as Jora stole one of their trikes—she took one last shot that sent the men and woman of Bloodstone Mine running for cover.

Fuel tanks blazed as the pistol ignited them to cover their escape. Pillars of fire shot skyward, and the stone walls of the camp lit up. Blinded by the sudden light, burned by the heat, the bandits looked to see where their quarry had gone but there was no sign of her. Only the sound of a bike and the smell of burning fuel.

Miles later, the truck, Jora, and Scar were back in the Strand. Scar assured the hunter they'd not been followed. The people they'd saved were welcomed into the town with open arms. The pair did not stay for thanks; they got their bounty and retreated to the edge of the town. No time for "thank-you" speeches or "well-done" platitudes.

Jora knew it wasn't over. She'd got them out, but things would not be OK until Ram was cold and dead. So, she turned and walked to the gate out of the Strand, and took the trike back to get her bike.

We find Ram and end him, she thought at the raptor.

No objections at all.

Good.

Time to hunt!

The roar of her bike on the open road and a trail of dust in the dark was all that remained in her wake. Pity Ram, with that pair of hunters on his heels. His life was about to get terminally short.

She'd even do this one for free.

— FOREVER —
by Robert J. Sawyer

E verything we know about dinosaurs comes from a skewed sample: the only specimens we have are of animals who happened to die at locations in which fossilization could occur; for instance, we have no fossils at all from areas that were mountainous during the Mesozoic.

Also, for us to find dinosaur fossils, the Mesozoic rocks have to be re-exposed in the present day—assuming, of course, that the rocks still exist; some have been completely destroyed through subduction beneath the Earth's crust.

From any specific point in time—such as what we believe to be the final million years of the age of dinosaurs—we have at most only a few hundred square miles of exposed rock to work with. It's entirely possible that forms of dinosaurs wildly different from those we're familiar with did exist, and it's also quite reasonable to suppose that some of these forms persisted for many millions of years after the end of the Cretaceous.

But, of course, we'll never know for sure.

—Jacob Coin, Ph.D.
Keynote Address,
A.D. 2018 Annual Meeting of the
Society of Vertebrate Paleontology

Five planets could be seen with the naked eye: Sunhugger, Silver, Red, High, and Slow; all five had been known since ancient times. In the two hundred years since the invention of the telescope, much had been discovered about them. Tiny Sunhugger and bright Silver went through phases, just like the moon did; Red had visible surface features, although exactly what they were was still open to considerable debate. High was banded, and had its own coterie of at least four moons, and Slow—Slow was the most beautiful of all, with a thin ring orbiting around its equator.

Almost a hundred years ago, Ixoor the Scaly had discovered a sixth planet—one that moved around the Sun at a more indolent pace than even Slow did; Slow took twenty-nine years to make an orbit, but Ixoor's World took an astonishing eighty-four.

Ixoor's World—yes, she had named it after herself, assuring her immortality. And ever since that discovery, the search had been on for more planets.

Cholo, an astronomer who lived in the capital city of Beskaltek, thought he'd found a new planet himself, about ten years ago. He'd been looking precisely where Raymer's law predicted an as-yet-undiscovered planet should exist, between the orbits of Red and High. But it soon became apparent that what Cholo had found was nothing more than a giant rock, an orbiting island. Others soon found additional rocks in approximately the same orbit. That made Cholo more determined than ever to continue scanning the heavens each night; he'd rather let a meatscooper swallow him whole than have his only claim to fame be the discovery of a boulder in space...

He searched and searched and searched, hoping to discover a seventh planet. And, one night, he did find something previously uncatalogued in the sky. His tail bounced up and down in delight, and he found himself hissing "Cholo's world" softly over and over again—it had a glorious sound to it.

But, as he continued to plot the object's orbit over many months, making notes with a claw dipped in ink by the light of a lamp burning sea-serpent oil, it became clear that it wasn't another planet at all.

Still, he had surely found his claim to immortality.

Assuming, of course, that anyone would be left alive after the impact to remember his name.

"You're saying this flying mountain will hit the Earth?" said Queen Kava, looking down her long green-and-yellow muzzle at Cholo.

The Queen's office had a huge window overlooking the courtyard. Cholo's gaze was momentarily distracted by the sight of a large, furry winger gliding by. He turned back to the queen. "I'm not completely thirty-six thirty-sixths certain, Your Highness," he said. "But, yes, I'd say it's highly likely."

Kava's tail, which, like all Shizoo tails, stuck straight out behind her horizontally held body, was resting on an intricately carved wooden mount. Her chest, meanwhile, was supported from beneath by a padded cradle. "And what will happen to the Earth when this giant rock hits us?"

Cholo was standing freely; no one was allowed to sit in the presence of the Queen. He tilted his torso backward from the hips, letting the tip of his stiff tail briefly touch the polished wooden floor of the throne room. "Doubtless Your Highness has seen sketches of the moon's surface, as observed through telescopes. We believe those craters were made by the impacts of similar minor planets, long ago."

"What if your flying rock hits one of our cities?"

"The city would be completely destroyed, of course," said Cholo. "Fortunately, Shizoo civilization only covers a tiny part of the globe. Anyway, odds are that it will impact the ocean. But if it does hit on land, the chances are minuscule that it will be in an inhabited area."

The Shizoo lived on an archipelago of equatorial islands. Although many kinds of small animals existed on the islands, the greatest beasts—wild shieldhorns, meatscoopers, the larger types of shovelbills—were not found here. Whenever the Shizoo had tried to establish a colony on the mainland, disaster ensued. Even those who had never ventured from the islands knew of the damage a lone meatscooper or a marauding pack of terrorclaws could inflict.

A nictitating membrane passed in front of Kava's golden eyes. "Then we have nothing to worry about," she said.

"If it hits the land," replied Cholo, "yes, we are probably safe. But if it hits the ocean, the waves it kicks up may overwhelm our islands. We have to be prepared for that."

Queen Kava's jaw dropped in astonishment, revealing her curved, serrated teeth.

Cholo predicted they had many months before the flying mountain would crash into the Earth. During that time, the Shizoo built embankments along the perimeters of their islands. Stones had to be imported from the mainland—Shizoo usually built with wood, but something stronger would be needed to withstand the waves.

There was much resistance at first. The tiny dot, visible only in a telescope, seemed so insignificant. How could it pose a threat to the proud and ancient Shizoo race?

But the dot grew. Eventually, it became visible with the naked eye. It swelled in size, night after night. On the last night it was seen, it had grown to rival the apparent diameter of the moon.

Cholo had no way to know for sure when the impact would occur. Indeed, he harbored a faint hope that the asteroid would disintegrate and vaporize in the atmosphere—he was sure that friction with the air was what caused shooting stars to streak across the firmament. But, of course, Cholo's rock was too big for that.

The sound of the asteroid's impact was heard early in the morning—a great thunderclap, off in the distance. But Cholo knew sound took time to travel—it would take three-quarters of a day for a sound to travel halfway around the world.

Most of the adult population had stayed up, unable to sleep. When the sound did come, some of the Shizoo hissed in contempt. A big noise; that was all. Hardly anything to worry about. Cholo had panicked everyone for no good reason; perhaps his tail should be cut off in punishment ...

But within a few days, Cholo was vindicated—in the worst possible way.

The storms came first—great gale-force winds that knocked down trees and blew apart huts. Cholo had been outdoors when the first high winds hit; he saw wingers crumple in the sky, and barely made it to shelter himself, entering a strongly built wooden shop.

A domesticated shieldhorn had been wandering down the same dirt road Cholo had been on; it dug in its four feet, and tipped its head back so that its neck shield wouldn't catch the wind. But five of its babies had been following along behind it, and Cholo saw them go flying into the air like so many leaves. The shieldhorn opened her mouth and was doubtless bellowing her outrage, but not even the cry of a great crested shovelbill would have been audible over the roar of this storm.

The wind was followed by giant waves, which barreled in toward the Shizoo islands; just as Cholo had feared, the asteroid had apparently hit the ocean.

The waves hammered the islands. On Elbar, the embankments gave way, and most of the population was swept out to sea. Much damage was done to the other islands, too, but—thank the Eggmother!—overall, casualties were surprisingly light.

It was half a month before the seas returned to normal; it was even longer before the heavens completely cleared. The sunsets were spectacular, stained red as though a giant meatscooper had ripped open the bowl of the sky.

"You have done the Shizoo people a great service," said Queen Kava. "Without your warning, we would all be dead." The monarch was wearing a golden necklace; it was the only adorn-ment on her yellowish-gray hide. "I wish to reward you."

Cholo, whose own hide was solid gray, tilted his head backward, exposing the underside of his neck in supplication. "Your thanks is reward enough." He paused, then lowered his head. "However..."

Kava clicked the claws on her left hand against those on her right. "Yes?"

"I wish to go in search of the impact site."

The waves had come from the west. Dekalt—the continent the Shizoo referred to as "the mainland"—was to the east. There was a land mass to the west, as well, but it was more than five times as far away. Shizoo boats had sailed there from time to time; fewer than half ever returned. There was no telling how far away the impact site was, or if there would be anything to see; the crater might be completely submerged, but Cholo hoped its rim might stick up above the waves.

Queen Kava flexed her claws in surprise. "We are recovering from the worst natural disaster in our history, Cholo. I need every able body here, and every ship for making supply runs to the mainland." She fell silent, then: "But if this is what you want..."

"It is."

Kava let air out in a protracted hiss. "It's not really a suitable reward. Yes, you may have the use of a ship; I won't deny you that. But while on your voyage, think of what you really want—something lasting, something of value."

"Thank you, Your Highness," said Cholo. "Thank you."

Kava disengaged her tail from the wooden mount, stepped away from her chest cradle, and walked over to the astronomer, placing the back of a hand, her claws bent up and away, gently on his shoulder. "Travel safely, Cholo."

They sailed for almost two months without finding any sign of the impact site. Cholo had tried to determine the correct heading based on the apparent direction from which the huge waves had come, plus his knowledge of the asteroid's path through the sky, but either he had miscalculated, or the ocean really had covered over all evidence of the impact. Still, they had come this far; he figured they might as well push on to the western continent.

The ship deployed its anchor about thirty-six bodylengths from the shore, and Cholo and two others rowed in aboard a small boat. The beach was covered with debris obviously washed in by giant waves—mountains of seaweed, millions of shells, coral, driftwood, several dead sea serpents, and more. Cholo had a hard time walking over all the material; he almost lost his balance several times.

The scouting party continued on, past the beach. The forest was charred and blackened—a huge fire had raged through here recently, leaving burnt-out trunks and a thick layer of ash underfoot. The asteroid would have heated up enormously coming through the atmosphere; even if it did hit the ocean, the air temperature might well have risen enough to set vegetation ablaze. Still, there were already signs of recovery: in a few places, new shoots were poking up through the ash.

Cholo and his team hiked for thousands of bodylengths. The crew had been looking forward to being on solid ground again, but there was no joy in their footsteps, no jaunty bouncing of tails; this burned-out landscape was oppressive.

Finally, they came to a river; its waters had apparently held back the expanding fire. On the opposite side, Cholo could see trees and fields of flowers. He looked at Garsk, the captain of the sailing ship. Garsk bobbed from her hips in agreement. The river was wide, but not raging. Cholo, Garsk, and three others entered its waters, their tails undulating from side to side, their legs and arms paddling until they reached the opposite shore.

As Cholo clambered up the river's far bank and out onto dry land, he startled a small animal that had been lurking in the underbrush.

It was a tiny mammal, a disgusting ball of fur.

Cholo had grown sick of sea serpent and fish on the long voyage; he was hoping to find something worth killing, something worth eating.

After about a twelfth of a day spent exploring, Cholo came across a giant shieldhorn skull protruding from the ground. At first he thought it was a victim of the recent catastrophe, but closer examination revealed the skull was ancient—hundreds, if not thousands, of years old. Shizoo legend said that long ago great herds of shieldhorns had roamed this continent, their footfalls like thunder, their facial spears glaring in the sunlight, but no one in living memory had seen such a herd; the numbers had long been diminishing.

Cholo and Garsk continued to search.

They saw small mammals.

They saw birds.

But nowhere did they see any greater beasts. At least, none that were still alive.

At one point, Cholo discovered the body of a meatscooper. From its warty snout to the tip of its tail, it measured more than four times as long as Cholo himself. When he approached the body, birds lifted into the air from it, and clouds of insects briefly dispersed. The stench of rotting meat was overpowering; the giant had been dead for a month or more. And yet there were hundreds of stoneweights worth of flesh still on the bones. If there had been any mid-sized scavengers left alive in the area, they would have long since picked the skeleton clean.

"So much death," said Garsk, her voice full of sadness.

Cholo bobbed in agreement, contemplating his own mortality.

Months later, Cholo at last returned to Queen Kava's chambers.

"And you found no great beasts at all?" said the Queen.

"None."

"But there are lots of them left on the mainland," said Kava. "While you were away, countless trips were made there to find wood and supplies to repair our cities."

"'Lots' is a relative term, Your Highness. If the legends are to believed—not to mention the fossil record—great beasts of all types were much more plentiful long ago. Their numbers have been thinning for some time. Perhaps, on the eastern continent, the aftermath of the asteroid was the gizzard stone that burst the thunderbeast's belly, finishing them off."

"Even the great may fall," said the Queen.

Cholo was quiet for a time, his own nictitating membranes dancing up and down. Finally, he spoke: "Queen Kava, before I left, you promised me another reward—whatever I wanted—for saving the Shizoo people."

"I did, yes."

"Well, I've decided what I'd like..."

The unveiling took place at noon six months later, in the large square outside the palace. The artist was Jozaza—the same Jozaza who had assured her own immortality through her stunning frieze on the palace wall depicting the Eggmother's six hunts.

Only a small crowd gathered for the ceremony, but that didn't bother Cholo. This wasn't for today—it was for the ages. It was for immortality.

Queen Kava herself made a short speech—there were many reasons why Kava was popular, and her brevity was certainly one of them. Then Jozaza came forward. As she turned around to face the audience, her tail swept through a wide arc. She made a much longer speech; Cholo was growing restless, hopping from foot to foot.

Finally the moment came. Jozaza bobbed her torso at four of her assistants. They each took hold of part of the giant leather sheet, and, on the count of three, they pulled it aside, revealing the statue.

It was made of white marble veined with gold that glistened in the sunlight. The statue was almost five times life size, rivaling the biggest meatscooper's length. The resemblance to Cholo was uncanny—it was him down to the very life; no one could mistake it for anyone else. Still, to assure that the statue fulfilled its purpose for generations to come, Cholo's name was carved into its base, along with a description of what he'd done for the Shizoo people.

Cholo stared up at the giant sculpture; the white stone was almost painfully bright in the glare of the sun.

A statue in his honor—a statue bigger than any other anywhere in the world. His nictitating membranes danced up and down.

He *would* be remembered. Not just now, not just tomorrow. He would be remembered for all time. A million years from now—nay, a hundred million hence, the Shizoo people would still know his name, still recall his deeds.

He would be remembered forever.

— TO MEGA THERION —
By Markisan Naso

The bone battle-axe came down on Phantar Ro's head like an unexpected rockslide. His weathered reflexes registered the strike at the last moment, and he managed to shift to his left as the cleaver breezed by the side of his face and bit into the top of his right, back horn. A second later the sound of the weapon ricocheting off the keratin pierced the air.

Phantar wrinkled the black and olive scales around his nose and cursed.

As the axe bounced up and to the right, the old euoplocephalus rolled beneath it, centered his gravity, and readied his stygian sword for a counter strike. The parry maneuver was something Phantar had practiced countless times since he was small. Three thousand? Five? He couldn't remember how many attacks he'd dodged over the course of his long life, or when he had even mastered the technique. At seventy-five years of age, every action he made was instinct now, as if all the ancient battlefield calculations puzzled out by his teachers had been implanted directly into his brain at birth. Phantar recalled his father Heiro often mentioning to his friends and neighbors that he came straight out of the egg ready to fight. He remembered the proud contours of his Dad's smile every time he said it, and sometimes Phantar even believed it was true. Sometimes he imagined himself bursting through that brittle orb, bits of speckled shell stuck to his spikes, blade in hand.

Phantar's sword burrowed into his opponent's abdomen, slowly traveling through rugged skin and dense thickets of sinew, then muscle, bone, and organs like a mutant tapeworm. He twisted his hard grip on the hilt, using both hands to push the blade deeper until the tip erupted through the back of the big majungasaurus, ruining the elegant red and gold swirl pattern of his hide.

Karnog inhaled slowly as the sword invaded him. He felt the cold sting of carbon steel beneath his ribs, but the pain was trivial compared to the rush of shame that flooded his heart. He'd failed. *Lord Phantar, please forgive me,* he thought, as he desperately searched for the face of the king he loved.

Phantar met Karnog's gaze and loosened his hold on the handle, then he watched the light behind his eyes start to escape into the universe.

"Death… death *will* come for you, my King," Kornog whispered affectionately as the last air exited his lungs. He bared his once fearsome teeth in a smile filled with gushing blood, like secret cave stalactites playing peekaboo behind a waterfall.

Karnog's corpse slid slowly down Phantar's blade, coating it in crimson, then collapsed into a bed of magnolias below. The old king looked at the lifeless body and suddenly felt the gash in his back spike. It had been twenty years since a challenger managed to cut him. Phantar envisioned putting a hand on the young warrior's shoulder and praising his courage and skill as their gaze met for the last time. *You fought magnificently. Your axe was fierce, and your heart was full of fire,* he thought. *That is what I should have said.*

Phantar attempted to speak the words posthumously, but his mouth failed to move. The moment was too far gone. Instead, he looked out upon the vast field where he stood and recalled that it was one of Karnog's favorite spots on the coast. The majunga-saurus had often taken his two daughters to this place. He loved to watch them chase each other through the tall grass and make up imaginary adventures as the summer breeze liberated pollen from the sea of nearby flowers, and the ocean pummeled the shore half a mile beneath their feet.

Phantar looked down at the body again, saddened by the sudden thought that Karnog's girls would never play here again. The next time they visited this field, it would be to say goodbye to the father they loved so dearly, and all the days after that they'd only return to grieve and remember him. Phantar hoped they would build a grand pyre and burn his body here, until the wind took his ashes over the cliff to the tidal arms of the sea.

It's a fine place to rest, nephew, Phantar thought lovingly. Then his mind grew quiet of reminiscences and future predictions, and he took a short walk to the edge of the earth.

The king stopped on a thin stretch of ridge and felt the swelte-ring, salted air blow up from the ocean. It entered his lungs like slow-moving magma as he withdrew a cloth from his belt pouch and carefully wiped the family blood from his sword.

Phantar was nineteen when he unexpectedly inherited his mother's barbaric, black blade. He received it days before she died and became a legend. As the longest serving soldier in the royal guard, Captain Davstana Ro lost her life to six assassins deter-mined to remove King Habon from power. Phantar's mother left the world as she tumbled down the imperial steps with ten knives and three spears sticking out of her massive nodosaurus frame like a demonic pin cushion. The mutineers, however, never came within six feet of the king's throne. Though she faced horrible odds and was mortally wounded early in the fight, Davstana simply refused to die until she plunged her blade into the beating organ of the last insurgent.

Phantar squinted at his mother's fabled sword. She had aptly named it The Black Curse. The blood of his own enemies had made the patina darker than it was when he received it, and darker still since the sword was forged two centuries ago in the southern iron-mine town where his great grandfather grew up.

Phantar pictured Davstana's hunter green face in his mind and held it there for a moment, recalling all the intricate, countenance lines he could. Then he wondered what his mother might think of him now if she were alive. Having never had children of his own, Phantar could not claim to know the internal mechanics of a parent's heart, but he often imagined that it might be filled with the same deep affection he felt for his mother when she gave her life for the crown and entered the annals of history. Phantar remembered the tears he shed that day. He remembered how he thought his ribs might burst apart as his chest swelled with pride.

Ever since the moment he learned of his mother's sacrifice, Phantar dedicated his life to following the legendary examples she set. In combat. In governance. In love. But in truth, his own bravery and accomplishments far eclipsed those of his mother ages ago. For nearly thirty years he had been revered by all dinosaurs as the greatest warrior of any generation. The acclaim, however, did not phase Phantar. It never went to his head or changed him. In his mind, he would always live in the shadow of Captain Davstana Ro, even if it was no longer cast upon him.

"All I wish is to honor your legacy and pass it on, mother," Phantar said, almost inaudibly. He let his hand glide softly above the blade of The Black Curse, as if acknowledging some sort of invisible energy emanating from its edge. "I had hoped to give your sword to Karnog today. I'm sorry."

Phantar placed The Black Curse in a handcrafted, black leather scabbard on his back, ornamented with red streaks of paint and a handful of archaeopteryx skulls, and stood silently atop the cliff. He remained there, motionless, for an hour and watched the sun slow dive into the ocean, as it made space for the impatient, twilight sky. When the horizon darkened to blue and then onyx, he decided to stay a bit longer and count the stars as they pricked pin holes of white light in the cosmic tapestry. He noticed one seem to grow stronger in brightness as time passed and chose it as his favorite.

When the night was finally still and the heavens fixed with fire, Phantar walked back to his nephew's stiffening body.

An hour after the duel, Phantar returned to his city of Callinus. A large crowd of villagers were waiting for him as he approached the sturdy bone and rock entrance gate, forged by the calloused hands of dinosaurs past. He could see hundreds of scaled and feathered faces light up with admiration in the gathering concourse. Not one of them was surprised to see their king walk back from the ocean. They expected his return, just as they expected the sun to soak the earth with light each morning.

Phantar had ruled the territory of Thrace for fifty-five years. No king nor queen in the Cretaceous period had reigned that long, or even come significantly close to approaching the time Phantar spent on the throne. A year after his mother died, and just three days before he entered his second decade, Phantar challenged her king. Habon was the most hated overlord in the history of the region. There wasn't anything particularly special about his cruelty during his fifteen-year rule, or his many failures as the sovereign of Thrace. Once a cunning spearman who rose up from poverty, the anserimimus became narcissistic and entitled just months after he came into power. He was the kind of king who was villainized and caricatured in story since story had been invented. Selfish decisions. Disregard for his subjects. Unnecessary taxes. A desire to see every dinosaur kneel before him and kiss the overly ornate ring on his red, wrinkled talon. Phantar's mother never once complained about being in his vile service, because she had sworn an oath to protect him as long as he reigned. But Phantar recalled one moment when she revealed her true thoughts to him and crystalized the feelings of nearly every dinosaur in Callinus at the time.

"Mother, is King Habon good?" seven-year old Phantar asked.

Davstana turned to her son and hesitated for a moment, then decided right there she would never lie to her little boy. *You will grow up knowing the truth of this world, even if my words aren't always easy to hear,* she thought. *I will teach you that this life can be unkind and your leaders cruel, even those chosen by the Gods. But you won't be, Phantar. You will be better. You will be more.* "No, son," she said at last, stroking his face. "He's the opposite of good."

Phantar was the complete opposite of Habon. His mother kept her pledge and pushed him hard to excel in all things, from the intricate use of a blade, to preparing a meal, to selflessly helping the community. When Phantar was ten, his mother forced him to haul rocks and logs from the Middle Fields to help strangers rebuild their homes after an earthquake rocked Callinus. At the time he grumbled constantly about the chore under heavy breath, but now he looked back on it as one of the proudest, most satisfying moments of his life. Davstana often expected her son to do things he did not want to do, or did not understand, but no matter what task he was given, she always praised him for his effort, even when he complained, struggled, or failed.

When Phantar dispatched Habon in under a minute and became ruler of Thrace, he instantly knelt and thanked his mother, large droplets falling from his blue eyes. Every single day after that, Phantar wished his mother could see what her lessons and her love had made him. The victory over Habon earned Phantar great respect from the Thracians because he had rid the world of a heinous tyrant at such a tender age, but it was his emotion and compassion that made them fall in love with him from the moment his armored knees hit the grass. In time, his kindness, fair nature, and resolve became as highly regarded as his unparalleled skill with The Black Curse.

Phantar carried Karnog's body on his shoulder through the heavily fortified entranceway toward the heart of Callinus. Under Phantar's stewardship the center of town had become a bustling hub for crafters and cooks, assorted dealers and peddlers. Moments earlier Callinus was pulsing with eager customers searching for deals in little vegetable stands, hardware stores, blacksmith shops, and pop-up restaurants. But now, the whole market was as silent as an ocean trench. Hundreds of dinosaur onlookers began to step back toward the edges of the square, making space for their king as he passed through the colorful thoroughfare.

Phantar felt half-mast eyes focus on him as he walked down the street he had known his whole life. After a few minutes, his measured stroll ended at a large rock slab on the back edge of the merchant square. The flat, granite altar was held in place four feet above the ground by a tangled bed of roots grown rogue from a nearby Araucaria tree. The surface of it was tattooed with decades old brownish-red blotches and dried, sanguine smears. Directly behind the slab and its arboreal chair stood an elaborate base, made of marble and cherry wood. The wood featured detailed etchings of bones and flowers, like a haunting battle of life and death was taking place inside the dark beauty of the grain.

The dinosaurs of Callinus had long desired to erect a statue of King Phantar atop the base while he was alive, so that he might know how much he meant to the city. Phantar refused the gesture, in part because it went against the tradition of creating a statue in memory of a fallen warrior, but also because he simply hated the idea of seeing his likeness every day. Despite the king's objection, the greatest stone worker and the greatest wood carver in

Callinus had conspired against him to craft the stand. After six months of chipping and whittling, it was placed in the square with immediate plans to create the sculpture portion atop the base in public, so everyone could watch the painstaking effort and passion the artisans planned to put into the work. Phantar immediately ordered the base removed and the statue cancelled, but hours before it was scheduled to be carted away, he rescinded his command. That day he found himself walking past the altar and noticed three children climbing on to the base, pretending to be great warriors worthy of glory and tribute. Phantar immediately felt a connection. As a toddler, he often had the same, lofty aspirations. Sometimes he would even refuse to go to school unless his father put a cape on his back, just like the one his mother wore with her royal guard uniform. "From the egg," his father had said. "From the egg." So Phantar let the beautiful base stand as a way for all the younglings to dream of battle and adventure, and becoming something more than they were.

Phantar thrust the Black Curse in the grass circle before the granite altar. As he stared at the slab, with his nephew still strewn over one of his broad shoulders, the king's six personal guards emerged from the crowd, dressed in ceremonial, scalloped blue armor and yellow cloaks clasped with black, archaeopteryx skull sigils like the ones that adorned Phantar's scabbard. These elite soldiers were highly skilled, greying fighters who had been by the king's side for years. They were all deeply trusted and would give their lives for Phantar without question, but they were also more than just protectors and allies to him—they were his chosen family. He could not count the number of times he fought beside them, celebrated significant events in their lives, or just shared pints of mead and laughter with them at the end of a trying day.

The king's guard approached Phantar from behind, familiar with the ritual that came next. Amytis, a deinonychus scythe-wielder, and Calliope the swift ornithomimosauria archer, gently removed Karnog's limp body from Phantar's clavicle. The king flexed his old trapezius muscles, trying to work out the kinks that formed from carrying a dinosaur almost twice his weight for a mile. Amytis and Calliope placed the body on the rock slab carefully, dismayed by the task. They both stared at their lost friend and remembered. Amytis recalled skipping rocks into the sea with Karnog the morning before he was married. Calliope thought of the day she and the king's nephew ate pawpaw fruit for the first time under a tree. They were just ten-years-old.

Two more guards set to work on Phantar's armor, removing the pieces and setting them aside on a black, woven cloth they had laid on the ground. Nephele's large green eyes began to water as she unfastened the king's breast plate. Her tiny, silver shuvuuia talons that had so often wielded knives with devilish precision, now trembled as they freed a black leather shin guard. She pictured Karnog's child-like expression when he was unanimously named to the royal guard, a perfect mixture of surprise and elation that had made her smile eight years ago. She looked up at Desma, now unable to muster anything more than gloom on her face. The hulking grey baronyx frowned back at her as he shifted the battle hammer in his belt and set to work on a gauntlet. He suddenly realized that he'd never hear Karnog's oversized laugh again.

When Phantar's armor was completely removed, the last pair of guards draped a red cloak lined with silver and orange velociraptor feathers over his powerful frame. The flowing cape had holes in it that exactly matched the spike pattern on the king's back and slipped on with ease. Lethia, the tarbosaurus captain of the guard and lethal sword master, received a nod of approval from his king as he straightened the cloak collar. His second-in-command, Sotiris, stretched his long, tan opisthocoelicaudia neck behind Phantar to ensure the spikes had indeed punched through properly. He spotted the damage Karnog had inflicted on the king's spike and for a split-second felt immense pride for his friend's accomplishment. But as quickly as the warmth of that reflection came, it faded and froze when he caught a glimpse of the body in his peripheral vision.

Phantar, now fully dressed in his ceremonial robes, placed a hand on Karnog's peaceful face and held it in his palm for a long moment. His elite guard lined up beside him, three on each side, like an armed wedding party waiting for the processional song to begin. Then the king turned around slowly to face all the dinosaurs of Callinus who were anxious to hear his words.

"Callinus," he spoke at last, his voice booming like thunder in a quiet field. "Today my heart feels like crumbled shale inside my chest. My nephew, Karnog, who many of you knew as one the noblest, finest dinosaurs in all of Thrace, fell to my sword today. He was..." The king broke off as his throat started to fail him and his eyes grew hot with grief. "He *was* like a son to me."

As Phantar paused, a deinonychus mother and her two, young daughters approached the altar. Their eyes appeared to be hollowed out and replaced with liquid pools. Phantar looked down at them and searched for his next words as he felt his shale heart plummet into his stomach and disintegrate. He put a hand on the pommel of his infamous sword, now a family slayer, a love destroyer.

"I very much wanted Karnog to be the one standing here now, holding up my sword as your new king," choked Phantar. "I trained him from birth. I gave him all the guidance and wisdom I had in me and more... and he excelled at everything. *Everything.* No matter what I threw at him, he rose to the challenge. He surprised and delighted me with his intelligence, his kindness and his prowess on the battlefield. I could not have been prouder of him."

Phantar stared vacantly at Sayina and her daughters, Zaida and Raewyn, who now stood before him, their frail maroon and teal feathered bodies in the elegant, silk dresses that Karnog had bought them. Their tiny legs somehow seemed weakened beneath the fabric, held up only by will and respect for their beloved husband and father. The king steadied himself and tried to again project his voice for all to hear, but no volume adjustment could escape the intimacy of his words. He was speaking to his family.

"But it wasn't enough. All his natural ability, and my knowledge and training... it wasn't enough to put him here, in my place."

Phantar looked out at the crowd. The faces of his onlookers mirrored, and even magnified, the anguish on his face as he spoke. There wasn't a dinosaur in the city who did not wish to comfort their leader with a delicate hug or lay a hand gently on his back, as Phantar's ice blue eyes welled up with tears like water threatening to rise above the rim of an ancient well.

"My mother called my sword The Black Curse, but today it feels like that name should be mine," Phantar said, as his fingers white-knuckled on the hilt and the moment overwhelmed him. "Forgive me, Karnog. Forgive me."

Today it had been fifteen years, the king thought as he asked his dead nephew to absolve him. Fifteen long years since he was supposed to die.

In the territory of Thrace, dinosaur kings and queens were honor bound to accept formal challenges to their leadership at age sixty and beyond. The outcome of such a challenge was determined by single combat to the death. The rules were fairly simple. No spectators were allowed to witness the battle for the crown, and the victory had to be earned. A dinosaur ruler could not willingly die. He was required to duel to the best of his abilities. If it was discovered that the conflict was anything less than a sincere fight to the death, the winner would be immediately killed and two members of the king's guard would be selected by the citizens of Callinus to vie for leadership. In the history of the great, burgeoning city, however, there had never been cause to believe a duel was false. Even horrible King Habon mostly respected and abided by the traditions set forth centuries ago.

At age twenty, Phantar was by far the youngest dinosaur to challenge for leadership and the youngest to ever succeed. Any dinosaur in Thrace could muster the courage to try and take the crown once they'd lived two decades, but it rarely happened. Most warriors invoked the rite of royal battle when they were seasoned fighters in their late thirties or forties. In fact, only one other dinosaur had been able to seize power in her twenties. Queen Syrvad, known throughout the continent as the Deltadromeus Demon, was twenty-nine when she became regent.

When kings and queens were forced to fight for their crown, they did not last very long. The majority were killed the first or second time they faced a challenger, simply due to their advanced age. The system, for all intents and purposes, was designed for this to occur. It was an immense honor for a ruler to die in combat during his twilight years. Most kings and queens did not live that long, so the rare opportunity to pass on the throne to a deserving warrior through death was revered. It was also a cause for celebration; it represented a pure change of direction and renewal for the city. As the blood of an old ruler flowed out into the fields, new energy and hope for the future flowed into Callinus.

There were, however, a few stubborn kings and queens who lasted a year or more beyond the intended retirement age. Along with Phantar, two others had been inducted into that prestigious club. Queen Manorn was sixty-three when she died. The amethyst and gold bambiraptor was widely considered the greatest warrior in Thrace before Phantar. Her wily, acrobatic nature and masterful defensive skills with a halberd made it difficult for challengers to get close enough to dispatch her. There was no doubt she would have continued to rule, if not for the stroke she suffered in her sixty-third year that unsteadied her left arm.

The heinous King Habon reigned until he was sixty-one-and-a-half. He only survived that long because he rigged the battlefield before each duel began. Habon relished the chance to outmaneuver his foes, and with each challenge, he got more creative with his deceptions. There were no specific rules against this practice, but even if there were, no dinosaur dared question the king's underhanded tactics. Speaking out against Habon usually meant death for any objector, as well as the death of any close relatives.

Habon had tried to gain an advantage over Phantar the night before their duel by instructing his minions to dig a hidden pit on the battlefield and fill it with tar. Phantar's mother had warned her son about the king's penchant for trickery years earlier when he asked about challenging for the crown. So, that evening, Phantar snuck out to the site and found Habon's lackeys setting up the trap. When they departed, snickering to themselves about the nefarious work they'd just completed, Phantar reversed their treachery by filling in the pit with limestone.

Now, at seventy-five years of age, Phantar stood alone as the greatest warrior king to ever live, unequaled in the history of all sentient dinosaurs. Although he had grown noticeably slower and more tired in the fifteen years since he was expected to die, his mind and his skills remained nearly as sharp as they were when he was thirty years younger. His ability to adapt to the physical limitations that continually crept into his battle-weathered body, as well as to the fighting styles of challengers he faced during the early years, made him seem absolutely terrifying to any potential foe.

No matter what was thrown at him, Phantar always managed to find a solution. Though his mother was fearless and taught him most of his skills, his father passed down the ability to problem solve. A healer and inventor of sorts, Heiro could not even muster rudimentary proficiency with a weapon, but he could think his way around any difficulty or impasse presented to him. He simply refused to believe in impossibility. Phantar did not always feel the same as his Dad, especially when he was a teenager full of self-doubt, but when he became king, he adopted his father's outlook. The instant the crown touched the dark green ridges on his head, he believed there was no obstacle he could not overcome. In the forty years after he cut down Habon, Phantar faced many arduous hurdles. Famine. The Yarrow Plague. The volcanic eruptions of Thrawsunblat. The siege of Keverra. He helped the dinosaurs of Thrace get through it all, even when desperation and fear threatened to destroy the world they'd built; even when it seemed like everything would be buried in blood and ash, he always managed to lift them back up.

When Phantar turned sixty, many dinosaurs thought it impossible that he would live to see another week, despite all his accomplishments, victories and grit. If history taught any lesson to the Thracians it was that their old leaders, even the most beloved, worked with finite time on the throne.

Ten years later at age seventy, the number of decimated opponents was piled so high that the challenges to Phantar's crown started drying up. Losing to the king in one-on-one combat became a certainty for any who dreamed of taking power. Phantar changed history; he changed the expectation for what could and could not be accomplished. The word "impossible" that dinosaurs once ascribed to their mighty king disappeared, and in its place now was the only one that made sense—mythic.

Phantar's hand went limp and fell from the hilt of his sword as Sayina's daughters ran to their father's corpse on the altar. They kissed his cold face over and over, somehow hoping they might heat him back to life if their affection proved strong enough. Sayina stared up at Phantar for a moment as if she might say something, but then simply embraced him. She pushed all her weight into the king and wailed uncontrollably into his chest. The growing dinosaur crowd of Callinus cried with her.

When Sayina ran out of breath, she stepped back, putting some distance between them. Her tears weighed down the bottom lids of her eyes, and she looked at Phantar with affection. Phantar peered back, then shifted his head slightly to the left, his gaze never leaving hers.

"Captain Lethia, remove the damaged spike from my back and hand it to me."

"My lord?" Lethia responded, surprised by the request.

Phantar broke his connection with Sayina and finished his head turn to emphasize the order with the deep cerulean of his eyes.

"Yes, King Phantar," Lethia replied.

The captain of the guard removed the dagger from his belt and cut around the slashed spike as the king held Sayina's hand. When Lethia finished the surgery, he twisted the spike and pulled it out carefully. The blood and separating tissue spilled slowly down Phantar's cloak like a stream flowing into an estuary. Sotiris quickly removed his own cape and pressed the yellow fabric into the fresh wound to stop the bleeding.

The king never winced as Lethia enacted his command. He just smiled at his nephew's bride until the task was complete. Lethia placed the severed spike in his king's hands, staring at it, as if it were a rare diamond excavated from a mountain cave. He resisted the urge to ask his king if he could have one too. Phantar handed it to Sayina.

"Karnog was magnificent. He nearly ended my life with this strike," Phantar said, the pride written in the lines of his face.

Sayina took the spike and held it to her face. Her eyes closed as the king stepped away and released her hand so he could address the crowd of Callinus for a final time.

"It has been my honor to be your king for fifty-five years. I love this city, and I love all of you deeply, but I fear I've lived far too long," he lamented. "Although the Gods see fit to keep me here, I cry out for the many good dinosaurs I've killed; dinosaurs with such great potential that will never be realized in this world."

Phantar's mind weighed heavily with thoughts of legacy in the last few years. Karnog had attempted to become king at age twenty-eight because Phantar openly and emphatically encouraged him to do so. He had handpicked his successor out of deepest love, but the selection was not without utmost merit. Phantar had spent nearly three decades preparing his nephew, just as his mother had prepared him. He had little doubt that Callinus and Thrace would flourish under Karnog's leadership and direction, and for nearly ten years he had desired to pass on the crown and fade into the stars. But he hesitated. He waited. He wanted to make sure Karnog was at his peak physical and intellectual abilities—but it was more than that. Sometimes he wrestled with the idea of leaving too soon. If no dinosaur could defeat him, was it his obligation to continue leading Thrace until his natural death? Must he see his reign through to ensure the Ro legacy? Was he setting an impossible standard for any who followed him?

Would his mother tell him to keep going?

"It's time to reset Thrace," Phantar decided. "Time to put someone new on the throne."

The crowd went very still as their king continued. "Tomorrow, I will die on the anniversary of my mother's death," Phantar stated with absolute surety. "I will return to the cliff where Karnog fell and face all six of my royal guard in combat, just as she faced the six assassins who took her life fifty-six years ago. I will fight to the best of my ability as I always have, but I know they will prevail. I have prepared them for this day," the king said confidently.

The citizens of Callinus, however, were not prepared for Phantar's words, nor the promise of his demise. The sounds of their heavy gasps carried to the altar like leaves in a wind storm.

"When it is done, they will toss The Black Curse into the ocean and you will all chose your next leader. You will start anew."

The crowd looked up at Phantar, completely stunned by his declaration, unable to speak any words that would somehow matter in such a staggering moment in history. Phantar looked back at the rainbow wave of dinosaurs before him and started naming each one in his head, as if trying to add them into an infinite memory basket.

Portz the butcher.

Dulemba the swordsmith.

Battoe the librarian.

Finley the flower shop girl...

He stood and stared at them all for a long time, cataloging their faces without saying a word. Then the greatest king of Thrace turned and walked away, blackened bloody sword in his stalwart grip. As he headed for the throne room, the dinosaurs of Callinus suddenly found their voice. It rang out in unison like a chorus song.

Thank you, Phantar!!! Thank you, Phantar!!!!

By the time the sun started to rise, Phantar was already standing on the cliff with his claws clasped behind his back, watching the sky get brushed with tangerine and red. The vibrant star he'd noticed last night was still visible and in the same place, but it appeared much larger now. It almost looked like there were two suns in the heavens. "A sign from the Gods?" Phantar wondered. "Perhaps they will finally come down to fetch me from this planet and bring me to the stars."

He wore no armor, only a black tunic and a short, dark red and hole-less cape with its ends jagged and frayed from fire and years of battle. It was the first cape his father had made him when he was young. The Black Curse was stabbed into the ground in front of him like a sentry marker for the sea.

When the sun completely escaped the ocean depths, Phantar heard the sound of leather and metal growing closer. He looked over his shoulder and his royal guard were there, dressed in the same ceremonial, blue scalloped armor and yellow capes from yesterday. For them, that night of honor never ended.

"We do not wish to kill you, Lord Phantar," Captain Lethia said as the guard stopped yards from their beloved king and knelt in respect. "Can we not wait another five or ten years instead, when you might require a cane?"

Phantar now faced his guard and put his hand on the hilt of The Black Curse. He smiled. He often thought Captain Lethia should change his name to Captain Levity.

"Heh. I'm sorry my friend," he said. "It's time. Rise and give me my death."

The wind blew delicately over the field and the six members of the royal guard stood as ordered. Then Nephele stepped forward slightly. Her wiry, long-muscled frame moved with confidence and grace, but the king could see a layer of melancholy wash over her as she spoke.

"King Phantar, the dinosaurs of Callinus put up a statue in your honor today. The stone chipper and wood carver worked on it for years in secret, and it's magnificent," she exclaimed, throwing her hands in the air to try and emphasize the grandeur of the monument. "They put it on the old wood and stone pedestal, and everyone is going up to it and thanking you for everything you've done. I thought you should know. We thought... we..." she said, stumbling in her sadness.

Amytis put a hand on his friend's shoulder as softly as he could and continued her sentence for her. "We wanted you to know how much you mean to Callinus. To Thrace. How much you matter to generations and generations of dinosaurs in this world, and always will."

Phantar considered the gesture. "A damn, secret statue of me," he muttered. It felt good to know he had been defied and defeated for once in his life.

The king pulled his blade from the earth and held it in front of him with one hand.

"Understand that I cannot fight any less than the best of my ability. Although I am ready to leave this world, I must always honor my Mother," he said in a deep, low voice. "Don't hold back or you will die. Do not attack me one-on-one or you will die. You must coordinate your offense as I have taught you if you wish to succeed."

Phantar clasped the hilt of his sword with both hands and held the deadly point straight at his loyal guard.

"Thank you for giving my life meaning and purpose," he said. Then the king steadied himself and prepared to fight the greatest battle of his long, decorated life.

Amytis engaged Phantar in combat first. His mammoth, battle scythe tumbled toward the king with uncanny speed. Phantar, who had received his fill of monstrous weapons crashing down on his head lately, dodged it easily with a side-step. The strike, however, was a distraction. Just as he escaped the reaper's blow, Phantar was greeted by a volley of three arrows from Calliope's bow. Each shaft was aimed at a different section of his body to prevent a sword block, but Phantar had long practiced avoiding hidden arrow attacks. When he evaded the scythe, he had also grabbed Amytis by the cape and pulled him down into the path of the anticipated bolts. The deinonychus was bent over from the momentum of his strike and was easily re-directed. Phantar went to one knee, heaving the surprised guard in front of his body. One arrow dug into Amytis' meaty left calf, the other embedded in his hip. The colossal dinosaur howled in pain. The third arrow, meant to rocket through Phantar's head, instead shattered against the flat side of The Black Curse.

Phantar wasted no time, swiftly drawing his sword across his body, then hurling it as hard as he could from his crouched position. In less than a second, the razor edge of his blade sliced neatly through Calliope's instinctively outstretched forearm, then burrowed into her chest. The impact took Calliope off her feet and she was thrust backwards several yards, blood spurting from her wounds like water from a drainage hose.

Sotiris and Nephele were instantly on top of the weaponless king. The ultra-fast shuvuuia got to him first, savagely unleashing her double-bladed knives straight at Phantar's chest. Phantar whipped his cape in front of him, and the quick strikes deflected off it, leaving needle holes in the red fabric.

"Damn. Chainmail inside!" Nephele bellowed, just before the king's bone-armored elbow struck her ear canal, cracking her skull around the opening, and throwing her equilibrium into complete chaos.

Sotiris' long neck craned over the disoriented Nephele, searching for a target. On his head was a helmet that looked like a torture device from an evil dungeon. Jutting straight out of the front of the mask were a series of deadly metal skewers, soldered 360 degrees around his tiny face. The opisthocoelicaudia had, in effect, turned himself into a massive morningstar. His neck served as the handle and chain. His head was the spiked ball.

Still in a low position, Phantar somersaulted beneath the first head strike, and then another. He felt the impact of the helmet hitting the ground where he'd been split-seconds earlier. As the king barreled away again, past the arrow-riddled Amytis, he picked up the scythe lying next to the wounded guard. With miraculous fluidity for a dinosaur his age, Phantar completed his roll and immediately sprang to his feet swinging the scythe in a giant, upward arc.

Sotiris' head tumbled off his ladder neck like a boulder released from loose mountain soil. It hit the field with a hollow thud as half the spikes embedded in the earth. The other half of the helmet's teeth stuck straight up in the morning sun. The headless body of Sotiris went limp and plummeted sideways, barely missing Nephele, who was wobbling around, trying to regain her wits and balance.

As Phantar completed the kill, he suddenly felt a hot sting in his leg. Amytis growled as he buried an arrow deep in his king's thigh. The hole in the lower leg of the deinonychus, where the arrow previously resided, gushed blood all over his shin and onto the grass. Phantar ignored the jolt of pain and brought the sole of his foot down on Amytis' face.

Desma entered the fray with a sideswipe of his war hammer. Phantar managed to bring the long handle of the scythe up in time with both hands and catch it between the square head and the fluted beak. The force of the blow buckled the king and nearly broke his weapon in half. Desma was stronger than Phantar had ever been in his prime, but the king had faced many behemoths in his life. He knew how to use his enemies' strength against them and overcome the disadvantage. He pushed back the hammer with enough force to separate the weapons, then he braced himself for the next blow. Desma immediately and savagely swung again, hoping to overwhelm the king with his power, but Phantar stepped to the left and caught the war hammer again with the shaft of the reaper. This time, he used his improved angle to turn the scythe handle over in his hands, forcing it to nestle beneath the flute spike, and popped the entire hammer from Desma's grip. A shocked Desma stepped back as the king swept the scythe at his defenseless ankles. The baronyx hopped over the curved blade in time, but the slice was not meant to cut off his feet. Phantar continued the attack motion, pivoting with the momentum of the swing so the scythe handle kept moving in the same direction. As Desma landed, the end of the reaper shaft caught him in the shins and knocked him off his feet. The severed, spiked head of Sotiris waited for him below.

King Phantar grabbed the war hammer lying near the convulsing, impaled body of Desma and walked toward Captain Lethia. He gripped the hammer in his right hand and the scythe in his left. In between his quarry, the bewildered Nephele, dripping blood and pus from her ear canal, was flailing about, trying to shake the irreversible damage off. Phantar drove the spike of the hammer through the top of her head without missing a step and let go of the handle. She crumbled.

Lethia liberated his twin swords from the scabbards on his back, as Phantar started running at him, scythe held tight. At the moment when it seemed they would collide like a ship and an iceberg, the king hit the ground in a slide, streaking past Lethia on his left as he held the scythe blade directly up. He hoped to catch the Captain off guard and sever an artery in his thigh. The move surprised Lethia, but his instincts kicked in and he managed to stop the crescent blade with his sabers in a coordinated cross-block. The Scythe clanged away.

The king knew there was only a small chance the maneuver would pay off and injure the captain of his guards. Lethia was one of the very best warriors he'd ever encountered. He would have been disappointed if the tarbosaurus failed to make the parry. But it was Phantar's secondary goal that really mattered. His slide took the king yards beyond Lethia in the exact trajectory of Calliope's body. As soon as he was past the Captain, he hustled over to her corpse, which lay rumpled in the grass twenty yards away. When he reached the body, he pulled his mother's fabled sword free.

"I suppose this is the big finale, my lord," Lethia shouted as Calliope's blood glistened on Phantar's blade. "It appears you've won again."

"Your strategy against me was very good, Captain. The spiked helmet on Sotiris was particularly creative."

"Yes, but not good enough. I'm sorry I failed you."

"It isn't over yet, Lethia," Phantar smiled, offering his friend a smidgen of hope.

Captain Lethia walked over to his king, swords drawn.

"No. But, I really don't like my chances."

The two best warriors in Thrace clashed swords, and the ding of metal on metal rang out with each connected slash. Almost instantly, Captain Lethia discovered what he already knew in his heart; he was nowhere near a match for the old king, even after twenty-plus years of sparring with him. He thought he had memorized all Phantar's techniques and could counter them. He thought that after all the time they spent together he was very nearly approaching the skill level of his lord. But the king he faced now was nothing like the one he knew from practice. Every move executed was something unexpected and innovative. Every turn of his blade offered a different twist on a strike perfected forty years earlier. Lethia was permanently on the defensive, unable to perform even one offensive maneuver. The king attacked mercilessly, keeping Lethia on his back foot, as the purple tarbo-saurus struggled to block the savage advance. With each sublime burst of violence that exploded against his swords, Lethia knew it was just a matter of seconds before he'd falter and forfeit his life.

Then the moment came. Lethia felt The Black Curse slice through his left, sword arm shoulder, then a roundhouse kick to the gut paralyzed his legs and pulled the air from his lungs like a weed extracted from dirt. He hit the ground on his right side, grimacing from the severe cut, as his sabers clattered away.

Phantar walked two steps toward the disarmed Captain, now determined to finish the fight he had very much hoped to lose. As he raised his weapon, point down with deadly purpose, he suddenly felt an awful sting in the upper part of his sword arm.

Amytis. Phantar thought he was as good as dead from the poison on Nephele's daggers. She always coated them in deadly Nerium toxin before a fight. But the resilient deinonychus wasn't quite finished. He'd crawled over to Nephele's body and retrieved two reserve knives from her sheathes. With the last bit of life left in him, he hurled the daggers at Phantar and collapsed.

The pain seared in the king's shoulder and bicep, and he instinctually tightened his grip on The Black Curse, as if to somehow ensure the wounds would not separate him from the blade. Lethia immediately seized on the moment, fumbling for one of his swords. Before Phantar could shake off the agony and recover, Lethia was on one knee slicing through the air with gritted teeth. The blade found a target just above Phantar's elbow. It connected with scale and flesh, then traveled through bone and muscle to the air again, bringing a wispy tail of blood with it.

Phantar's severed forearm slid from the upper meat, claws still tightly gripping the hilt of the sword, and plopped on the ground. The shock of the dissected limb forced the great king down to the earth as well. He crashed on his back into a bed of green.

Phantar felt a brutal, aching throb where his arm once was and stared into the sky as he lay motionless in the tall grass. His favorite star wasn't even a star any longer. It had become a massive, blazing entity, closing in on the atmosphere. Was he imagining it? Was it really the Gods come to whisk him away? Was this the end?

The king suddenly recalled his father telling him, just days before his heart gave out, "You know, son... when this world ends one day, even the greatest legacy will be lost."

Then his mind wandered to a time when he was ten years old. He had just failed to qualify for his first sword tournament after months of doing nothing but preparing, and his father sat him down to explain his place in the universe. "I know how much you wanted to participate in the tournament, Phantar," he told his boy sympathetically. "And I know how much you want to make your mark. There's nothing wrong with that. There's nothing wrong with honoring your mother. But if you spend all your time trying to live up to someone else's accomplishments, you won't ever be satisfied with your own."

You were right, father, Phantar thought as he pictured him in his workshop, tinkering. *These last few years, I've been trying so hard to ensure mother's legacy will live on when I die. But it has. It has for a long while now. If this is my final day... if all that I've done burns away... it's enough,* he thought. *I've done enough.*

Captain Lethia was on his feet now and glanced up to see what Phantar was witnessing. The flash of the approaching object prickled his eyes. He shielded them and quickly looked away. Unable to fully comprehend or process what he saw, Lethia returned his focus to fulfilling the king's wish. He stood over Phantar as the light above his head intensified and a crackling sound began to drown out the ebb and flow of the ocean.

"Goodbye, king of kings," Lethia said, pausing for a slight moment to pay his respects. He raised his sword slowly.

The Captain of the guards hesitated a fraction too long. Phantar pushed himself up with his bleeding stump. Clutching his amputated limb by the wrist with his intact hand, he thrust The Black Death into Lethia's exposed stomach. The king twisted the appendage, and the sword rotated inside the Captain. Then the dead claws released their grip on the hilt and Lethia collapsed.

"Goodbye," Phantar said in a low voice, as he tossed his severed arm away. "I'll see you again in the stars."

The king slowly staggered to his feet, as blood and bits of tattered meat spit out of his ruined limb. He ripped The Black Curse from Lethia's gut and held it down by his side, as the liquid proof of his final victory ran off the blade in steady drips. The pain from the poison arrow in his leg and the daggers still planted in the remains of his arm, began to dull. He closed his eyes and inhaled the primordial sea air, as the crackling sounds above grew louder, like worn tendons popping over an old joint. Then the mythic king opened his deep blue eyes, looked up, and smiled as his long-awaited death rocketed down from the cosmos.

King Phantar Ro pushed his mother's sword through the snarled and bloody grass for the last time, and watched the sky disappear in white, hot fire.

— DROMA STATION —
by Alexandra Pitchford

The distress call had come from nowhere, a sudden blaring alarm disrupting the night-cycle aboard the *Icarus*. Jaina groaned as the lights flickered on in her quarters, the influx of light and sound jarring her from sleep and forcing her to clench her eyes tightly, arm thrown across her face.

"Someone will deal with it," she grumbled to herself as she rolled over in her bunk and drew the covers up over her head. A moment later, the blaring alarm stopped, only to be replaced by the crackle of the intercom.

"Captain?"

"Go away," she grunted, tightening the covers around herself. Not that the person on the other end would have heard her. The silence stretched for several blessed moments, but it didn't last.

"Captain Deckard? You're gonna want to hear this."

Jaina sighed, throwing off the covers and grimacing as the light stung her eyes again. She flailed her hand toward the wall panel beside the bunk, catching the switch mostly by chance, and was rewarded with a soft click as the mic activated.

"I'm coming. Gimme a few..."

Jaina pushed herself from the bunk, taking a few moments to dress and tie her hair back before she stumbled toward the bridge. The space was cramped, for a ship the size of the *Icarus* -—something common to the line of low-grade cargo runners. It meant she'd gotten it for a steal, but that the technology was probably half a century out of date and required constant tinkering and repair to keep it running. As she entered, Marcus jumped to his feet, recoiling halfway through a quick salute as his head thudded against one of the button-filled panels above him.

"You okay?" Jaina asked, but her pilot waved her off, collapsing back into his chair and rubbing his head.

"Yeah, Jay. I'm fine. Not the first time I've done that."

"Also, not the first time I've told you not to salute me. This isn't a military ship." Jaina slipped into the chair next to his, briefly glancing over the readouts. "So, what set all the alarms off?"

"This." Marcus's fingers flew over the console, a flickering projection of a star map appearing on the viewport glass in front of them. "A few minutes ago, we received some kind of signal from here, although whatever's sending it doesn't seem to be in our database." He tapped the screen, indicating a sharply blinking light a short distance from the icon that represented their ship.

"That's in the middle of an asteroid field......do you think some other hauler broke down out there?"

"I thought that, but no. There's no trade route through that field, and besides..." Marcus pressed another button, and a string of code appeared beneath the beacon on the map. "Every ship, every station, has an identity code, right? Well, the first few bits of this code indicate a military facility. The rest, though......it's nonsense. Back when I flew for the Central Systems, I memorized as much of the code book as I could, but I've never seen one like this."

"So, what do you recommend?"

The pilot shrugged, brow furrowing. "Let's take a look. We approach, scan from a distance, and if things look suspicious, we jump away. That way, if it's legitimate, whoever it is will get help."

"All right, then. Take us there. I'll go get geared up," Jaina said, smirking when Marcus gave her an odd look. "If we need to land somewhere, I'd rather be armed."

Approaching from the edge of the asteroid field, Marcus piloted the *Icarus* closer to where the sensors indicated the source of the signal to be. Built into the side of a small, rocky body was a squat structure protruding out into the void, exterior lights flickering madly in the endless dark.

"I've seen structures like this. The Central Systems tend to build modularly, so that building likely extends into the asteroid. Not sure why in the Void they'd build one out here, though." Marcus leaned over the console, peering out into space, the blinking glow of the buttons casting eerie shadows across his face. "But it seems like they're really in trouble. Scans show that the power is on the fritz."

Feet kicked up on the other half of the console, Jaina nodded, her gaze fixed on the station as well.

"Can you bring us in? If the docking hatch is still functioning, we might be able to get inside. Take a look around."

"You got it."

The *Icarus* inched closer, drawing near enough to engage the docking clamps -—the ship jerking as they locked down on the exterior. When the deck settled, Jaina jumped to her feet, heading toward the airlock at the ship's rear. She paused in front of the hatch, checking her pistol in its holster and settling an earpiece over her ear. A single tap brought the familiar crackle of the old tech.

"All right, I'm heading inside. Keep the engine running."

"Sure thing, Jay. Don't get dead."

"That's the plan." She hit the release, the hatch hissing open to reveal a dark corridor beyond. Scans had said that the air inside was largely breathable, and that the scrubbers *should* have been functioning, but the air that hit her had an odd musty stink that made Jaina crinkle her nose. It was a thick smell that reminded the woman of the Protein Farms she'd seen. Like animals kept in close quarters, combined with a sharp, metallic tang. "Oh, that's not good..."

Reaching for a glow-orb on her belt, she held it up near her head and activated it -—the globe shedding light around her and hanging in the air when she released it, hovering along beside her. The corridor was lined with blank, metal bulkheads that extended off beyond the range of her light, the sense of the place cold and unsettling enough that Jaina drew her pistol and trained it ahead as she began to make her way down the hall away from the airlock.

In the distance, a slow thump sounded down the corridor. Blood smeared the wall to her left in a long line at her shoulder-level. Jaina paused, touching the smear and pulling her fingers away coated in tacky red.

"What in the Void happened here...?"

Again, a metallic thump. She was closer, now, the sound echoing dully down the empty hall. Wiping her hand on her pant leg, Jaina lifted her gun again and made her way forward, following the sound of the clanking -—passing sealed door after sealed door until she was right on top of it. Blood was smeared across an access panel beside another sealed hatch, the panel sparking when Jaina pressed the button to unseal the room.

"No power......Marcus, you hear me?"

"I'm here," the pilot's voice responded, crackling and distorted. "Whatcha got for me?"

"There's something behind one of these doors. Might be a survivor. Can you restore power to…" She turned, shining her light around the hall. "Section C-6, Access Panel 12."

"Sure. I think some of the old codes might at least let me access the power systems near the docking port. Whatever happened has the system glitching like crazy, or I doubt I'd even be able to do that much."

The comm went quiet, and Jaina stood in silence for several moments before the panel sparked again, then flickered to life.

"Thanks, Marcus." When she hit the button, the hatch hissed open to reveal a room lined with rows of tables and benches. The lights in the room were on, likely due to whatever Marcus did with the power, flickering dimly in their recessed apertures. She heard the thump again from within, coming from behind a line of heat tables against the back wall. Keeping her pistol ready, Jaina moved around them, her light illuminating a man slumped to the floor with his back against the tables, staring off into space as he lifted a bloodied wrench and dropped it back against the deck again—resulting in that metallic thump that had brought her to the room.

"Hey…sir? Are you okay?" She stepped closer, reaching up to switch off her light as she kept her eyes on the man. He was older, his hair greying and thin at the top, a pair of cracked spectacles resting on his nose. His clothing—some sort of military uniform—was torn and bloodied, some of it appearing to be his own. He didn't respond, his eyes unfocused and distant. "Sir?"

Jaina touched a hand to his shoulder, and the man jerked and swung the wrench at her with a strangled scream. She threw herself backward, landing on her back and lashing out with a foot—her boot connecting with the man's wrist as he tried to bring his makeshift weapon down on her head. It clattered across the floor, and the man cried out and scurried behind a table - , hunkering down and trembling.

"What happened to you...?" Jaina asked, inching closer while holstering her pistol. The man didn't respond, simply rocking back and forth where he sat. She reached out again, though stopped short of touching him -—instead, waiting for him to lift his head and finally meet her gaze. "I won't hurt you, I promise, sir. I'm here to help."

"It...it all went to hell," he stammered in reply. "They got out... killed everyone..."

"Who got out? What are you talking about?"

Behind her, there was a soft hiss of the hatch opening again, and the man's eyes widened in horror. He let out a yelp, scrambling from beneath the table and throwing himself behind the counter again, leaving Jaina dumbfounded. She spun, barely ducking aside as a muscular, scaled shape the size of a man threw itself at her, only to slam into the table and jerking it noisily across the floor. Jaina's gun was out in an instant, but she froze, the sight of the creature registering as impossible in her panicked mind. It was easily as tall as she was, carrying itself on a pair of thick legs that ended in a number of sharply-clawed toes, one of which on each foot was poised and curved like a sickle. Cold, reptilian eyes leered at her as the raptor managed to right itself, its small hands flexing as it clawed and scuffed at the deck under its feet. There was more to the creature than the simple impossibility of it, a dinosaur on a floating hunk of rock in the middle of deep space -—parts of it had been replaced, armored metal plates secured over its head and back, and part of its tail replaced with a segmented metal appendage that ended in thick barbs. Its eyes narrowed, and the raptor leaned in -—ready to pounce again as it let out a metallic, distorted screech that broke Jaina from her trance.

"You have got to be kidding me!" she shouted, firing off a blast from her pistol that missed the mark, deflected from the armor plates that covered the beast's head. She moved, even as the creature leapt, landing on her side behind the countertop and right in front of the huddled scientist. "That!? That's what you were doing here!?" she snapped at him, causing the man to cringe. They had to leave, that much was clear. Pushing herself up, she grabbed the scientist by his arm and hauled him to his feet.

"Come on!"

The raptor rounded on them as Jaina ran and dragged the scientist behind her, screeching in frustration and running after them. Hazarding a glance back, she saw that it was too close for her to slow enough to try sealing it in the room, so she kept running -—pushing herself as fast as she could go back toward the docking port. Rounding a corner, a strange whirring noise caused her to look back again -—cursing when plates on the raptor's back slid away to allow a pair of arm-mounted blasters to train themselves on the fleeing pair. Jaina pulled the scientist around a corner that veered off from the main hall just as a flurry of glimmering energy bolts raked the deck and bulkheads. She wanted to laugh from the absurdity of it, but instead she tightened her grip on her pistol and braced herself.

"We're going to die..." the scientist moaned, and Jaina shot him a sharp look before peeking out far enough to fire back at the modified creature.

"No, we're not. But whose brilliant idea was to give a bloody Velociraptor a gun!?" She shouted, ducking back again to avoid another volley of bolts.

"Utah..."

"What?" Jaina looked at the scientist. He wasn't looking at her—instead, staring off into the distance, his eyes unfocused.

"They...they're Utahraptors. Velociraptors are...small, the size of a dog. It's a common mistake."

"Do you think I really give a shit right now?" She tapped her earpiece. "Marcus, there's some...weird...cyborg dinosaur here! It's got us pinned down. Can you give us a new route back to the dock?"

The radio crackled, but no reply came back. Uttering another curse, Jaina fired a few more bolts at the angry raptor before grabbing the scientist again and running down the side corridor they'd ducked into. They'd have to find another way themselves.

"Wh...where are we...?" the scientist managed.

"Route's bad. I've got a ship docked, but we need a new way to get there. Please tell me you know the layout and can get us there!"

The man nodded mutely, stumbling and forcing Jaina to grip harder just to keep him on his feet. As they ran, he motioned toward another corridor that led off from the one they were on.

"That way. That...should take us back toward the main dock."

Jaina didn't bother to respond, turning down the hall even as she heard the heavy hammering of the raptor's gait behind them. It was fast, and closing, though if it hadn't caught up to them already, the various modifications made to it must have been slowing it down. Either that, or they weren't as fast as Jaina had been led to believe as a child. Either way, she was grateful.

"Marcus! Dammit, if you can hear me, ready the ship to leave, now. We're coming in hot!"

Again, only static. Jaina didn't have the time to dwell on it, and only hoped the pilot had heard her as the familiar airlock hatch came into view. She increased speed, even with her lungs and legs burning from the exertion—only to skid to a halt, the scientist crashing into her, as another raptor emerged from the open hatchway into the ship. Its muzzle was slick with blood, and its small arms had been replaced with robotic appendages that ended in razor-like claws. They were cut off; the way into the *Icarus* blocked. The raptor screeched when it caught sight of them, a cry from behind the pair coming in response.

Maybe they *were* going to die.

The blood-smeared raptor screeched again, lunging at them faster than Jaina could follow. The scientist shoved her, causing her to stumble enough that the creature's razor claws missed her, though it still bore down on her—pinning her to the deck. She lifted her left arm, the raptor's teeth slicing through the sleeve of her jacket and digging in deep—then jerked when the limb began to twitch and spark. Before it could pull back, Jaina pressed her pistol against the underside of its jaw, barrel pointed toward where she assumed its brain should be and hoping whoever had made these things hadn't thought far enough ahead to move or armor it from below.

"See? You're not the only one with surprises," she spat, pulling the trigger. Her pistol roared, and the raptor released her arm as it collapsed to the deck, twitching and screeching in its last few moments. The balding scientist rushed back over to her, dragging her to her feet by her good arm and moving down the hall. Any desire Jaina had for a moment to catch her breath vanished when she heard another cry from the first raptor, close enough now to see them and spray bolts of energy at the fleeing pair.

Jaina cradled her prosthetic arm against her chest as she ran, only stopping when the scientist did—the man grunted, forcing open a pair of lift doors to reveal an empty shaft that led deeper into the facility.

"Come on. There's......there's another way out, I think. If it's still there."

"If what's still there?" Jaina asked, though the man didn't respond, disappearing into the pitch black of the shaft. With one last glance down the corridor, Jaina slipped in after him, hoping to whatever God was listening that the damn raptor didn't have an easy way to follow them.

Jaina's damaged prosthetic made the descent difficult, her progress slow as they followed the shaft down into the depths of the station inside of the asteroid. At the bottom, the scientist was waiting to help her down to the deck. Using her good arm, she helped pry the lift doors open far enough to let the pair slip out into a lightless corridor, their breath misting in the air.

"Thank you. You...never gave me your name, I think..."

"To be fair, you never asked, but given the circumstances..." The man shrugged. "It didn't seem terribly important, in the moment. I'm Doctor Barnes......I, uh......wasn't working on the cyborg Utahraptor project, if that makes any difference."

Jaina laughed, even if it didn't feel like the right time for it. She couldn't really help it. The entire situation was absurd. She was trapped in a secret military base on an asteroid, being pursued by half-robotic dinosaurs, and her crewmate was quite possibly dead. Laughter, at least, was better than letting herself fall apart any further.

"Jaina Deckard. It's nice to meet you, Doctor. You said there was another way out?"

Barnes nodded again, exhaling a thin cloud of mist.

"Yes. The project I was working on was an experimental ship. It was nearly ready, when the bioweapon experiments escaped. Though I suppose it could be worse..."

"Worse? What's worse than cyborg lizards chasing us around an asteroid?"

Barnes shook his head, adjusting his glasses and motioning down the corridor. "We should go this way. I'd rather not think about anything else getting out."

Jaina shrugged, directing her hovering light to shine down the hall in the direction the Doctor had indicated. The whole mess was insane, but if the man who knew more about this place than she did felt there were worse things than the murder-lizard-bots, she'd trust him on it.

"So...this facility had cyborg dinosaurs and experimental spaceships being worked on in the same place? Seems really broad..." Jaina kept her pistol raised, filling the nervous silence as they walked through the dark and cold.

"It's a large facility, Ms. Deckard. Numerous teams working for the Central Systems on myriad projects. Did you study the experiments of the governments of Earth, in the past? It is filled with a thousand things more ridiculous than 'cyborg utahraptors,' I promise you. Bat bombs and death rays…" Barnes stopped, brushing a layer of frost from a wall panel and pausing to rub his hands together in a vain attempt to warm them. "But I fear we won't have time to remain amused by them if we can't get the environmental controls on this deck functioning again. I am already losing feeling in my extremities."

He breathed into his cupped palms, then tapped the panel until it flickered to life—allowing him to begin entering a series of numbers and letters. The doctor wasn't wrong—Jaina felt the chill even through her thick clothing. Being deep inside the asteroid was probably the only thing insulating the level they were on from the unbearable chill in space.

"Just tell me where we need to go."

Barnes nodded, finally bringing up a map of their level, indicating a room that lit up beneath his finger.

"The environmental controls are here. If we keep moving, we should be able to make it before we freeze. Might I borrow your globe?" He indicated her light, and Jaina nodded, a mental command transferring the floating orb's control to the doctor. Barnes reached up to touch the light, which turned green and brightened, floating away from them at a quickened pace. "There. I've synced it to the level's layout. It should lead us there."

Taking off at a jog, they followed the green orb past sealed hatches and the slumped bodies of scientists, soldiers, and even a few more dinosaurs -—small ones, which Barnes pointed out were Compsognathus, the minute dinosaurs modified to serve as scouts and spies. Jaina tried to wrap her head around the idea, but finally pushed it aside. Dwelling on what she found silly about any of this was only a detriment. The creeping chill only got worse as they ran, barely held at bay by their exertion and making her weapon feel heavy and her fingers thick and stiff. Finally, the orb stopped, bobbing in front of another hatch where Barnes set immediately to bypassing the locking mechanism.

"Hurry it up, or I'm gonna need to replace my good arm, too…"

"Ms. Deckard, if I weren't going as quickly as I am, we would have both frozen to death by now. Please…let me work…"

The rebuke made Jaina bristle, but she gave the man the silence he needed to work. It didn't take long before the door jerked slightly as it was unlatched. Barnes motioned for her to help him, and she holstered her pistol to use her good hand—however clumsy it felt—to pry the door open. They were met with a rush of humid, hot air from the other side, along with a thick animal reek.

"No…no no no…" Barnes stammered, rushing into the control room. The air was thick, rank, with strange vines climbing the walls and coiling along the decking. Here and there, the metal plates of the floor were even pushed up, making way for odd flowers and other plants that Jaina didn't recognize. The doctor ignored all of it, heading instead for a control panel that most certainly no longer worked. More vines had cracked the casing, disappearing into it in one place and re-emerging through the corner of a damaged glass panel elsewhere. "Close that door! Oh Void…"

Jaina followed the command, bracing her damaged prosthetic against the door and pushing with her good hand to shut it again. Light filtered down through the mass of plants that had covered the ceiling, yellow and diffuse, but at least enough to see by.

"Guess whatever made the controls shut down on the rest of the level, made them go out of control in here," she said, tentatively stepping across the vine-matted floor. The odd squelch of her feet on the plant matter made her skin crawl; the vines oozed an odd, red liquid that looked far too much like blood for her taste. "But what's with the plants?"

"Experiments in rapid growth plant life for the purposes of terraforming. Not my forte, either, and not what I would consider 'successful.'"

Crouching, Barnes pried the front panel from the console, revealing the tangle of wires, vines, and shattered components inside of it. He cursed, fumbling at his belt for one of his tools before leaning in and beginning to pick at the damage.

"Keep an eye out, would you? Void knows what might be lurking in this mess. If this climate extends to the rest of climate control, anything that escaped could have found their way here before they froze to death."

"Oh...that's comforting..."

Jaina hefted her broken arm again, locking the mechanism in place against her chest and drawing her pistol. She would be more than glad to be out of here. Until then, she couldn't let herself get distracted, couldn't dwell on what had already gone wrong. Still, she was tense, expecting some small lizard or something far worse to leap out at them from the tangle of plants at any moment. To her left, something moved—caught from the corner of her eye. She shifted her weight, turning enough to point her gun toward the sound. Whatever it was, the plants hid it from view.

"This place is getting to me..." She muttered, jumping with an audible gasp when something clanged sharply just behind her. Barnes cursed shortly after, crawling back out of the console and rubbing his head, and Jaina felt the icy grip on her heart release. "Void...Doctor Barnes, are you all right?" She started to move toward him, stopping when he waved her off.

"I'll be fine. I'm not so sheltered that I haven't had my bell rung a time or two. Now..." The man activated the console, the panel flickering to life weakly. "Once I get this started, we need to move. Quickly. Hopefully, everything outside Environmental Control succumbed to the cold, but I hold no illusions that they all perished out there. When I reactivate the system for this level, the noise will likely bring most anything that's left coming right for us."

"Good. That's...good." Jaina exhaled, tightening her grip on her pistol and nodding for Barnes to go ahead. The scientist nodded back and reset the system, plunging the room into darkness as an awful, clanking whirr began somewhere nearby. A moment later, chittering rose from all around them, pairs of red dots glimmering from behind the rough tangle of vines. The moment the lights flickered back on, the sound became a dull roar, and Barnes turned quickly from the console to rush for the door—striking the panel to open it and whirling back to face her.

"Go!"

Jaina ran, even as a swarm of small, scaled creatures that resembled the frozen bodies from the corridor outside boiled into the room from somewhere behind the walls of plant matter, chittering and screeching. Too many to count. The moment she was beyond the door, Barnes slipped through as well and sealed it, motioning for her to follow.

"Void...how many of those things did they make!?"

"Truthfully, Ms. Deckard, I have no damn idea. We need to go, however." Their breath still misted in the air, but the cold had less of a bite to it. It wasn't much, but it was something. "Whatever programming they had, it's made them as vicious as their larger friends, and these can fit through air ducts. So... shall we?"

Letting Barnes take the lead, Jaina followed him through the twisting corridors, any attempt at figuring out the place's layout failing. Around them, she could hear the clatter of those little monsters in the vents. Compsognathus, the doctor had called them. Compies. At every vent opening they passed, small forms slammed themselves against the grating, tiny clawed arms -— some cybernetic, some biological—sticking through the gaps and flailing at them. One creature wasn't strong enough to open the grating, but there were enough trying to get through that the panels creaked ominously. Neither of them was given a moment to relax, not until Barnes stopped before a much larger hatch and punched a code into the key pad beside it. The door hissed, venting steam as its hydraulics pulled the halves apart to reveal a massive hangar behind it, covered in darkness save for small lights that ran the length of a narrow catwalk that ringed the chamber.

"Try not to touch anything," Barnes said, letting her through and shutting the hatch behind them with another hiss of hydraulics. "If you'll just give me a moment to find the lights...ah... here..." As he trailed off, there was a sharp clack above them, followed by the hum of electricity and a dim flicker of light. One by one, heralded by the same sound, the lights came on—Jaina gasping as the darkness receded and her gaze fell on the ship in the hangar's center. It was at least as large as the *Icarus*, with its cargo pods attached, and shaped like a wedge, the engines in the rear far larger than Jaina had ever seen on a ship its size. She walked down the catwalk, heedless of the doctor or anything else for the moment, simply taking in the beautifully sleek shape of the wings, the slope of the cockpit windows made of crystal-clear transparent steel. The whole thing was state of the art, every inch of it pristine.

"Where have you been all my life, gorgeous...?" she murmured, pausing in front of the ship's sealed hatch.

"Don't get too attached, Ms. Deckard. This ship still belongs to the Central Systems military, and once we get out of here, I intend to return it to them." Barnes stepped up beside her, pressing his palm to the hull plating. The panel beneath his hand lit up, scanning his hand and releasing the ramp, the older man smiling at Jaina and ducking into a low bow. "After you, my dear."

Jaina gave him an odd look. The man had been acting more confident, since their flight from the upper decks, but there was something about his sudden shift in demeanor she found unnerving. Still, she glanced away, starting up the ramp into the ship—and stopped cold when she heard the sound of metal against leather and felt the shift of weight as her gun was drawn from its holster at her hip.

"You know…" She murmured, slowly lifting her good hand in the air. "I gotta stop trusting people when it's really obvious I shouldn't."

"It *is* a bad habit, isn't it? Now, turn around, Ms. Deckard. Please. I do hate to do this, and I have certainly appreciated your help, but you must understand…" Barnes smiled as she turned as she'd been told, keeping her hand up. "I went to quite a bit of trouble to lure someone here that could help me, and now that we're here, I'd rather not have someone around that knew about…well…all of this…" He kept her gun fixed on her as he motioned around them with his other hand.

"Ah…" It clicked together for her. "You wanted to steal the ship, so you let all the nasties out…but you got stuck, yeah? Needed some dupe to come bail you out?"

"I'm not about to monologue by plan, Ms. Deckard. So please, do forgive me…" He raised the barrel a touch more, aiming the blaster at her head. Before he could depress the trigger, a loud metallic crash rang out behind them, causing Barnes to spin toward the sound. The moment his back was turned, Jaina lunged, kicking the man's knee from the side hard enough to hear bone crack. He cried out, toppling to the deck and sending the gun spinning away across the catwalk. Jaina leaped over him and scooped up the pistol before turning back to face him.

"Smart. Not doing the monologue. I totally get that." She fired, Barnes cringing when the bolt struck the catwalk beside his head. "Now, what do I need to fly this thing? Your hand? Because at this point, I am more than willing to take it and leave you here."

Paling, the doctor shook his head, undoing a band around his wrist that had been hidden under his sleeve.

"No. Not at all. I… just have this. The identity bracelet will make the system think you're me, and then you can fly the ship. I'll give it to you, of course. Just…please don't leave me here?"

He gave her a sickeningly sweet smile, and Jaina just shook her head. Fool her once, and all that.

"Not a chance, Doc. Set it down, and slink away. Then, maybe, we can talk about you hitching a ride." When he complied, whining in pain as he was forced to move his injured leg, Jaina took the bracelet and stepped sidelong toward the ramp leading back into the ship. Before she'd managed to get all the way up, something lurched in the darkness underneath the catwalk, the dim lighting keeping the lower portion of the hangar cloaked in shadow. Barnes cried out in fear, and Jaina raised her pistol, ready to fire—even as human hands gripped the catwalk railing and a familiar face, smeared in grease and blood, popped over the side.

"Man, Jay…you gonna lower that?" Marcus asked, sparing a brief glance at Barnes before hoisting himself over, moving gingerly on one leg. His other leg was bloody and torn, pants ripped through by claws and teeth, but otherwise the man seemed fine if incredibly filthy. Jaina cried out happily, moving to throw her good arm around her friend and practically knocking him back against the rail.

"Marcus! You're alive!"

"Barely. Some freaky lizard robot thing got onto the ship, since *someone* left the damn hatch open. Some kind of dino fragged the main console trying to get at me. Don't think she's gonna fly any time soon." Marcus gave Jaina a dour look, but smiled a moment later. "You owe me a leg, Jay."

Jaina nodded, lowering her shoulder to put Marcus' arm over and guide him toward the ramp.

"I'll make good on that, promise. And next time, we are *not* answering weird distress calls…"

As they hobbled to the top of the ramp, Barnes whimpered, and Jaina spared a glance back over her shoulder at the man. He'd pulled himself up, leaning heavily against the rail with wet eyes locked on the two of them.

"Please...please don't leave me here!" he wailed, lurching away from the rail and toward the ramp. Jaina readied herself to have to fight him off, and she even felt Marcus tense—but something else had heard Barnes' cries. Moving sinuously from below, a dark shape slid up over the rail and lunged. A massive length of black, reflective chitin and uncountable legs slammed into the scientist, mandibles clamping into his sides and piercing deep into the flesh. He screamed, thrashing and kicking, but the shape dragged him back toward the edge, the monstrous centipede pulling him into the dark. His wails rose, and then abruptly cut off with a wet crunch, leaving Jaina and Marcus both staring out into the hangar in mute shock.

"...nope." Jaina finally said, hefting Marcus over to lean against the bulkhead and hitting button to seal the hatch. "Just...nope."

"Yeah...let's get the hell out of here," Marcus grunted, letting her help him up again and into the cockpit at the other end of the ship. He let out a low whistle when she lowered him into the pilot's chair and took the chair beside his, finally feeling the tension slough from her body. The bracelet worked like a charm, the entire hangar rumbling when the signal was sent to open the doors to the empty black beyond. Other asteroids spun slowly in the glittering dark, and the sight made her smile.

With only a little coaxing, the new *Icarus* lifted off, sliding out into the void like a dream. Jaina gazed out the viewport as they passed the original *Icarus*, an indistinct shape slipping past one of the ship's windows backlit by flickering light.

"Sorry to leave you out here to rot, old girl."

"Oh, she won't rot. When I thought we were all gonna die, I left a little surprise on board." Marcus grinned, waiting until they had put more distance between themselves and the station before producing a jury-rigged remote and pressing the button. In the distance, the *Icarus* bloomed into a sphere of radiant fire, flashing out a moment later. The ship was gone, and with it most of the asteroid and the station hidden within it.

"I knew I kept you around for a reason," Jaina said with a laugh. "Put some parsecs between us and this disaster."

— WHAT CAME FIRST —
by Kimberly Pauley

I t all started with the hardboiled egg. It was an unremarkable organic free-range brown egg from a carton with a picture of a happy looking chicken plastered on it, even though the particular hen that this egg had come from was prone to fits of ennui. The egg had two yolks, but no one would ever know that because it wound up being digested approximately 70 million years before it was laid.

The egg was supposed to have been part of Henry Lee's midnight snack as he worked late at the cosmology lab at Duke University, as per usual, but he had been interrupted, also as per usual, by his friend Edwin Klurg.

They were both scientists, though from different fields. They had both done their undergrad at M.I.T. and might not have met at all if their mothers hadn't insisted they join a club and at least *try* to meet people. So, they had met when they both joined the Laboratory for Chocolate Science club their freshman year, partly because they both liked sweets, but mostly because it had sounded ridiculous enough to be appealing.

It was a club dedicated to the appreciation and scientific investigation of chocolate, and consistently went through more than 500 pounds of the stuff a year. They learned how to make truffles, the best way to melt chocolate without burning it, and the challenging socio-economic conditions of chocolate farmers around the world.

Henry had liked chocolate more than Edwin back then, but he also loved hardboiled eggs, which Edwin hated. Edwin always said they smelled like something only the devil should eat. To Henry, they reminded him of the lunch boxes his mother would pack for him when he was young, so for him it was the smell of childhood, not Hell.

Food was just one of the many things they argued about. Their few fellow friends said they bickered like an old married couple. They called Edwin the husband and Henry the wife, though the only thing about their relationship that was remotely romantic was their shared love of Keanu Reeves and an obscure comic called *Kid Eternity* from the 1940s.

It was an entirely different, non-food related argument that made Henry throw the egg at Edwin and miss out on his late-night snack.

And it was a gallimimus bullatus that ate the egg, some 70 million years earlier in the late Cretaceous period. The gallimimus was the largest of the ornithomimids and had a long snout and toothless jaws that looked fairly impressive, but three-fingered hands so weak they were only capable of grasping small things, like eggs. It was an opportunistic scavenger.

It had never eaten a cooked egg before and definitely never one that had come out of nowhere. It liked it. For the rest of its life, every time it bit into an egg, it was disappointed. But Henry had only the one egg to throw at Edwin. All the other food he'd brought had come in a bag, and they'd already eaten it all besides.

Edwin was at that point of drunkenness just past tipsy but before the room was spinning when the argument with Henry began. He was also happier than he had ever been before, which made him argue all the harder. It was their favorite and most frequent argument, in fact; a well-traveled road that always ended in the same way (though not usually with an egg being lobbed at his head). He and Henry would politely agree to disagree, until the next time. No winners, no losers. It was, perhaps, Edwin's favorite argument because Henry had never decisively won it. It was the kind of argument that no one won.

They had been having this quarrel about what came first, the chicken or the egg, since their long-ago days at university. It was as philosophical as they ever allowed themselves to get, and somehow, it was an argument that nearly always lent itself to beer and late-night snacks and celebrations. Most of those occasions had been for Henry's small triumphs, but this time it was for Edwin. It was, in fact, the first time Edwin had really ever had anything to celebrate since being accepted at M.I.T. Life had been a downhill slide since then.

Edwin didn't even have to duck for the egg to miss him. That's how well things were going for him, for once. It was usually only Henry that had decent things happen to him.

Henry was an astrophysicist. He had tenure at a private university. He was regularly published in scientific journals, though his name was usually listed second or third. He monitored dying stars and dreamed of alerting the media to a planet-killer asteroid and basking, however briefly, in the fame that would bring. He had once prematurely called Edwin to celebrate the discovery of a comet until he had realized it was actually only one of his own exceptionally long eyelashes that had fallen onto the telescope.

Edwin liked to bring that up. A lot.

Henry usually drank beer, only occasionally, and had the tolerance of a man who had never drunk a drop before in his life. He blamed that on his Chinese heritage. Drinking anything gave him a wicked case of Asian flush. When he threw the egg at Edwin, he was halfway to looking like a tomato.

His stance had always been, like Neil deGrasse Tyson, that the egg *must* have come first. An egg, of course, that had *not* been laid by a chicken. It was the only thing that made sense. Lots of scientists agreed with him.

Edwin, on the other hand, had been a mostly theoretical physicist until recently, when things had taken a very practical turn. He preferred a nice stout or a porter on a regular day, or a tumbler of whiskey, neat, for a celebration. He'd always argued for the chicken partly because he enjoyed them fried, but also because he knew it drove Henry crazy. Driving Henry crazy was one of the few pleasures in his otherwise—up to now—generally boring life.

Henry regretted tossing the egg at Edwin almost immediately. He was hungry. Drinking always made him hungry, and he had polished off an entire six pack on his own, something he hadn't done since his last girlfriend had broken up with him. She'd given him the news after baking him a chocolate birthday cake, complete with thirty-four candles and a knock-off figurine of One Punch Man stuck on top. She'd said it would have been worse if she'd broken it off before his birthday, but it had nearly ruined chocolate for him. Now candy bars left a bitter taste in his mouth that only alcohol could get rid of.

Neither of them realized, for a few moments, where the egg had actually rolled after it missed Edwin's head, the shell sustaining only hairline cracks from hitting the floor. It had been well boiled. It looked remarkably normal and innocent for being the thing that changed everything.

But it wasn't really the egg's fault. It was the time machine that actually started it. It was, after all, the reason they were both well on the way to being drunk at two a.m. on a school night.

Because the time machine had finally worked.

The time machine didn't look much like a machine at all. It was really more of a small window, a roughly round hole in the center of the lab about the diameter of a child's hula hoop. It hovered in the air about two inches off the lab floor, the edges of it hazy and indistinct.

No matter which side you viewed the time machine from, it looked the same, like a piece of somewhere else had been torn away from wherever it was meant to be and plunked down in the lab. But it wasn't just *somewhere* else. It was *some when* else. Currently, that when was the late Cretaceous period, because Edwin had always wanted to see a dinosaur. Some kids liked cars. Some liked dinosaurs. Henry had liked constellations.

Edwin hadn't seen a dinosaur yet; the window was hard to control and not very big. It had taken him hours of fiddling to get it focused on a spot that wasn't inside the ground, up in the air, or inside what he could only assume was the middle of a mountain but could have been the inside of an argentinosaurus, the largest land dinosaur known to man at 100 metric tons and 40 meters long. The inside of anything was pretty dark.

Henry had been the first person Edwin called to share his success with. Actually, he was the *only* person Edwin had rung. He was the only person Edwin *had* to call since his mother had died five years before.

It took Henry a few moments longer than it should have to trace the trajectory of the egg after he missed Edwin with it. He wasn't sporty, which was one of the reasons he had wound up as an astrophysicist. His mother had always told him to shoot for the stars, not to keep his eye on the ball.

When he saw the egg, he let out a giggle. "Look, Ed, I told you I was right!" He pointed. There was the egg, a small brown spot among some lush green vegetation somewhere in what would one day become Mongolia. "See, the egg did come first!" Henry laughed so hard that he fell over. Empty cans and bottles scattered across the lab floor. Everything was funnier when you were drunk.

The hardboiled egg was the very first thing to go through the time machine.

In fact, up until that moment, Edwin wasn't even sure if anything *could* go through. It had been enough, that morning, that he had been able to open a window at all. And, after that, to be able to control *when*. The first crack in time he had managed at exactly 8:02 a.m. had been the size of a fifty cent piece and had showed a window looking back at some point in the 1970s, or so he had assumed based on the glimpse he'd had of someone's bellbottoms. Now he was looking millions of years into the past through a hole big enough to stick his head through.

The thought was strangely exhilarating. Stupid, certainly, at this stage of the project, but maybe someday. Oh, to be able to smell what the air had been like back then with his own nose! Was it supercharged with high oxygen levels like Brenner and Landis had deduced from pockets of air trapped in amber? Or had it been lower than modern levels, like in Tappert's study? He could find out. He. Him. Edwin Klurg. Inventor of the Time Machine.

It made it all worth it. The low paying non-tenure track position at a public state university, while Henry had his cushy job at Duke. Having to teach Solar System Astronomy to non-science majors, where half the class thought they were there for astrology, while Henry got to teach Supernovae and Cosmic Rays. The lab space he'd fought hard for, only to be grudgingly given a disused storage room far away from the main campus in amongst the agricultural studies out buildings. He was practically next door to a cow field.

Ten years of hard work, miles worth of whiteboard scribblings, countless late nights, all while enduring the ridicule of so many in the scientific community that had vocally (and in subtly barbed papers published in respected journals) insisted that what he wanted to do wasn't possible. He didn't even have a grad student for an assistant. They had given him a choice between one or a coffee maker, and he had needed the caffeine. But they would eat their words now.

Edwin's go-to response had always been to quote Richard Feynman: "We are trying to prove ourselves wrong as quickly as possible, because only in that way can we find progress."

He had been wrong for so many years. It was so nice to finally be right.

Feynman was his hero. Feynman, in fact, probably would have looked at the egg, lying there in the late Cretaceous period, and done the exact same thing as Edwin, especially if he was drunk.

Edwin laughed with utter joy. Then he hiccupped. And then he poured himself another dram of whiskey and proposed a toast to Henry, paraphrasing Feynman again.

"To all those who said, 'I could do that, but I won't,' which was just another way of saying they couldn't. To hell with you all! *I* did it!"

Henry grudgingly raised his own glass in a half-hearted salute. He had expected, when Edwin had called him earlier that night and told him to bring as much booze as he could carry, that things had somehow gone badly. Perhaps he had lost his meagre funding or had stepped in cow poop again. He hadn't expected *this* Edwin, grinning madly and exuberantly like Cesar Romero's Joker. Edwin had always been more like the Heath Ledger or even Joaquin Phoenix's Joker, with their smiles full of pain and anger.

The next time they looked, the egg was gone and so was half a bottle of Johnnie Walker Blue. They had missed the cockroach, surprisingly recognisable compared to its modern-day counterpart, that had crawled over the egg and decided it wasn't worth bothering with, as well as the gallimimus that had eaten it with such joy. Edwin still hadn't seen a dinosaur.

"Egg's gone. I'm telling you, it's the chicken that came first," said Edwin, poking Henry in the shoulder with an unsteady finger.

They both swayed as they sat. They argued some more, Henry with exhaustion and Edwin with fervour.

Henry was the color of a fire truck from the tips of his ears to his nose. He stuck by the egg theory. He trusted Neil deGrasse Tyson even more, now that it was approaching 3 a.m. You had to trust a man with that kind of face. *He* didn't smile like the Joker. Tyson had a smile as trustworthy as Mr. Rogers.

Edwin was nearly blind drunk when he sent the first chicken through the time machine and had exhausted himself of quotable Feynman, which was not an easy task.

He had managed to break into the lab across the hall, which had not been very difficult to get into as they often forgot to lock it. If it had been locked, he never would have succeeded. He probably couldn't have even found it if it had been in a different building.

While Edwin was stealing a sleepy hen, Henry was furiously scribbling on a whiteboard. There was a picture of an egg and a picture of a badly drawn chicken and, inexplicably, a rocket ship wearing a tutu. He was trying to prove a point, but he wasn't even sure what that point was anymore. He just knew he had to prove it. He couldn't let Edwin win. Not this Edwin. Maybe normal Edwin, but not this smug, confident, self-satisfied Edwin. The Edwin that had reminded him three times in the last thirty minutes about the comet that hadn't been a comet.

The scientists who worked in the lab across the hall were a practical lot, nothing theoretical about them at all. They were all home in bed. When they were in the lab, they studied *in ovo* vaccination in Rhode Island Reds and were well funded by the poultry industry. They had an entire wall of chickens of various ages, as well as incubators full of eggs. Like the chicken that had laid Henry's egg, these hens also often suffered from depression, even though the scientists played them Mozart on a regular basis.

"Did you know," said Edwin, after he returned triumphant from the hunt, "that the color of a chicken's ear is what determines the color of their egg?" He had memorized that particular fact after finding out where his lab would be located, in the hopes it would give him something to talk about with those working near him. But he'd never managed to work it into a conversation until now.

He prodded the hen towards the time machine with a ruler. Even drunk, he didn't like to touch feathers. He liked his chickens already plucked.

"Really?" asked Henry, eyes wide and unfocused. He dropped the whiteboard marker, leaving behind a half-completed astro-chicken coming out of the rocket ship. He'd completely forgotten where he was going with the drawing, now that a real chicken was in the room.

And, unlike Edwin, who tended to produce more and more random factoids the drunker he became, Henry just became increasingly excitable. He waved goodbye to the hen with both hands as it crossed through the almost invisible barrier between times.

"Yes!" Edwin laughed, triumphantly. "You can't argue with SCIENCE! There, my friend, is the chicken. The chicken came first." He clapped Henry on the back, nearly knocking him over. "Concede!" Henry shoved him away, annoyed, and threw a punch that didn't land anywhere.

The hen wouldn't have noticed the scuffle, even if it could have heard them over the distance of time. It was confused. Five minutes before it had been fast asleep and dreaming of chicken feed. It had definitely been nighttime in the lab; overhead lights off, the low hum of the air conditioner, the glowing, blinking indicators showing that the incubators were on and at the right temperature.

Now it was somewhere it had never been before. Somewhere with dirt, which it had never touched, having been born in the lab, unlike some of the chickens in other parts of the complex. Here was somewhere with plants and bugs and sounds and smells. Lots of smells. Things that smelled like *food*.

It took a hesitant, jerky step forward in that way that chickens do. It scratched at the rich, loamy ground, uncovering a reddish worm-like thing the likes of which it had never seen. It was, in fact, the first creature from beyond the Cretaceous period to ever see it, as worms left almost no trace in the fossil record, and this type in particular had left behind no mark at all that a human being had ever catalogued.

The hen ate it.

It was much, much tastier than mass-produced chicken feed, even for a creature that had only roughly 350 taste buds, compared to the 10,000 of a human being. It scratched around for more, wandering farther and farther away from the time window.

Meanwhile, Henry and Edwin were still arguing, which mostly involved Edwin spouting increasingly unrelated facts and Henry flapping his hands about and periodically shouting out "The egg!"

"The chicken is one of the closest things we even have to a dinosaur today! Just look at Bhullar's research!" Edwin cackled and pointed to the hen happily scrabbling in the dirt. "Besides, proof positive right there in front of your eyes! Or are you, sir, denying the evidence of your own eyes?!" He drew himself up like he imagined a distinguished scientist of yesteryear might have done. Tall. Proud. Chin in the air. A man that makes history.

It was actually daytime, back when the chicken was. The sun shone hot, dust motes and spores dancing in the air. The light filtered through large ferns, dappling the ground. The air itself was heavy with the smell of leaf mold and damp and half-rotted logs. Something trilled every few minutes, a lonely sound that hung on for longer than it should before being absorbed into the stillness.

There were a lot of bugs and worms. The chicken was happy, perhaps for the first time in her short life. She ate an ant, larger than its modern-day counterpart, with segments as plump as blueberries. She cluck-clucked to herself, oblivious to Edwin pointing in her general direction proudly, as if she were his first grandchild.

Neither of them noticed the tarbosaurus bataar as it approached from the side, though the chicken should have, as the dinosaur weighed nearly four metric tons and made the ground shake. The chicken didn't notice because she'd never seen a predator before. For its size, the tarbosaurus might as well have been a truck to her. She'd never seen one of those either. Edwin didn't notice because he had bent down to fumble on the floor for the nearly empty bottle of whisky.

Henry did notice, but he was two beers past the point of a quick reaction. He flapped his hands and let out a garbled noise that sounded like a bagpipe being strangled by an angry cat.

The tarbosaurus was an apex predator, similar to the tyrannosaurus made familiar in nearly every movie that ever featured a dinosaur. It, too, was bipedal and had a wide, grinning mouth that held sixty very large teeth. It had small, useless arms with two tiny fingered forelimbs. The tarbosaurus didn't mind. It didn't eat with its arms. And there wasn't anything around it had ever felt the need to pick up, even if it had been able to, that it couldn't make do with its mouth.

This one wasn't particularly fussy about what it ate. It was old and slowing down, glad that its mere size was usually enough to discourage anything from bothering it. It would happily scavenge from already-dead carcasses or snap up anything that looked like it might not put up a fight. The easier, the better.

Its ears were still keen, as was its sense of smell, though its already weak eyesight was beginning to fail. The chicken looked like any small reddish blur as it cluck-clucked to itself. This prey smelled…different. It stopped to get a good sniff. The chicken pecked at one of the dinosaur's clawed toes, found it didn't appear to be edible, and wandered back toward where it had found the first worm.

The tarbosaurus leaned down, whiffed, blowing the chicken's feathers about, and ate the hen in one bite. It had a satisfying crunch. It cast its head around looking for more. When it didn't find any, it moved on, accidentally stomping right through a clutch of eggs laid by an oviraptor, which was smart enough to relocate itself instead of complaining.

"Hey," said Edwin, who had finally found the bottle, "where'd the chicken go?" He didn't notice the few feathers that littered the ground, all that was left of the hen. Or the footprint left behind by the tarbosaurus.

Henry could only gesture wildly. "Egg," he said sadly, after a moment to collect himself.

"Chicken," said Edwin, firmly.

"Egg," whispered Henry, popping open the last beer and holding it up in a toast to the unfortunate hen.

"Chicken!" Edwin drank the last few sips directly from the bottle and flung it away. It crashed into the wall and bounced off not very far from Henry's head, but didn't shatter.

Henry didn't like this Edwin. He barely liked normal Edwin, even if they were best friends. He drew himself up as tall as he could. "The egg," he said, trying very hard not to slur, "was *first*. It went through over an hour ago!" There was more to his argument, but that was as much as he got out.

Edwin stopped. The room spun. Henry was right. The egg had gone through first. His shoulders drooped. Was this it? Had Henry finally won this argument too?

But no. He had a time machine.

Edwin stumbled over to the controls he had built out of a couple of old Xbox controllers. He fiddled with the D-pad and the right stick, the scene in the time window blurring and shifting with the slightest movement of his fingers. Henry watched, at first fascinated and then increasingly nauseous as the scenery seemed to blur and swirl, faster and faster. The deep green of woods, the red orange of an all-encompassing fire, the dark of night, a sky full of stars he didn't recognise as they flew past. Stars he'd never seen before because they were long dead and extinguished. He threw up into his backpack and closed his eyes as the scene finally stabilized. Daytime. Unnaturally large flowers. The edge of a small lake. Reed-like plants waving in a breeze. Approximately 71 million years ago, but only 5 million years away from the Cretaceous–Tertiary extinction event that killed off three quarters of life on Earth and everything that weighed over 25 kilograms.

"Just you wait," said Edwin, and ran out of the lab, bouncing off the doorway and ping-ponging down the hall. Left wall, right wall, left wall. Door to the right, the lab next to his, the one with the bars on the outside windows. His lab didn't even have a window. But the inside door was normal, with a glass panel that broke with one solid hit from the Johnnie Walker Blue bottle.

More chickens. These were a mix of different breeds, some of whom were very loud, selected and bred for their intelligence. Edwin hated them. The sound of their satisfied cluck-clucking that he could hear at all hours of the day through the thin wall that lay between this shiny lab full of new equipment and his own. The smell of chicken shit layered with the reek of antibacterial cleaning products that seemed to permeate everything. He had often fantasized about breaking in and stealing one to roast at home but had never done it. He couldn't afford to rock the roost; not when poultry was the state's leading agricultural industry. North Carolina was the home of Butterball. And his university had well-defined mutually beneficial ties to the industry.

But now…what was more important? Some stupid chickens? Or the man who had invented the time machine?

He opened a cage and grabbed a small Bantam hen by the neck, not even minding the feathers. It was so surprised it didn't even let out a squawk. It was so tiny, he simply tucked it under his arm and went on to the next cage. He pulled a buff-colored Orpington from that one. The label on the cage indicated it had come from England from a small farm outside Surrey and had consistently tested well on mazes. He had room for one more in his arms and grabbed a Delaware hen with a ring of black feathers like a necklace against its white feathered body. A handwritten label on her cage said "Princess." He didn't know it, but she was the one who always chose to peck the button that would feed her fellow chickens over food only for herself.

He took them back to his lab, only stumbling once as he tried to step over Henry, and chucked them through the time window without any fanfare.

He shook Henry awake and pushed him into a sitting position and propped him up on a cabinet. "Henry. Look." He pointed at the three hens, who were cowering together under a bush, beady-eyed. Henry just blinked, slowly.

"I win," said Edwin. "Just admit it." He shook Henry again, but that only made his head loll from side to side. Edwin let go and Henry collapsed in slow motion back onto the floor.

"Egg..." said Henry, who was dreaming of his lost snack.

Edwin screamed and ran back to the chicken lab, grabbing the last bottle Henry had brought with him. Jägermeister. He hated liquorice and Henry knew that, but he opened the bottle and drank a gulp down anyway. He had work to do.

Edwin was slurring, stumbling, drop dead drunk when he sent the rooster through. He didn't even feel it when Evil Red—for that was what everyone called the rooster, even though his official name was a number—pecked his hand until it bled as Edwin hurled him into the window through time.

Evil Red forgot his anger almost immediately. The rooster had watched, concerned, as the white lab-coated human had swept into the lab time after time, sometimes giggling, sometimes nearly crying, nearly always babbling something, though the only word Evil Red had understood out of it was "chicken." He was the smartest bird in the lab by far, but his English was limited to a handful of words and most of them had to do with food.

He'd squawked in anger as the man had taken one hen after another, including one he'd had his eye on for weeks. He was a very frustrated rooster, who was only allowed limited access to what he wanted when the humans wanted him to have it but now, now…

He let out a loud, triumphant crow. They were here. They were all here. His flock. His brood. No bars between them. No mazes. No lights. No buttons. No humans. He flapped his wings, fully extending them and puffed out his chest. He hightailed it into the densest brush, not looking back. The confused hens, glad to have a leader show them the way, followed him. A stream of multicolored feathers. The smartest chickens collected from around the world. Wyandottes, Araucanas, Jersey Giants, Plymouth Rocks, even a lone Silkie, with feathers as soft as fur.

Behind them, panting and exhausted, Edwin fell to his knees and then forward onto his face. It was 4:30 a.m.

Edwin woke up first. His head was pounding and felt rather like his skull was filled with a combination of raw meat and the inside of a lava lamp. He was face down on the floor of the lab. The insistent buzz of the fluorescent light sounded like a chain saw. He turned his head and saw Henry, curled into a ball, his head tucked into a dark corner by a cabinet like he'd tried to escape from something. He was twitching in his sleep, like he was having a bad dream. Probably the chasing one. Henry had been having that one since college. It was always something big, lumbering after him, while he ran as fast as he could, feeling like he was wading through molasses.

"Henry, wake up." Edwin tried to clear his throat. What in the world had he done last night? The inside of his mouth tasted like gravel and rotten worms. Even his voice was wrong, high pitched but croaky at the same time. He couldn't have crowed if he'd wanted to and he'd already missed daybreak anyway. He could feel it. The sun was well up by now.

Henry groaned and rolled himself around until he was back on his feet. He shook himself, feathers flying. He snapped his beak tentatively, like he was checking to see if it were still there.

"Ed, I had that dream about the egg again."

— ABOUT THE AUTHORS —

Alana Joli Abbott is an editor and author, whose multiple choice novels, including *Choice of the Pirate* and *Blackstone Academy for Magical Beginners*, are published by Choice of Games. She is the author of three novels, several short stories, and role playing game supplements. As Editor in Chief of Outland Entertainment, she edits fantasy anthologies, including *Knaves: A Blackguards Anthology* and *Where the Veil Is Thin*. You can find her online at VirgilandBeatrice.com.

J. A. Cummings has been playing RPGs since she was a college freshman all the way back in 1987. Today, she's still playing every chance she gets. She is currently running a Pathfinder Adventure Path for her friends.

August Hahn is an American (mostly) writer of science fiction, fantasy, and roleplaying materials. Between his work with the RPGA (Roleplaying Gaming Association) and multiple personal campaigns, he has been roleplaying for very nearly three decades and is both proud and profoundly depressed by that fact.

Andrew J Lucas has contributed to books published by Fasa, Dream Pod Nine, White Wolf Games, Rebel Minis and Atlas Games among others. He has twelve solo books for various publishers and while his creative output is often blunted by his day job and the enthusiasm of his young daughter for distracting him, he does manage to get produce a few prime works each year. The last few years he has written and line produced books for

Rebel Minis, as well as contributed five short stories to various short story anthologies. Andrew has also been writing poetry and fiction for many years and had a number of poems and stories successfully published in that time. He enjoys biting off more than he can chew and often writes for emerging markets and RPG publishers he finds cool... When not working or writing he paints his wargame armies and occasionally finds time to field them in battle. He lives in Langley BC Canada likes cats but has none.

Gwendolyn N. Nix has been an editor, casting producer, scientist, and social media manager, but always a writer. A born seeker of adventure, she saw her first beached humpback whale on a windy day in New York, met a ghost in a Paris train station, and had Odin answer her prayers on a mountain in Scotland. *The Falling Dawn*, her first fantasy novel, released in 2018 and her short fiction has appeared in *StarShip Sofa*, and anthologies such as *Where the Veil Is Thin* and *The Sisterhood of the Blade*. She lives in Missoula, MT. Find out more at www.gwendolynnix.com.

Markisan Naso is an accomplished writer and editor based in Honolulu. He's the writer of the critically-acclaimed comic book series, VORACIOUS, for Action Lab Entertainment, and has authored hundreds of features in print and on the web, covering subjects as diverse as EF5 tornadoes, death metal and Superman. Markisan has also edited dozens of books including *The Anatomy of Zur-en-Arrh: Understanding Grant Morrison's Batman* for the Sequart Organization, and revitalized national publications such as *Knowledge Quest* and *School Library Research* for the American Library Association. Markisan loves spoiling his cat, Zoso, devouring pie and talking heavy metal every month as a host on the METALHEADS Podcast. To find out more about Markisan, visit his website: www.markisan.com.

Kimberly Pauley wanted to grow up to be Douglas Adams, Robert Heinlein, or Edgar Allen Poe when she was little, but has since settled for being herself and writing her own brand of funny quirky fantasy. Born in California, she has lived everywhere from Florida to Chicago and has now gone international to live in the UK with her husband (a numbers man) and son (her geeky partner in crime). She is the award-winning author of four young adult novels and 2020 marks her debut as a middle grade novelist with *The Accidental Wizard*.

Darren W. Pearce is a British fantasy and sci-fi author, game designer, and has worked with the likes of Joe Dever, Cubicle 7, and is the lead writer on the *Shaintar* setting designed by Sean Patrick Fannon. He's one of the Savage Mojo Family and wrote the Set Rising setting for Suzerain. He's also a regular at the UK Games Expo. His work on the Core Box 11 for the *Doctor Who* RPG won him a Gold Ennie in 2013. He won an Epic E-Book Award 2011 (Best Anthology) for his anthology work on *Bad A$$ Faeries 3*.

Alexandra Pitchford is an author and freelance game designer who has written material for game settings like *Shadowrun* and *Vampire: The Masquerade*, as well as third-party material for *Pathfinder 1st Edition*. Originally from the US, she currently lives in Australia with her partner.

Jennifer Lee Rossman is a queer, autistic, and disabled parasaurolophus disguised as a human. She quotes *Jurassic Park* any chance she gets, and she believes that life...uh...finds a way. Read her stories on her blog http://jenniferleerossman.blogspot.com and follow her on Twitter @JenLRossman.

Robert J. Sawyer is one of only eight writers ever to win all three of the world's top awards for best science-fiction novel of the year: the Hugo, the Nebula, and the John W. Campbell Memorial Award. He has also won the Robert A. Heinlein Award, the Edward E. Smith Memorial Award, and the Hal Clement Memorial Award; the top SF awards in China, Japan, France, and Spain; and a record-setting sixteen Canadian Science Fiction and Fantasy Awards ("Auroras"). Rob's novel *FlashForward* was the basis for the ABC TV series of the same name, and he was a scriptwriter for that program. He also scripted the two-part finale for the popular web series Star Trek Continues. He is a Member of the Order of Canada, the highest honor bestowed by the Canadian government, as well as the Order of Ontario, the highest honor given by his home province; he was also one of the initial inductees into the Canadian Science Fiction and Fantasy Hall of Fame. Rob lives just outside Toronto. His website and blog are at sfwriter.com, and on Facebook, Twitter, and Patreon he's RobertJSawyer.

Lee F. Szczepanik, Jr. has been writing professionally for nearly 30 years. In addition to fiction, he's worked as an editor for various publishers, and has written bestselling role-playing games for over a decade.

Jonathan M. Thompson is an author, a trained historian and an amateur paleontologist. He has a house full of his first love, dinosaurs. His love of dinosaurs goes back from the age of eight. He collects books, memorabilia for several hobbies, including science fiction, anime, superheroes and gaming. For the last twenty years he has run the Ennie award winning small press role playing game publishing company, Battlefield Press International, and has co-written several settings for the Savage Worlds game engine, including the recent releases of *Robotech Macross* and *The Dinosaur Protocol*. His love of gaming goes back nearly as far as his love of dinosaurs, and proudly wears a shirt that proclaims that if history repeats itself, he's getting a dinosaur. Jonathan lives in Shreveport, Louisiana with his son and three cats.

D.W. Vogel is a veterinarian, board game developer, marathon runner, SCUBA diver, and cancer survivor. She was raised on Cincinnati chili and is a really terrible bowler. Her bestselling *Horizon Alpha* sci-fi series is set on a dinosaur planet; other novels include *Super Dungeon: The Forgotten King*. President of Cincinnati Fiction Writers, she is represented by Alice Speilburg of Alice Speilburg Literary Agency. She lives in Cincinnati with her husband Andrew and a houseful of medical disaster pets.

LaShawn M. Wanak grew up on the south side of Chicago and now lives in Wisconsin with her husband and son. Her works have been published in *Fireside Magazine, FIYAH,* and many others. She is the editor of *GigaNotoSaurus* and reviews books for *Lightspeed Magazine*. Writing stories keeps her sane. Also, pie. Visit her blog at tbonecafe.wordpress.com.

love of dinosaurs, and proudly wears a shirt that proclaims that if history repeats itself, he's getting a dinosaur. Jonathan lives in Shreveport, Louisiana with his son and three cats.

D.W. Vogel is a veterinarian, board game developer, marathon runner, SCUBA diver, and cancer survivor. She was raised on Cincinnati chili and is a really terrible bowler. Her bestselling *Horizon Alpha* sci-fi series is set on a dinosaur planet; other novels include *Super Dungeon: The Forgotten King*. President of Cincinnati Fiction Writers, she is represented by Alice Speilburg of Alice Speilburg Literary Agency. She lives in Cincinnati with her husband Andrew and a houseful of medical disaster pets.

LaShawn M. Wanak grew up on the south side of Chicago and now lives in Wisconsin with her husband and son. Her works have been published in *Fireside Magazine*, *FIYAH*, and many others. She is the editor of *GigaNotoSaurus* and reviews books for *Lightspeed Magazine*. Writing stories keeps her sane. Also, pie. Visit her blog at tbonecafe.wordpress.com.